T. ALLEN DIAZ

Lunatic City: Prince of Tithes

First published by Blackened Shield Entertainment 2019

Second edition

This book was professionally typeset on Reedsy.
Find out more at reedsy.com

To Tom Campbell, the voice of Frank Parker.

Contents

Chapter One

I knew it was coming and was glad it wasn't a gun. Pricilla "Prissy" Vanderwal lunged with the knife she'd produced from the kitchenette. The overflowing sink from which she'd drawn the blade was ground zero for the stench permeating the nasty, ramshackle flat.

Prissy was the only sister and last surviving relative of Terrance "T-Van" Vanderwal. He'd been killed in a Pandrom prison shower, beaten by a battalion of Lunatic gang members, presumably while the Third Region guards provided lookout.

Her full, brown cheeks were wet with shed tears, and her bloodshot, coffee-colored eyes were wild with rage. "You killed him, you fucking pig!"

I sidestepped the blade, locked her arm, and grabbed her wrist in the vise of my thumb and forefinger. She cried out and dropped the weapon. I put my foot over it and stole a glance; it was a short-bladed paring knife covered with enough food residue to give me a nasty infection.

I pushed her away to create some separation and glanced at her friend. Winnie Odili was an emaciated woman with midnight skin and shorn scalp. She sat at the counter on a stool, arms folded and legs crossed, bored disinterest on her world-weary face.

"I didn't hurt him. What sense would that make? I needed him as a witness. Information I wanted died with him."

Prissy pointed an accusing finger, the flab of her arm sagging in the weak Lunar gravity. "But you got him killed askin' around. Didn't you?"

There was truth in her accusation. I remembered T-Van laughing in my face when the Third Region guards detained me for Rodson's bullshit material witness warrant. Well, he wasn't laughing anymore.

"And *that* is all you care about! Would you even give a shit about who killed him, if it didn't lead to your bullshit partner?"

I made no effort to deny it. T-Van had set Rick up. What possible reason could I have for giving a damn about this punk? "That doesn't change the fact that I'm trying to find his killer. Does that matter to you, at all?"

"Shit! I care about feeding my babies, about how I'm gonna keep the lights on. It sucks that T-Van got his ashes scattered, but I got my own problems."

How sisterly. I reached for my Fillamayum cards. "Well, Rocamora and his crew put him down. You wanna do something about that, you let me know."

"Do you even know it was de Rock?"

I stared at her. "A death squad of Lunatics went berserk on him in the shower. You have other thoughts on what that means, I'm all ears."

Her chuckle was bitter. "I meant your boy. Loonies ain't the only friends T-Van had, you know. Might've been someone else, someone he trusted a whole lot."

I met her eyes, searching for deceit, but something about her smug righteousness brought back my last moments with T-Van.

"The cops don't give a damn about Dave Carson! Nobody does."

"Did you go to them?"

"Didn't have to. They came to me."

I hid behind my two decades on the street. "I'm considering all possibilities."

She laughed at that, as if cops were incapable of looking at their own. And, maybe she was onto something. I drew a Fillamayum card for each of them. "I just want to know what you know about that day. Anything you can provide would be appreciated."

She didn't reach out to take it. Winnie didn't even look at me. I left the cards on the counter next to the roach I'd thought was a stain. I paid it no mind. Years working flats like this can rid a person of a lot of phobias. "Let me know if you hear anything."

Neither responded, and I picked my way across a floor cluttered with clothes and boxes and other trash. I closed the door behind me and looked down at a pair of angry eyes staring up. One of Prissy's babies, I presumed. He was closing on ten, but no older, and wore dirty, holey clothes. I offered a smile. He didn't.

I left and strode through the gloom of the Lower City, a kerchief over my face to keep out the dust and obscure my features. Three Loonies joked on the walkway ahead, catcalling women and hassling weaker passersby. They stood in front of a dirt-stained storefront that resembled all the dirt-stained storefronts in the Lower City. They were a motley bunch: jeans, T-shirts, and wild facial tats with crazy hair.

Lemon-lime eyes looked out from their leader's dark green face. A shock of bright green hair had been combed straight back and stood out like he might've just pissed on a power coupling. One of his partners had a pale blue face with long silver hair. The other sported a black and white tribal pattern that ran vertically across each of his mismatched brown and blue eyes. They angled back at the jaw and down each side of his neck.

Each brandished short sticks taped at one end for a better grip. The way they stalked back and forth and glared out at the crowd said they'd all used them before, and they weren't afraid to do it again. One might think they were Satan's own clowns, but I'd seen more than a few get pinched and cry like babies for their mammas. Loonies were like any other street thugs; better at dishing it out than taking it.

The gangsters were perfectly situated in the gorge of moonboard and concrete to exert maximum influence on the passing crowd. I stayed my course and kept my posture, trying to find that perfect mix of swagger and anonymity. Green Hair looked at me, and I turned my eyes without changing direction.

I passed close enough to smell the Purple K they were smoking. Purple K was a drug engineered to enhance the neural connection to the subject's pReC. The Personal Retinal Communicator was a companion computer wired into almost every human on Luna. Purple K was an enhancer for software highs and gave the user delusions of invincibility. I didn't care about a little drug usage. What I did care about was getting out of the Lower City alive.

"Hey!" I knew he was talking to me. I stood upright and turned back to the crew. Green Hair was already strolling over like he was next up at bat. His friends moved in on either flank. They weren't especially muscular, but they were tall—Satan's clowns. "I know you?"

I was careful to hold his eyes and not look away. I'd taken three Loonies down at once, but they'd been busy exploiting a pair of girls at the time. This was gonna be different. I was front and center, and if any of these Mensa candidates thought to check their pReC, I was a dead man. "Nah, lost my job at an Upper City casino, looking for something down here."

The one with the mismatched eyes laughed. "Ain't that somethin', J? Looking for a job."

J's yellow-green eyes never left mine. He drew a deep hit from the ornate purple dragon in his hand. He held the toke for several long moments and turned his head to blow it over his shoulder, those eyes never leaving me. "Job, huh?" His voice didn't sound like he was expecting a resume. "What kind of job?" His friends picked up on his lead and stepped forward to crowd me on either side. "Pull down that dust rag and let's see the rest of that face, Mr. Job Seeker."

Damn it! I was pulling my rag down when my eyes fell on a lonely figure standing on the far side of the chasm. I grinned beneath the cover, and said, "Ken!" I pushed through the clowns, hoping they didn't cut me down right there for disrespecting them. But they watched, openmouthed, as I strode past and said, "What the hell brings you here?"

Ken Scholar stood at the mouth of an alley. He wasn't wearing his embroidered pullover that identified him as the Tycho City detective sergeant he was. He did wear a mortified expression more at home on the face of a man banging his sister instead of spying on a fully clothed man from an alley. He spoke with his nasal tenor. "Hello, Frank."

"Where's Dana?"

Scholar shrugged and rested his hand on the one thing that did ID him as a cop: the Kholar ten-mil on his hip. He gazed past me at the clowns over my shoulder. "Who the hell knows? Not my day to watch her."

I laughed like he was the funniest guy in the Lower City. "Well, these gentlemen were just asking me where I was going and what I was doing down here. Tell me, as a man of the law. Is it illegal for me to be down here?"

Now, it was the Loonies' turn to look guilty.

Scholar shifted his gaze to me. "Depends. You got any new writs out on you?"

I grinned and glanced at the Lunatics. They seemed to be having a rec discussion between them. "Not yet, but the day is young."

Scholar turned to the Loonies. "How about you boys? Any warrants on you?"

The threesome stepped back, their interest in me suddenly evaporating. "Man," said Green Hair. "We got places to be."

They moved away and disappeared around the corner. I frowned at

Scholar. That was twice the prick had helped me out, and I hated him for it. "Thanks."

He regarded me with baggy, bloodshot eyes. "You think I did that for you?"

"I don't care who you did it for."

He nodded as if we had a cosmic understanding. "I'd go that way," he said, gesturing the direction I'd come with his head. "It might turn out their interest in you was more than casual."

I thought of Green Hair's lemon-lime stare. "Yeah." I turned and left him standing in the street. He never even asked me any questions. I climbed the six levels, past laundry lines strung across dusty chasms and women selling young, nubile bodies under empty, hollow-eyed faces. Another group of Loonies on Sylvester Street was too busy playing dice to pay me any mind, and I took care not to change that.

I passed through the queue for the trains without incident. Another day Fate was tempted, another day she came up empty. A dour woman in her twenties processed me. She glared with suspicion at my status as a suspended Tycho City police officer. If something smarmy occurred to her she was professional enough to keep it to herself, something I couldn't say about others. "Where's my buddy, Virgil?"

"You friends with Virg?"

That was overstating things. "I've seen him in my travels."

"He's not here today." She turned to the next person in the queue, a not-so-subtle sign our conversation was over. I nodded and moved to the train that would take me to the hub and lost myself in thought.

"Might've been someone else, someone he trusted a whole lot." Cops. There was no mistaking the implication. Could cops have set him up? I didn't want to think so but... I thought of the look on Scholar's face when I caught him watching me *"Loonies ain't the only friends T-Van had,"* Prissy had said. She hadn't just said it, she'd lorded it over me, as if she had a dark secret I wasn't gonna like.

The train came to a stop. I disembarked and rode the escalator into Upper Tycho City, rising from the dirty, grimy, destitute poverty below into garishly framed, modern sophistication above. Flashing lights and holograms shined down on clean, neat, well-maintained streets. I stared up at the gawdy display and smiled. I was home.

Chapter Two

I pushed through the front door of the office of Janet Foxx, Esquire. James, her assistant, sat at a desk big enough to host the work area of four TCPD detectives. His smile was as flawless as his hair, and I sometimes wondered if he wouldn't make the perfect holographic avatar. "Hello, Detective Parker."

I'd told the kid to call me Frank, but he refused. I couldn't fault him, though. Foxx demanded a certain decorum from her people. "Hello, Jimmy." He'd never told me to call him Jimmy, but one of us was gonna be casual. "Janet in?"

He smiled like I'd told him he was getting a thousand-bill bonus. "She asked me to send you in as soon as you returned."

"I hope it's not a deal. I'm pulling a night shift at the casino." I was working off a favor by entertainment mogul Angelo Katsaros. It was his way of stalling while he searched for a graceful way to get rid of me. My family lived under his protection. Though whose interests were being protected by having them under Katsaros's thumb was an open secret.

"I think that shift is getting cancelled." Foxx stood in the double doors to her expansive office. Her face was still swollen and a snotty shade of yellow green.

"I had a run in with a Lunatic who had a face like that."

"Aren't you the fucking comedian?"

I chuckled, crossed the plush outer office, and entered her inner sanctum. It was posh and had been completely redone since a Loonie hit squad had paid Janet a visit looking for my family. Katsaros had been pissed because she'd stood up to him and had put them on the scent. I hadn't told her and wasn't sure she knew, but, while Janet Foxx could be many things, stupid wasn't one of them.

The original desk was still here, but almost everything was different, including the heavy, magnetically secured doors that felt more like they belonged on a prison cell than a lawyer's office. I watched her pull them closed and raised an eyebrow. "How are you?"

"It'll take more than a couple of Loonie thugs to get the better of Janet Foxx." I tried to see some sign of the grizzled lawyer who promised to emasculate Simon Frost in this very office but saw only empty bravado. "No luck with the sister?"

I shrugged. "Who can blame her? The cops have never been a friend to her or hers."

"Be careful, I'll turn you into a defense attorney before too long."

I laughed at that. "Fat chance."

She grinned, and I thought it the first genuine pleasure I'd seen her show since the attack. "Turner and Grace came by to see you today."

Turner and Grace was a show streamed on one of the Lunar services. It was a police procedural about a pair of Tycho City detectives. Foxx had given the label to Sergeant Darren Norrington and Detective Lacy Hammond. The pair was hot on my trail for a murder I didn't commit. They seemed like good cops, but their tenaciousness was a pain in my ass. "Yeah? Come to tell me how wrong they've been all this time?"

She laughed. It was good to see. "I think that girl's hatred of you is clinical."

"I noticed that. I suppose I'd hate the murderer of an escaped sex slave trying to get out of a trap she had nothing to do with." The room came back to me—the gloomy light, the dark blood, and Lenny Marquez's glowing pale skin.

"You're doing a lot of good out here, you know. Garrett Latham and his family have a new lease on life. He's been given full immunity for the ritual, and I bet they get off-world once the trial is over."

I didn't look at her. "And Lenny Marquez? She gettin' a new lease on life? Anyone offering her immunity from Katsaros's thugs?"

"Beyond your control."

"I take it this means you still haven't sent the packet, yet." I had prepped a letter and supporting evidence of the illegal things I'd done as a cop, including fabricating evidence on one Kelly "G" Gordon.

"I keep meaning to, but the attorney in me keeps thinking you should listen to the professional paid to look out for your best interests." I thought of Allison Kramer, mutilated by her brother because I framed the wrong man. Foxx seemed to read my thoughts. "Self-awareness is one thing, Frank. Self-loathing is another. You may be able to get your daughter put into protection, but what's it going to do to her to never see you again? What's that gonna do to you? I think you deserve better." I took comfort in her words, but not in her next ones. "I hate to bring more anxiety to your day, but your master beckons."

"Katsaros?" Janet nodded. "That bastard only thinks he's my master."

"Either way, he wants to see you ASAP."

"He say why?"

"I suspect it involves a job."

I thought about the last time I'd worked for Angelo Katsaros and the broken trail that had led to the corpse of Lenny Marquez. "Great."

* * *

Simon Frost was waiting on the landing pad. He'd slipped his athletic frame into a charcoal, tailored two-piece over a white crewneck. The thick brush of the garden at his back swayed in the rotor wash of the air car's turbines. He turned his head and leaned away but held his ground.

The rotors wound down, and the gangway dropped. He resumed his full height, looking at me with disappointed eyes. "Aw! You made it. I was hoping you'd decided to refuse."

"Looking forward to doing something other than sitting in Katsaros's lap?"

Frost's muscular face tensed around his narrowed brown eyes, but the insincere cordiality returned. "Funny for a man with your problems." A satisfied smile spread over his face. "Paid your girlfriend a visit at the hospital this weekend. Fell down the steps, you know."

It took me a second. Allyssa Ramacci had helped me find my family's hidden location, but Frost had been waiting with a small army of thugs. He'd promised bad tidings for the madam and threatened Suzanne and Mattie if I warned her. The livid understanding on my face fueled his glee. "Yep, fell down the stairs. Though between you and me, I think that's a cover story. Stairs don't do that kind of damage. Know what I mean?"

"I'm here to see Katsaros."

Frost led us across the garden to the glass and gold elevator. The doors shut, the car rose, and I gazed out at the city below, its flashing neon contrasting with the gloom of my mood. Allyssa Ramacci wasn't a perfect woman, and I couldn't say I loved her, but we'd commiserated over our flawed lives in a brief, not quite enjoyable, affair. We were kindred spirits; awash in regret, and unable to change the road we found ourselves on. She deserved better than being beaten half to death by Simon Frost for succumbing to my extortion.

The car stopped, the doors opened, and it was time to put aside my self-pity. Katsaros's pyramid penthouse was the same as it always was, gloomy with wood floors and an impressive bar. The fireplace was dark and cold, and the wood floor cracked and popped beneath our weight as we strode across its width.

Angelo Katsaros sat under the same tree he always seemed to be under, and I wondered if he sat anywhere else, but one glance up at the great blue and white crescent hanging in the black sea of stars, and I doubted I would sit anywhere else, either. He let the tinkle of the infinity pool fill the space between us.

A servant appeared with a silver tray and coffee pot. The white-gloved man poured a healthy heaping and left the silver creamer and bowl of real sugar for me to help myself. I stared hard at the setup, and Katsaros gestured with his hand. "Please, be seated, Detective."

I hesitated but sat. "Foxx says you wanted to see me."

"I have a case for you. Your favorite kind: a missing person."

My first sip of earth-grown coffee turned to piss in my mouth, but I choked it down. "Is that supposed to be funny?" Frost's grin said someone found it funny. I offered him a severe glance. "Last time I took a missing persons' gig from you— "

"I know. It hurt your delicate police sensibilities, but this one is different."

"Oh? You promise not to murder this one in front of me?"

Katsaros gave Frost an exasperated glance, and I had the impression they'd discussed this scenario before my arrival. The "I told you so" look on Frost's face said he had predicted my response. Katsaros turened back to me. "It's a friend's son. He's been missing for two weeks or so, and the family's delirious with grief."

I drew a long, pensive breath. "Kidnapping?"

Katsaros shrugged. "We don't think so—at least not a snatching."

I nodded. "How old?"

"Twenty."

"Twenty? As in grown-ass twenty-year-old man?" Katsaros nodded. "Did he steal an heirloom, too?"

"Droll. I don't know of any theft, but he has disappeared, and Margaret is beside herself. She asked for you specifically."

"Margaret who?"

"Mellenburg."

I managed not to drop my coffee. "Maggie Mellenburg of Mellenburg Land Development, Mellenburg?"

"Could you imagine me consorting with any other?"

I decided I couldn't. "Why the hell would she want me?"

"Two words: Garrett Latham."

"I'm honored." The Latham Case had made quite a splash in the media, and the shootout between me and three Sixty-first Street Assassins had been recorded by security cameras and could still be found on the net.

"I hope you don't treat Maggie with this kind of insolence."

I sipped coffee. "It's dispensed proportionate to the amount I receive."

Katsaros acted as if I hadn't spoken. "Obviously, Maggie is a woman of means. So, discretion is at a premium."

I smirked and drew another sip. It made Joe Obradovich's special blend taste like floor cleaner. "What about our time together leads you to believe me discreet?"

He glared at my tone and responded with an edge in his own. "I told her you'd be very delicate and that you'd start today."

"I don't suppose I can refuse?"

He offered a dangerous grin and pulled a pulp envelope from the inside pocket of his ash grey suit. "I have a letter from Mattie, here." Mattie! I hid behind the same mask I'd used on the Loonies but had the feeling it was a vain effort. "She seems to be doing quite well. This whole kerfuffle has worked out for her benefit. Most kids of her standing don't have access to the tutelage she's getting in the Upper City. All right into her pReC in the security of our safehouse."

I held the letter and admired the tall, loose script: Daddy. The heartache blossomed like a supernova, but I pushed hard against the tears trying to rise. It took effort, and I'm sure both Katsaros and Frost reveled at the display. I cleared my throat and looked him in the eye. "Give me her address."

Chapter Three

I left the Olympian on foot. Cars are great for show, but they're not especially practical in our city of mass transit. The crowds were the same; rich Earthers and wannabe rich Earthers who were looking to mark Tycho City off some kind of bucket list. Some were single and too intoxicated on booze or designer drugs to know what solar system they were in. Others were families staring out with wide-eyed wonder.

This latter group was especially notorious for wearing shirts like "I'm Over the Moon for Tycho City" and "Call me Loonie, but I Love Tycho City." The cheesy slogans never stopped, and the people never stopped buying them, often in triplicate, so the whole family could look like they stepped out of a cloning facility rather than a trans-system shuttle.

I found a mostly empty diner, sat in a booth in the corner, and ordered a coffee from a waitress named Rene. She smiled and repeated the order. I thought of the brewed delicacy Katsaros had fed me and reconsidered. "Make it a water."

She offered a smile in need of cleaning. "Food?"

I wondered if I'd have the stomach. "What's the special?"

"Algae steak and hash."

"Any good?"

She pursed her lips in thought. "You'll get better in other places, but it won't make you sick."

Well, when she put it that way... "I'll take it."

I pulled out Mattie's letter, slipped it from the envelope, and read:

Daddy,

The streams are all covering what you did for those people and how you saved their lives. I've watched it over and over! Even Mom admits you're pretty amazing.

Every time I stream the story, I think, "That's my dad!"

But please be careful, The footage of you getting shot at and beat up is hard to watch. I miss you, Daddy, and I think Mom misses you, too.

Hugs and Kisses!

Mattie

The grief came from nowhere, and I started to shake in silence, racked by the aching pain of being separated from my daughter, the mess my family was in, and the certainty I would never see them again. I turned my face to the wall to hide my anguish. I clasped my fist and clenched my jaw, but the sobs still came. I think I kept them quiet, but I'm sure Rene saw, because she didn't return until I'd dried my tears and stopped sniffling.

"Here you go, hun, algae and hash with a side of water." I forced a smile, folded the paper, and slipped it into the envelope. I don't know if she read the letter or me. "Got a boy, myself. Tangled up with M-plant."

I nodded, not sure I wanted to commiserate with this stranger. "That's tough. He in rehab?"

M-plant rehab was both expensive and notorious for its low success rate. She gave me a sad smile and shook her head. "No. Last I heard he was in the Lower City doing what he could to afford his habit."

I gave a grim nod of my head. There were few ways to earn M-plant money, and none of them promised longevity. I motioned to the letter. "It's my daughter. She's with her mother." I tried to find more words, but they weren't there.

"It's hard, being away from your kids." She hesitated. "Is there any way to follow her?"

I looked through the window and locked eyes with a hooded stranger across the boulevard. Pedestrians shuffled between us, and he was gone. I frowned. "It's complicated."

The waitress seemed to make something of that and returned to the counter. I looked back out at the street, searching for that face but found nothing. There had been intent behind his stare, I was sure of it, but what? A Loonie hireling? TCPD surveillance? Some new group I'd pissed off in the last week? All were possibilities.

I did my best to shrug it off and eat. I didn't want it, and it wasn't very good. But my other option was to be hungry later, and if twenty years as a cop taught me one thing, it was to eat when you could.

A coffee slid onto the table next to me. Rene smiled at my perplexed expression. "On the house."

She must've read my reticence to order coffee as financial, not that water was much cheaper. "Thank you, Rene."

The smile she gave me dammed a river of torment. "Take it from someone who knows, mister. Uncomplicate what's standing between you and your daughter before it's too late."

Rene turned, walking towards the counter with purpose. She crossed the counter pass-through and disappeared into the kitchen. I got the feeling she would be going to the back to do some sobbing of her own. I sipped the third-rate coffee and looked at the letter in my hand. I had left this situation to Fate for too long. I would have to uncomplicate it, and soon.

* * *

Maggie Mellenburg owned an apartment that would make Garrett Latham green with envy. It consumed the top three floors closest to the canyon rim. I managed not to gape openmouthed at the plush ostentation of bamboo floors imported from earth under a real white-and-blue Persian rug.

The furniture was all custom white linen over stained maple, complete with two ottomans. The accent furniture was white against a sapphire blue wall. White-framed family pictures looked out, showing smiling faces and happier times: Maggie and her son, no father. White tulle curtains had been cast from large glass doors. The doors were open to the balcony outside. A glow from the valley of the crater hinted at the sprawling metropolis beyond my view.

My eyes lingered, hoping for a glance, and then met Maggie Mellenburg's grey stare. She was dressed in a comfortable linen dress a less discerning eye might consider cheap, but the way it accentuated the youth in Maggie's middle-aged frame hinted at a custom design. "Detective Parker," she said.

"Miss Mellenburg."

"Call me Maggie."

"Okay, Maggie." She offered a seat on the couch. I took it. "I understand your son is missing."

She glanced at the portrait that was now over my shoulder. "Yes." She cleared her throat and found some volume. "This is so unlike Bertrand. He's been such a good boy." I resisted the urge to ask if she named him Bertrand on purpose. "Even if his grades were—weak at times."

"Grades in high school?"

She shrugged. "College, too. It took creativity to get him there."

I nodded. "What's his major?"

"Failing," said a new voice. A slim man leaned on the banister at the top of the wrought iron spiral staircase with the air of a king. His sinewy body looked to be half Maggie's age. An ivory smile contrasted with his bronze face, projecting warmth, friendship, and sincerity. But it was too perfect and had just enough confidence to feel cocky. "I wish I could say he was chasing skirts, but, if he is—"

"He's not telling us," said Maggie. "Detective, this is my husband, Dick Chandler."

You don't say. His white collared shirt, baggy shorts, and athletic shoes said he was late to the tennis courts, but the intrigue in his pale eyes said he was going nowhere. Sometimes I had all the luck.

I turned back to Maggie. "How about other interests? Friends?"

Maggie shook her head. "Not that he told us."

"Was he always this way?"

"A bad student?"

I nodded. "And secretive about his personal life."

Dick had reached the bottom of the stairs. "As long as I can remember."

I ignored him and held Maggie in my gaze. "Mostly for the last five years or so."

"It's typical teenage bullshit," said Dick. "I'm sure you see it all the time. Am I right?"

I thought of all the shitty, selfish people I'd come across in two decades of police work and looked in his eyes. "All the time."

Maggie frowned. "My son didn't run away. We have our differences, but we—he still loves me."

I thought of Mattie. "The bond between parent and child can endure a lot." She smiled and nodded. "So, Dick isn't his father."

She watched him take the seat next to her. "No. Dick and I have been together for six years, married for two of them."

I nodded. "Loyal to his father?"

She chuckled. "Hardly. Carlo was too busy trying to headline at the

Olympian to be an important factor in Bertrand's life. Though they did 'reunite' recently."

I glanced at the sour expression on Dick's face and decided to push the envelope. "Was this because of your relationship with Mr. Chandler?"

"Hey, what kind of question is that?" Dick stood in a way that suggested I should watch my mouth, and I ignored him in a way that suggested he should sit down.

"It wasn't just Dick. You know how teens can be."

Dick took this as validation. "Yeah, that's what I said, kid bullshit. You know, I pay your salary!"

I offered a tight smile and looked at Maggie. "Tell me about your relationship from before things started falling apart."

"Oh, we were very close. After his father, I wanted nothing to do with men, and providing was never an issue."

I nodded. "So, he starts getting older..."

She glanced at Dick. "He started staying away with friends and started not being around." I nodded again but let her continue. "That's when I met Dick, and Bertrand went into open rebellion."

"So, how do we know he's missing and not staying away? He is a grown man, you know."

She grimaced. "That's what the cops keep telling me. He's stayed away before, but never without talking to me. And he hasn't been to class in over a week."

"And that's unusual?"

"He cuts class from time to time, but not like this. And, to not at least rec me? Never."

I nodded again. "Maybe he met a girl."

Dick snickered at that. Maggie shot him a glance. "But to not answer me? He's reconfigured his pReC!"

Reconfiguring a pReC wasn't as invasive as it sounded. Bertrand had changed his NIC, Net Interface Code. The code served as a network address and allowed people to be recognized. It wasn't illegal, but it was an all-or-nothing proposition, meaning everything and everyone in your old life would be broken off clean—no cookies, no pReC recall. Because of this, authorities viewed it with suspicion, and the process required both technical savvy and money to do it right. If Bertrand had reconfigured, it was an ominous sign for his relationship with his mother. "Have you talked to his father to see if he knows anything?"

"Two nights ago. He hasn't seen him, either. That's when I remembered Angelo bragging at a party about how he'd helped solve the Garrett Latham case." I managed not to laugh out loud. "So, I asked him to reach out and see if you'd help."

I nodded again. "Can I see his room?"

* * *

Bertrand Mellenburg had a room on the second floor overlooking the city. The entire wall opposite where I stood was a giant glass face. The spacious chamber looked even bigger thanks to the barren floors and sparse furnishings. A king-sized bed had been pushed into the back-right corner from where I stood, affording it a great view. A solitary bureau had been pressed against the wall to my left.

I tried to take it all in. The lack of pics or posters, the empty emerald carpet that could've served as a bed unto itself, and the lack of personal items anywhere. "Was he always this neat?"

Another snicker from Dick. Maggie said, "I keep it clean."

I nodded, expected nothing less. "I assume you've looked for clues as to where he might be?"

She stiffened. "We—I try to respect his privacy." I gave her a long, tell me the truth look, and she deflated. "I found prophylactics, pamphlets from school, and some love letters."

"Love letters?" I tried to keep the accusation out of my voice.

Apparently, I failed.

"It's not the kind of thing a mother wants to read about her son, and it's certainly not the kind of thing I want to share with a stranger."

I let my gaze linger for a moment before opening a tidy closet with clothes hung and objects organized on the shelf. "I'm not a stranger. I'm an investigator, *your* investigator. If I'm going to find Bertrand, I need to know everything about him; what classes he took, who his friends were"—I paused and turned my cop's gaze on her—"who he was intimate with, anything that might give me insight on where to look for him. Understood?"

She nodded, and I added, "I'm not going to judge him. He's a kid, and, as Mr. Chandler said, I'm exposed to a lot in this business. The exploits of a frisky college kid are mild when put in that collection."

Maggie's smile carried a note of gratitude. She turned to the bureau and drew out several pulp letters. They were all different pastel colors—blues, greens, yellows—but seemed to have come from the same notepad. Each page was fourteen by twenty-two centimeters or so with the same distinctive gold leaf around the edge.

The broad, looping script seemed female, and I could smell the perfume: an airy scent with a hint of something floral—rosewater. I read the one on top.

My Dearest Bernie,

I hope this letter finds you well and as hungry for me as I am you. This afternoon was amazing, but it's only made me want you more.

You have become more than a love in these weeks. You've become an addiction, and I crave to have you here with me, where I can touch you, feel you, taste you.

Don't worry about a world where no one cares or parents who don't understand. What we have is right, and we have our own truth. Keep me in your thoughts as I keep you in mine.

M.

I looked at Maggie. "M?"

She looked away and shrugged. "He never mentioned her."

I glanced through the rest of the letters and understood her embarrassment. They read like a trashy novel, or the "private letters" some porn streams still put to film. I folded them with care and slipped them into my pocket.

"What are you doing with those?" I had forgotten Dick was even here.

"Keeping them for later."

"No one said you could have them."

I didn't remember asking. I directed my response to Maggie. "These letters are considered clues, and I'm taking them to review later."

She nodded, and I returned to my search. His closet was clean. Clothes that were fashionably expensive, boxes of old models and toys, and actual pulp books. The bed and nightstand were clear except for condoms and lube. "So, Bertrand brought girls home?"

Maggie didn't seem to like the question. "He was a grown adult, Detective. I knew what he was doing but respected his privacy."

I nodded. "Did you happen upon any of these women's names while you were respecting his privacy?"

She blushed and kept her eyes on a spot on the carpet. "Early on, but not in a year or more."

"So, this agreement goes back to high school?"

"Yes."

I rechecked between the bed and mattress and stripped the sheets. This offended Dick. "She told you we already checked there."

I patted the letters in my pocket. "She also told me she didn't know anything about a girlfriend."

He glared and was about to say something when Maggie placed a hand on his arm. I turned to the bureau. More designer clothes. T-shirts and socks. Even his underwear was designer. I pulled them all out, checked pockets, and looked into the empty drawers for signs of letters, jewelry, electronic devices, anything that might give me insight into Bertrand. I swept the naked drawers with my hands: flat and smooth.

I frowned and turned to a desk I had missed at first glance. It had been recessed into a cubby in the front corner opposite the closet. The desktop was folded against a wall that held two rows of drawers on either side of a gap meant for a reader's legs. It was a tiny unobtrusive work area.

I pulled at a drawer. Pens, a stylet. An old notebook. The pages had started to yellow, giving the impression this might be left over from high school. I held it skyward and leafed through the top pages; no imprints of a previous message. I frowned and thumbed through the rest of the pages. Empty. I dropped it back inside and closed the drawers.

The others were the same. A lot of nothing; dust, paperclips, and batteries to a palm computer or other electronic device that had probably been sent to the recycler long ago. I closed the last drawer and looked at the underside of the folded desktop. I drew it down and saw a pulp pamphlet.

I picked it up and looked at a familiar face with bright green eyes over sharp cheekbones and chin. He had perfect auburn hair to go with that perfect salesman's smile. I read the message aloud. "Come find joy with us."

Maggie glanced at the pamphlet. "Church?"

I displayed it for her and Dick's benefit. "Church? The New Sunrise Tabernacle is *the* church in town. Never heard of it?"

The disdain on Maggie's face said she recognized it. "I know him. We've never attended, and I can't imagine Bertrand giving this charlatan the time of day."

I smiled. It seemed Maggie and I shared some world views. "Perhaps, but I'll keep this, too. You never know where the case will take you."

Maggie suppressed a smile. "If you don't take it, I'll toss it in the recycler."

"Thanks, Maggie. Let me know if anything new comes up." I glanced at Dick and showed myself out.

Chapter Four

Harper Ellis University was nestled in the eastern part of the Upper City. It catered to Tycho's wealthy, didn't offer Lower City scholarships, and sold itself as *the* school for Tycho City's elite. That didn't make it easy on a Lower City detective.

"It's illegal to share this information with you."

I leaned on the counter and held the pudgy-faced woman in my gaze. "Look, there are laws and there are laws. The fat-cat mamma who's paying for this magnificent education *and* has donated generously to this institution is worried something terrible has happened to her son. How's it gonna look on your recruitment brochures if it later turns out tragedy could have been avoided and you did nothing to help me?"

The woman stared for several long moments. "I can't give them over to you on your word"—she held up the card—"and this."

"No, but you can rec the guarantor of his tuition and confirm I'm who I say I am."

The notion must've tasted like week-old milk. "I'll be back." She disappeared into a back room, and I looked the lobby over. It was a nice waiting room, as nice as any such place could be and still be practical: cushioned chairs, modest wall treatments, and moonwalk-tiled floors. But it struck me as lacking after spending time in Maggie Mellenburg's home.

"Here you are, Mr. Parker." The woman offered a short stack of pulp papers. "Please feel free to come back, if you need anything further." I was surprised the words didn't choke her to death.

"Thanks," I said, allowing some of the victory to slip into my smile. "You have a glorious day."

I took the papers, sat down in one of their comfortable chairs, and looked them over in full view of the choking secretary. Maggie had been generous. Bertrand's grades were sliding from bad to dismal. He'd been hit with academic probation, and was staring at dismissal if he didn't get it together.

I read a letter officially banning him from the Student Union Against Repressive Treatment, a club dedicated to activism and championing the dispossessed. It wasn't the kind of club I'd expect in a school that catered to well-to-do rich kids with a silver spoons in their mouths, but here it was, with a thriving membership. The letter was addressed to a Camilla Zimmerman, professor of Sociology and Community Engineering. I glanced at the schedule and accessed the university database with my pReC to plan my day.

* * *

I rapped on the wall next to the open office door. "Professor Hauser?"

A round woman with full cheeks looked up, her big, walnut eyes made bigger by the large glasses she peered through. "Yes?"

"May I have a moment of your time?"

She looked around the office cluttered with books and papers. College professors, it seemed, liked their papers more than lawyers did. "Sure. I'd offer you a chair, but that one belongs to Kyle." Kyle Warren was an English prof who happened to teach Bertrand's English Lit class. I'd caught him heading into his ten-thirty twenty minutes ago.

"That's fine. I won't take much of your time. Bertrand Mellenburg is missing, and I'm trying to find him. Can you tell me anything about him?"

She frowned, as if trying to decide what to say. "He's failing. I wouldn't know anything about him being missing. He's attended"—her eyes rolled in a way that suggested she was accessing her pReC—"four of my eleven classes, not counting the one he's sure to miss tomorrow morning. When he does show up, he doesn't participate."

I nodded. None of this was news. The rest of his professors said the same; Bertrand was on his way out. "Did you ever see him around campus, note any of his friends—girlfriends?"

"Seen him around campus with the misfits."

I nodded. More of the same from the other professors. I looked at the gold nameplate on her desk and the round, frumpy professor. I tried to imagine her having an affair with a student and being the author of those letters and failed. Still... Mary Hauser. *M.* "Any girlfriends? Lovers?"

She shook her head. "I'm sure I've seen him with girls, but he's one of scores of students in my Tuesday/Thursday. I wouldn't know who he was at all if he wasn't failing out."

"How about faculty members he was close to?"

"Like I said..." There was a note of exasperation in her voice.

I nodded. "Okay, one last question. Can you think of anyone or anything that could give me a place to start?"

She shook her head in slow, measured beats. "Noth—Oh! He was a member of a club—one of the social activism—StUART!"

"Student Union Against Repressive Treatment."

"That's right." Then, more to herself, she said, "Camilla runs that club."

"Camilla Zimmerman."

She nodded. "That's right." She didn't ask if that was all, but it hung in the air between us.

"Thank you, Professor, I'll be going." She nodded and returned to her desk.

* * *

I caught Camilla Zimmerman stepping out of Room H135. She carried a sleek handbag with room for an electronic tablet. A professor who's joined the twenty-second century. Hurray! "Miss Zimmerman?"

There was a street savvy in Zimmerman's cognac eyes I didn't associate with academia. She pursed her lips, turning her wariness into condescension.

"You mean Dr. Zimmerman?"

Great, one of those. "Of course. My apologies. I wondered if I could talk to you for a moment?"

She continued her journey, leading me down a corridor of moonboard walls and a cold, tiled floor.

"About?"

"A missing person."

"You a cop?"

"Private."

"Well, I really don't have time. Besides, my students are all adults, if—"

"We're worried that something has happened to one of your students and are trying to help him. The university has pledged its cooperation. Are you going to help me, or do we need to take this to the dean?"

Zimmerman stopped, which gave me my first good look at her. She was young, early thirties. Her use of makeup was judicious but accentuated the right parts of her face: a little enhancement for her thin eyebrows, some red to help the lips stand out from a dusky face, and some help for her long lashes. She was also unreadable. If she was still working on tenure, I might have a little leverage. But, if she wasn't, I'd probably ended this interview before it started.

"Who?"

"Bertrand Mellenburg."

She offered no sign of recognition. "What class is he in?"

"Cultural Authoritarianism and the Myth of Order."

"Ah, yes." Zimmerman turned, and we resumed our walk.

I gave her several meters to speak. "And?"

She offered an exaggerated sigh, and I assumed she was checking her pReC. "Yes, he's one of fifty-seven people in my Monday/Wednesday afternoon."

"So, do you know him?"

"Not by name." I passed her the hard copy of a pic in Angelo's original package. She took it. "Familiar, but this looks old."

"It is."

"Is that the best his worried family could do, a dated pic? Doesn't exactly scream tight-knit." I thought of Dick and suspected I had an answer for that. "Seems like they sent him here to get him out of their hair. So, why care now?"

"They care enough to hire me."

"Care." Her husky contralto mocked the word. "Most of the people in my CA class are misfits. They wear polymorph tats, steel jewelry, and black clothes. I could probably paint a portrait of your boy without a word of description."

I nodded. "And StUART?"

She stopped and looked at me for the second time. "StUART?"

"Student Union Against Repressive Treatment."

She barked out a laugh that echoed in the harsh acoustics of the hallway. "You mean the Union! I don't spend much time with that, these days."

I produced the letter addressed to her, informing her of Bertrand's suspension. She looked it over. "I have a club secretary for this, but, yes, this communication looks familiar, as would scores of others I've received in the last month."

I forced a smile. That sounded a lot like the truth. "I see. And, this secretary?"

"She's a student."

I nodded my understanding. "I'm sure the registrar can help me."

She offered another sigh. "Carrie, Carrie DiPompo. You can probably find her in the Student Union."

* * *

I left the Humanities building and took in the scene of Harper Ellis. A concrete path meandered across a lush bed of green grass and under great oaks that brought to mind the garden on Katsaro's roof. It was getting on in the afternoon, and I was getting hungry. Maybe there'd be something to eat at the student union.

I noted its location on my pReC, started walking along the path, and recced an old but unwilling ally. A brown face framed by short, chestnut hair stared into my retina. Suspicion filled her honey eyes. "What do you want, Frank?"

"Cyndi! Still loving that exclusive I got you?"

"Yesterday's news."

I put on a pout. "What have you done for me lately? How positively cynical of you."

"Thanks to men like you."

I didn't think she meant that, but my relationship with Cyndi Travis could be hot and cold. "How about I put you onto some 'today news'?"

I turned left at a gazebo, where a suspiciously innocent-looking couple sat and stared at the greenery. Another student in a pale grey hoodie had stepped onto the path behind me, his attention focused on the tablet in his hand.

"Why do I feel like this is gonna cost me?"

I grinned and turned back to my conversation. "Just a little leg work."

"You mean the important stuff?"

"Absolutely!"

She chuckled. "Brenda still hates you." Brenda was Cyndi's girlfriend.

"Who can blame her? I'd probably hate me, too, but you and I understand the passion we share for the truth."

I could see the snarky response on her face, but it died unspoken. "What do you need, Frank?"

I arrived at the end of the trail and passed over a dry streambed that had probably never seen water. This wasn't the place for that kind of extravagance. A town square of restaurants and stores catering to students had sprouted up here. I strode across the green, past a handful of kids lazing in the grass or on the benches, harsh sunlamps on the rooflines warming them and the grass.

"Can you give me background on a pair of Harper Ellis faculty."

"Just two?"

"For now. Dr. Camilla Zimmerman, a humanities professor."

"Doctor, huh?"

"Yeah, a strong woman type. You'd love her."

"You really know how to talk to people, Frank. You know that?"

I smiled at her barb. "So I've been told. The other is Professor Mary Hauser."

"No doctor?"

"Nope, just a loser with an MBA."

"Okay, that's it?"

"One other thing. I might need some background on the New Sunrise Tabernacle."

"I'm sorry, what?"

"I found one of their pamphlets in my missing person's drawer. Might be something. Might not."

A long, tense pause stretched between us. "That church isn't the ray of sunshine it wants the world to believe it is, Frank." I'd heard rumors, but the religious beat wasn't my thing. "I know reporters who've done exposés on Petrovich."

"And?"

"And, they leave the story unfinished, buried in nondisclosure agreements and restraining orders." She paused. "Some of them still believe they're being followed."

"I'm just looking for background, Cyndi. I'm not asking you to take on a six-month undercover gig. You give me a little background. I give you dibs on any story that comes out of this. You in?"

She pondered the question a long time. When she did speak, there was real fear in her voice. "I'll get what's on the very superficial public record, but no deep dives on this one."

I reached the narrow lane I wanted. Smaller trees, maples, rose from holes in the concrete on either side, lining the path with green. The storefronts here were quaint, like the others: some had a slate feel, others brick, some even had a faux wood veneer. All had an abundance of glass in their faces.

"And, I expect a bonus on this one."

"A night out for you and Brenda on me."

"That's it?"

"I seem to recall more gratitude the last time I made this offer."

"Last time, you weren't asking me to spy on the Devil."

"He's a preacher, Cyndi; a rich and powerful one, I'll grant you, but New Sunrise isn't the Loonies."

"He might be worse, Frank." Spoken like a woman who lived behind a keyboard.

"Oh, can I get one more lookup?"

She sighed, but the exasperation was faked. "You're pushing it, Frank. What is it?"

"Carlo Izquierda, a failed bar singer. He's the kid's old man."

"Old man? You mean father?"

"Come on, Cyndi."

"All right, I'll see what I can do."

"Thanks, Cyndi. You're the be—" My eyes trailed to a reflection in the glass of a storefront on the far side of the pathway. There was a grey hoodie behind me. I couldn't see his face, but the hood was leaning forward and his stride was purposeful. "Gotta go. Rec me."

She was still speaking when I cut the connection.

The man's hand was in the pocket of his jacket, and his height and build brought to mind the figure outside the diner where I read Mattie's letter. He was close, six paces or so. His body shifted, and I knew there wouldn't be a move to be made if I waited.

I turned and leapt at him through the weak Lunar gravity. We collided before his hand had fully cleared the pocket, and we crashed into one of those thin maples. The loud crack from the man's body coincided with his pained grunt. I heard a metallic clatter I hoped was his gun skittering across the pavement.

I slashed his head with a well-placed elbow and glimpsed a clean-shaven face of light brown skin with a smallish nose. But the hood stretched, preventing a good look. My nose caught a familiar scent, triggering a powerful wave of déjà vu, and I lost half a beat trying to trap the memory.

It was enough. His fist clocked me in the nose, filling my eyes with tears. An elbow crashed into my jaw. The blow rocked me back, allowing him to slip his feet between us. They caught me in the chest and sent me soaring. I skittered along the walkway, smashing through an iron table and chairs set for outdoor diners. I rolled to a stop in front of a glass door and looked at my opponent. The man had found his knees and was reaching for his gun.

I gained my knees, grabbed the door, and rolled inside. The man had found the gun and was pointing it at me, but he didn't fire. He glanced at the crowd around him and ran, disappearing at the end of the block.

Chapter Five

I sat outside Arturo's Ice Cream and Gelato Shoppe with a cold compress held to my face. I'm pretty sure the iron chair I was sitting in was the same one that left a painful bruise across my back, but that didn't keep me from sitting in it.

"I don't think you have any permanent damage," said a paramedic with a thin, triangular face and sapphire eyes that complemented her inky-blue bob cut hair. "But that nose is gonna throb for the next couple of days."

I grinned. "They teach this compassion to all paramedics?"

The medic grinned. "You, of all people, should know when to duck, Officer."

I laughed at that. "I guess he taught me!"

She offered me a tablet. "Sign here, please."

It was the standard hold harmless agreement absolving her of any blame in the event I woke up dead or pissing my pants in the morning. I'd witnessed hundreds of such signings in my life, but this was the first time I'd scratched my signature as a patient. She looked it over and turned to a short, bald man in a Third Region collared shirt.

"So." Detective Sergeant Jorge Gomez stood on the far side of the table; a foot propped in the chair across from me. He was scooping ice cream he'd purchased from Arturo's from a paper cup. "What brings you to my campus?"

"That's your first question? What am I doing here? I am the vic, you know."

Gomez took a bite of his ice cream, his astute brown eyes glancing at my card on the table. "Well, while you were receiving the tender mercies of the campus medics, I chatted it up with a Detective Sergeant Norrington. You know him?" I frowned and looked out at the crowd still gathered on the far side of the walkway. "You *do* know him. He sure knows you! Says you were a witness, and are still a person of interest, in the murder of a runaway in the Southeast District; a witness who found a corpse at the Jinx Hotel, and was an active participant in two Upper City shoot-'em-ups in two hours." He spread his arms and gestured around him. "Now, you spend an afternoon interviewing our staff and someone takes a poke at you right here in the open."

It sounded bad when he put it that way. "A case."

"A case," he repeated. "Were you working cases at these other instances?"

"Some of them."

"Some of them." He stared hard. "Now, you bring those old cases here and that baggage of yours follows?"

"There's nothing—"

"You know what Harper Ellis is, Mr. Parker? The elite of Tycho's youth, the future of the colony. Now, you bring this shit from who knows what part of your past to do battle with a gunman on our campus?" He shook his head in disgust. "The TCPD might put up with that shit, but I promise you, we don't."

The smell! It was from my apartment, the night I was shot and almost burned to death! Gomez was talking to me. I focused on his round face. "What?"

"Everything okay in there?"

"You're right. It was someone who'd tried to kill me in the past. Happy?" The comment put Gomez on his back foot. "But I don't know the first thing about who he is, the danger has passed, and I have a job to do. Can I go?"

Gomez's eyebrows knotted on his bald head. "Go on. Right off this campus, Mr. Parker, and don't come back." I stood, and my back protested. "I mean it," he said. "I catch you on this campus, I'll haul you into our jail and let you spend some quality time with Lacy Hammond." My annoyance must've shown. "That's right, Parker. I talked to her, too. She *really* likes you."

I turned and left, still thinking about the scent. The same scent from my apartment the night it burned down. I had always assumed it had been a Lunatic hit, but I realized now how that had never fit. The Loonies might hire out work in the Upper City, but the Lower City was their domain. Hiding behind an anonymous hit man was beneath their dignity.

Now, I had a new mystery. If this guy wasn't working for the Lunatics, where was he from? Katsaros? Rick's murderer? Coconspirator? If it was one of Rick's murderers, and they weren't the Lunatics, who did that leave to kill Rick? T-Van's voice reached from beyond the grave. "... *The cops don't give a damn about Dave Carson! Nobody does."*

"Did you go to them?"

"Didn't have to. They came to me."

Cuff 'em or cut 'em. That's what T-Van had called them, Rocamora's cabal of dirty cops. How many were there? Did I know them? Was it possible I didn't? I recalled my run-in with the Loonies and Ken Scholar's fortuitous appearance at the mouth of the alley. Could *that* be chalked up to coincidence?

Then I remembered Dana from the night Rick was murdered. *"Well, you're gonna have to hold down the fort. Scholar and I just picked up a fresh kill..."*

That "fresh kill" was Rick. Had Scholar set the whole thing up? Had he made sure he would be assigned the case to cover the killer's tracks?

Had he been the killer? I thought of the scent from the apartment and my tussle with this new mystery man on the campus grounds.

If Scholar was involved, he was with others. Cuff 'em or cut 'em. I was going to have to operate on the assumption this mystery man was a dirty cop, part of this ring of dirty cops. The big question was how did this network operate and who was part of it? I looked out at the pretty scenery and wondered if I wanted to know.

I strode off campus and found a gift shop off one of the main boulevards. It was a loud place with the scratchy pulse of what passed for music these days blaring from overhead speakers.

I flashed a grin at the rotund figure with pink hair behind the counter and tried to find something low-key. What I found was a black T-shirt with a picture of Luna, a red arrow pointing at Tycho Crater, and white lettering that read, "You are Here." I added a white-and-black plaid shirt with an iron-on Luna on the left breast.

"This it?" said the pink-haired girl.

I glanced over her shoulder. "I'll take the hat on the top shelf and the wraparounds."

She pulled them from the shelves and set them in front of me. I paid with my pReC and asked for a changing room. She gave me a quizzical glance and said, "In the back."

I walked to the back and found the white louvered doors. I stepped inside, pulled my collared shirt off, drew the T-shirt over my head, and slipped the button-down over my arms. I left it open and rolled up the sleeves. Both were baggy enough to afford me good movement, and I felt sure I would pass a cursory glance, but if Gomez remained vigilant, this could end badly.

* * *

The student union was still open when I strode in at eight forty-five.

"Not here," said a spikey-haired girl with more metal in her face than went into the average handgun. She propped her head on a hand festooned with silvery rings of steel, boredom and fatigue competing for ownership of what might've once been a pretty face.

"Do you know where she might be?" I was doing my best to sound official, but the look I'd been forced to take on took too much gravity out of my presence.

"You got a writ?"

I offered an unpleasant smile. "Prelaw?"

"What?"

"You prelaw? Is that why you're asking about a warrant?"

Her tiny, grey eyes widened at the tone of my voice. "No I-I—"

"I'm looking for Carrie DiPompo. The administration promised its full cooperation. You interested in helping me, or shall I go back to them and say"—I looked for the name plate—"Denise at the student union wouldn't help me?"

She sighed and stared at the room behind me. "I don't know where they are..."

"But..." I said.

She sighed again. "The Dead Lizards are playing at the Mine Shaft."

"Mine Shaft?"

"It's a student bar just off campus."

I nodded. Off campus was good. "Thanks!" I left Denise to stare daggers I could almost feel into my back. The stroll to the western edge of campus was scenic, and I might've enjoyed it had I not been searching for signs of a hitman lurking among the pleasant walkways and storefronts.

There was twice as much foot traffic, now that classes were over, and students gathered in all the places you would expect. Girls sitting on their boyfriends' laps. Others standing around smoking or drinking. I assumed they were nonalcoholic beverages, given the campus rules, but some of those drinks were sure to be spiked.

Almost every student watched me pass, and those who didn't had me called to their attention by those who did. Changing my look had been a good idea in theory, but a grim, middle-aged man in tourist gear was going to stand out on a college campus.

I left the last green piece of Harper Ellis behind me and turned onto Fairway Boulevard. The Mine Shaft was on the opposite side and looked out at the school whose students it served. I followed the screeching wail of angry guitars to the crowd of college kids overflowing into the walkway outside.

Their dress was so similar, they could've constituted gang colors. Black over black, lots of metal in flesh. It was a look that never went away; the ultimate symbol of rebellion. I wondered how many of these angry rebels bought this metal with mom and dad's account. One glance at the expensive, brand-name clothing and I had my answer.

A bouncer with a broad chest and broader arms blocked my entry. He made a show of looking over my tourist motif. "You ain't the normal crowd, here, friend."

I tried my hand at a disarming smile. "Just looking to pass the time with one of the patrons here."

He gestured at a sign: MANAGEMENT RESERVES THE RIGHT TO REFUSE SERVICE TO ANYONE. "That means you, mister tourist."

The disarming smile became something more severe. I handed him a card and leaned into his face. "I'm here on behalf of the university, looking into a missing student. You wanna give me a hard time, maybe I start looking into how many of these fresh faces are freshmen and sophomores and put *that* in my report instead. The choice is yours."

The big man's face curdled and shifted in a way that said he was on his pReC. When he was done, he looked at me and said, "Who you looking for?"

"DiPompo, Carrie DiPompo."

He shook his head. "Don't know her."

I raised my eyebrows, glanced at the space he was taking up, and the open door behind him. He frowned and stepped aside. I slipped a twenty-bill note into his hand. "Thanks."

He slipped it into his pocket and nodded.

The interior of the Mine Shaft was painted black and projected a hole-in-the-wall air that was more contrivance than fact. It was bigger on the inside than it looked on the outside, taking up three of the building's street-level occupancies. The band—as they were being euphemistically called—made loud noise on the stage and gave the standing room only crowd something like a beat to jump to.

My ears ached beneath the assault, and I had a feeling I would pay for this tomorrow. I used my pReC to pull Carrie's face from the StUART page on the university site. The pic had been taken in the student union, in front of the very desk where Denise and I had conversed. Short, but thick, hair had been dyed midnight black, framing a pale face with a button nose and bloodless lips. I expected the blue-and-white Harper Ellis collared shirt to be replaced with something more rebel-chic at this hour.

The Dead Lizards stretched the fifteen minutes or so it took me to find her corner table into six to ten hours. It was a round high top with room for four, but a fifth had been pulled up. She was talking as fast as her black-painted lips could move, a broad smile on her face. The massive mug of beer in front of her was down to its last couple of centimeters, and she blew clouds of sweet-smelling vapor into the air above her table.

I stood in the aisle, pretending to watch the reptile wannabes, and assessed her mates. A skinny boy with a shock of platinum hair draped over his left eye sat next to her, his left arm dangling across her shoulders as if claiming proprietorship. He seemed to be the target of her words, but nothing about his demeanor said the boy was listening.

His pouty lips were pursed in bored disinterest as crystal blue eyes roamed the inside of the bar, stopping every so often on a shapely ass or pair of tits. They passed over me and kept moving. I wasn't on the menu.

The others were like the bar—more affect than reality. Black designer clothes and expensive tattoos standing in for actual grit. The music started to wind down, and I turned to their table. The feedback from the dying song still screeched when I spoke. "Hey, Carrie! I've been looking everywhere for you."

She looked up at me openmouthed. "Excuse me?"

"You're Carrie DiPompo, Secretary of StUART?"

Blondie answered for her. "That's right. Why do you care?"

I didn't look at him. "I'm wondering if you remember anything about Bertrand Mellenburg."

Blondie stood, all sixty-five Earth kilos of him. "I said, what's it to you?"

I stopped, looked at him, and realized he might be the largest single threat to me. I could beat some Lunatic into a bloody pulp without so much as a peep from the system, but this kid was someone's son, a rich someone. If I so much as brushed one of those platinum hairs, I'd be drawn and quartered. So, I chose a different tactic. "Nice jacket. Sampson and Sons. Your daddy buy that for you?"

Carrie put an arm across his chest. "Eugene!"

Eugene! I might be ready to fight the world, too. No one else moved, and I looked over the table. No one looked back. On stage, the Lizards were soothing their damaged throats with something cold and wet. "You do the secretary work for StUART?"

Eugene tried to speak. "I told you—"

I placed a firm hand on his chest without looking away from Carrie. It was as far as I dared go, but I didn't want him to know that.

She watched him sit with wide eyes. "I-I—he's in our club."

"Active?" I said. Eugene chose discretion.

"Uh—he's officially suspended. Bu-but we just pretend he's not there."

You rebels, you. "When's the last time you saw him?"

"Aaaallllright," said the man posing as a lead singer. "You guys ready for another?"

The crowd roared with approval. Carrie ignored him. "A-a week or two."

"That unusual?"

Eugene was finding his courage. "She don't have to talk to you!"

The head lizard spoke. "How about a little 'Downtown Pounddown'?"

The crowd cheered. I almost turned my head at that, but my tight window was getting tighter. "Is it unusual for him to be away for so long?"

She stared at the stage, and I could see Eugene drawing power and inspiration from her nervousness. "I've never known it to happen before."

"How about a girl? Had he met someone, maybe?" On stage they were counting in. "I'm a private cop with a considerable expense account."

"Your money means nothing to us." Eugene pulled Carrie to him. He was taking his toy away and wanted me to know it. The noise from the stage resumed.

I leaned close and shouted. "We're worried about him and just want to make sure he's okay. That seems reasonable. Doesn't it?"

"Seems like a damned lie," Eugene yelled back.

Carrie looked up at me. "H-he was around all the ti"—the music hit its stride and the hoarse angry lizard started on vocals—"er."

"What?"

I could see she regretted whatever she'd said to me. Getting her to repeat it was going to take some doing. But Eugene was on his feet. It was time to go. I passed my card around, and Eugene made a show of throwing them on the floor. He stared at me, those glittering, blue crystal eyes daring me to do something about it.

I frowned and left, frustrated with my results, but glad to be free of the Dead Lizards.

Chapter Six

I left the Mine Shaft, ears ringing in the relative quiet, and tried to get a picture of Bertrand Mellenburg. He was failing out of school with such commitment he wasn't likely to finish the semester. His friendships were casual and meaningless. That crew surrounding Carrie DiPompo couldn't have cared less if he'd hopped the next shuttle to Mars or fell between the streets into the Lower City.

Eugene didn't seem to have much use for him, but his bite came in the form of daddy and his lawyers. There was nothing of substance to his game. And there was M. I was no closer to finding M than I had been before. Mary Hauser? A student? A member of the Harper Ellis staff? Someone totally unrelated? Carrie knew something, and, if Carrie knew, others knew. I just had to keep at it.

I returned to the pamphlet found in the desk. What role did the New Sunrise Tabernacle play in this kid's life? Maybe I would find this M there. Maybe she would fall out of the sky and land in my lap, if I attended service. I smiled at the thought of that; a gift from heaven.

My second sight flashed, and Janet Foxx's sour face looked back at me. "Janet. I take it this isn't a social call."

"Sorry, Frank. It's not." The gravity of her voice filled me with dread. "You know I like to keep plugged into the public database in case clients come in front of a judge without my permission." I knew. It had bailed me out of trouble on one occasion. "Well, I didn't get a defendant hit, but the cops just responded to Pricilla Vanderwal's place."

I prickled with cold fear and thought of the run-in I'd had with the Loonies on K Street. Maybe they weren't random hooligans. Maybe they were surveillance. Or, maybe Ken Scholar's presence had been less fortuitous for Prissy than it had been for me. "What happened?"

"Assault. I don't have a lot of details or even a victim name."

I nodded. That kind of thing was never public record. "Okay. Did the ambulance transport anyone?"

"Tycho General."

"Thanks, Janet."

"Frank." I paused. "It's not your fault."

Easy for you to say. "Thanks, Janet."

* * *

I recced the hospital AI en route and was told Pricilla Vanderwal was on the seventeenth floor in ICU-D. It was a familiar ward. I had slept at Janet's side here three weeks ago. Four weeks before that, I had left here after spending time as a patient.

So, it came as no surprise when Mina Cho looked up from the nurses' desk and said, "You're becoming a common sight around here, Frank!"

"I'm just a regular angel of mercy."

A smile broke across her round face, but another voice broke our bonding moment. "More like angel of death. Ain't it, Sarge?"

My smile fell. "Detective Hammond. I thought I smelled brimstone."

"Funny, Parker." Lacy Hammond stood in the hallway on the far side of the nurses' station, looking as polished as always. Her tailored pantsuit complimented a not quite athletic frame that would have been downright pleasing in other attire. Her hazelnut hair had been cut short since the last time I saw her, hanging just past her earlobes.

Darren Norrington's squat form sat in a rigid chair by the door of a room I was certain hosted Prissy Vanderwal. He grinned and let Lacy press on.

"I hear you had a little trouble down at Harper Ellis."

"Nothing to speak of."

"Someone trying to tie up loose ends, Parker?"

The thought had occurred to me. "Jealous husband."

There was no mirth in Hammond's grin. "That's funny coming from a man staring down divorce."

"What do you want, Lacy?"

"Sarge and I have POI inquiries out on you. The moment your name hits our system." She pointed to her temple. "Right to the rec."

I looked at Norrington. "You in on this, too, Sarge?"

He shrugged. "I told you where I stood, but a lot changes in two weeks."

Hammond held up my card. "Like another Tycho City citizen beaten to a pulp after talking to you." She looked at Norrington. "Counting the lawyer and hooker, and all the dead people, we're talking what? A dozen?" Not by my count, but it was close. "I say we put Frank here in protective custody."

"I don't need your protection."

Hammond walked around the nurses' desk. She didn't speak again until her nose was touching mine, the soft smell of her peppermint breath ticking my nostrils. "I'm worried about protecting *them*." She motioned toward the room. "You wanna tell us what you talked about?"

I looked at Norrington. He was making a show of looking at a tablet in his lap. "The same thing I discussed with her brother. Rick."

"You aren't a cop anymore, Parker. Don't forget that."

That wasn't the complete truth. "I don't have to be. Still got my PI license."

"Thanks to Katsaros. I know. Is he the one who put the hit out on Lenny Marquez?" My face twisted in discomfort. "You might have plausible deniability, but this trail of destruction you're casting is gonna stop. One way, or the other."

I thought of a few cute retorts, but I needed to stay out of lockup, and I admired their persistence, even if it was getting on my nerves. Hammond continued, "You might not know this, Parker, but there are a lot of people not happy about the way a rogue like you took down one of our best for shit you pulled all the time."

I met her fierce gaze. "Wash almost put an innocent man in the airlock. Was I supposed to keep quiet about that?"

"And, Gordon? What's that all about, Detective? Word is Professional Standards is opening a new file on you over that one. What's that? Ten? Twelve?" I didn't offer a reply. "Well, maybe if you help us with Lenny Marquez, I can find my way to help you with that."

Lacy Hammond would sooner shoot me herself than help me with anything. "I have a lawyer. Take any plea deals up with her. Okay?"

"We're not here to plead. We're here to let you know the noose is tightening, and you have no friends in this police force anymore."

I thought about Dana Cooper. "That it?"

"For now." She stalked past me, toward the elevators.

Norrington put aside the tablet and followed her. I glared as he passed. He returned it with an "I tried to tell you" look.

Mina Cho had become engrossed in something on her desk. I frowned and walked to Prissy's room. Her head seemed three sizes too big; its mocha skin stretched and dark with bruising. A machine pushed air into her body through a tube in her mouth, the woman's life reduced to a series of beeps and squiggly lines on a monitor. She didn't know I was here, and something told me she never would. I walked away.

* * *

I left the hospital, weighed down by fatigue and depression. It was hard not to feel like a harbinger when everyone I talked to seemed to end up in the hospital or the morgue. But I wasn't the one being fed oxygen through a tube, and there were people counting on me. My pReC interrupted my thoughts. "What's up, Cyndi?"

"Well, it didn't take much to verify the reach of the New Sunrise Tabernacle's tentacles, but I wanted a current image."

I glanced over the crowded street. No familiar faces. "A regular spiritual advisor to the stars."

"I'm not talking spirituality, Frank. Tommy was one of those reporters I told you about. He was looking into dirty shit: extortion, bribery, sex trafficking. All on a level that would make the Lunatics green with envy." I remembered the packet Allyssa had provided me during my search for Lenny Marquez listing Petrovich as a client. "I've heard things."

"Well, he was digging, but got stonewalled everywhere he went. He finally gave up after getting mugged right on New Castle." New Castle Avenue was a north-south drag on the west end of the Upper City.

"Petrovich?"

Her avatar shrugged. "Tommy didn't like to talk about it, but whatever happened scared him. And he didn't scare easy."

I thought about the chances he took for Lenny Marquez and agreed. "So, what do you think?"

"Everyone knows about the church's obscene wealth. Most people assume it comes from his Upper City clientele, but Petrovich gets lots of donations from his Lower City temples." I considered that. Bilking the rich was one thing but conning the poor out of what little they had so you could live in style was a whole new level of depraved.

"They also run a number of New Sunrise Outreach centers all over the Upper and Lower City, scooping up lost kids and reshaping them into whole new people. I told you about the allegations of cult-like indoctrination, but nothing sticks."

I nodded. The only joke bigger than Wayne Petrovich's sincerity was the robotic loyalty of his parishioners. "They ever do any investigations?"

"Officially? No. Religion is a fickle thing, and government tends to stay out so long as the skeletons stay in the closet. His outreach centers produce productive, if somewhat weird, contributors to society. Besides, half the city council either goes to his church or his many functions."

I told Cyndi how Petrovich appeared on Lyssa's list of clients. "You think Tommy was looking into those parties?"

"That or the outreach centers." Her voice took on a transitory note. "Which brings me to your doctor. The records I can find suggest Camilla Zimmerman was straight-up Lower City hustler. She may or may not have hooked, but it's no exaggeration to say she lived by her own devices: petty larceny, small-time drug sales, con artistry."

I followed along in the file she'd sent me. "How did you get this? It's juvie stuff."

She smiled. "I have growing influence since Latham."

"You're welcome."

Her smile fell, and her honey eyes hardened. "It was earned, not given."

"Fair enough. What else have you got?"

"A court order sent her to the Ink Garden center as part of a plea deal. She was sixteen."

"Ink Garden," I repeated. Jacques Adrieux, Garrett Latham, and their brood had hailed from the Ink Garden. "Was she in with the Assassins?"

"Nothing on the record, but it was hard to make a living on the street without paying protection." I nodded, and she continued. "She's been on the straight and narrow ever since—at least on the record. Got the Grace Scholarship to attend Tycho City College, where she excelled. Went to Harper Ellis for her post grad and doctorate work."

"And now she teaches a bunch of wealthy, malcontent students and sponsors their clubs."

She nodded. "Kids ripe for reeducation. Anything about her strike you as radical?"

I remembered the edge in Zimmerman's eyes when she first looked at me. "She has a certain street savvy feel to her, but nothing about her screams zealot."

"Well, the church wouldn't give her a full ride unless she was doing 'God's work.' It's not that kind of charity."

I nodded at her insight. "She appear on any charters or as an officer in any church documents?"

"Petrovich hides behind his status as a religious figure. Nothing leaves church protection that isn't required by law."

I grunted my disgust. "What do your instincts say?"

"It's all a hell of a coincidence, but it's also pretty thin."

I remembered how Zimmerman denied even knowing Bertrand. "What's her middle name?"

"Cate."

"I was hoping for an 'M.'"

"Well, maybe it's her Reborn Name."

"Reborn Name?"

"Yeah, part of becoming your new better self at Sunrise Outreach is the Reborn Name, a new identity that leaves the old one in the past."

"Creepy."

"I told you; cult indoctrination."

"What about Hauser? Her name starts with an 'M.'"

"Not as much on her. Born in the Upper City to a midlevel casino manager and former dancer."

"Dancer, huh?"

"Not that kind, you perv; the legit, costumed kind on a family stage. Seems to have gotten into college on her own merits and is up for tenure.

No trouble, no record, and nothing in her public persona to indicate she had even a passing association with the church."

I felt M slipping through my fingers. Maybe I had to look elsewhere.

"Izquierda has an extensive history. When he's not getting into bar fights, he likes to get picked up on the walkways. He's bounced around to a number of jobs, mostly entry-level casino gigs. He once served as a bouncer in a Lower City bar called Adam's Treehouse."

Adam's was a gay bar that poked fun at the Christian icon of the same name. "He gay?"

Cyndi's eyes narrowed as if I'd just labeled everyone who'd ever had interest in the same sex. "He worked at a gay bar, so he had to be gay?"

I shrugged. "People like to spend their time in familiar surroundings."

Her glare lost some of its edge. "This isn't an in-depth bio, but I don't think so. My guess is he was campaigning for a singing gig." That made sense. "I'm sending his last known address and latest booking."

I pulled up the file. "AJ's Bar and Lounge."

"From what I've gathered, he's lucky to have that."

"Okay, you've been a big help. Thanks, Cyndi."

"Don't forget—"

"You'll be the first to know if I break this open."

"I'd better," she said, and was gone.

* * *

Janet Foxx was in the foyer when I got back. I glanced at the time. She was standing in front of the coffee maker, filling the entire office with that amazing, life-giving aroma. I savored a deep breath. "Don't you ever go home?"

She grinned and winced. Apparently, it hurt to smile. "There's no one waiting at home. Oscar is off chasing his next conquest. I can be just as lonely here." I tried to smile, but it fell flat. Janet pretended not to notice. "But here, I can charge five hundred bills an hour. How's the girl?"

"In a coma. They're not hopeful."

A heaviness settled between us. "But for the grace of God go I."

"Wouldn't have figured you for the religious type."

"Type? I don't know what type I am, but a higher power has to have guided us monkeys this far in the universe."

We both got a chuckle out of that. "Speaking of religions," I said, "what do *you* know about Petrovich?"

"The preacher?" I nodded. She handed me a coffee. "His status as a charlatan aside, he's one of the most ruthless figures in Tycho City."

"I'm starting to think he might have something to do with my Katsaros job."

"Oh, boy."

"Yeah. I may soon run afoul of his sense of privacy."

"Well, you do pick 'em, Frank." She tilted her head to analyze my face. "Is your nose twice its size?"

I pinched the bridge. It hurt. "Yeah. I think the guy who burned down my apartment took another poke at me."

"The Lunatic?"

I revisited my thoughts about how an assassin in the Lower City wasn't their schtick, how Scholar had shown up during my run-in with the Loonies outside Prissy Vanderwal's place, and T-Van's cuff 'em or cut 'em crew. *What were you doing there, Ken?* "I'm not so sure about that, anymore. Not their MO."

Foxx nodded, but it had the absent-minded quality of someone agreeing out of duty. "Oh, got a communiqué from the city attorney. New meeting about your job next Monday."

I drew my first sip of coffee. "I should have Bertrand Mellenburg chased down by then."

"Bertrand Mellenburg, Maggie Mellenburg's son?"

I cursed my carelessness and sighed. "Yeah. You know him?"

"Only his name."

I took another sip. "Well, he fell off the grid in the last two weeks or so, and she wants me to find him."

"What's Petrovich's involvement?"

"I found a church pamphlet in his room and the boy's professor used to attend the outreach center."

"That's not exactly a smoking gun."

"I didn't say I was ready to indict, Janet."

"Touchy, aren't we?"

She was right. "I'm sorry. Been a day."

"Aren't they all." She sipped at her cup. "Gonna go over a couple of cases and crash in the office."

I motioned down the hallway toward my quarters. "Gonna shower and do the same."

She smiled. "Good night, then."

"Good night."

"Oh, sometime in the next week, I need you to look over your case and discuss our strategy. I'd still like to get something in exchange for your newfound introspection." She tried to make it sound snarky, but I could hear admiration in her tone.

* * *

I soaked under the hot jet of water, thinking about everything I'd gathered. Bertrand spent a lot of time in with StUART. StUART was run by Camilla Zimmerman, who says she didn't recognize his name. She'd seemed truthful at the time, but now that I knew her history and paired it with that savvy look in her eye, maybe she was playing me.

On the other hand, there were these letters by M reliving carnal pleasures that would make Allyssa Ramacci blush. I thought of M and pictured frumpy Mary Hauser. It didn't feel right. Ca-milla—Milla? Maybe. I thought about the incomprehensible message Carrie DiPompo had tried to pass through the Dead Lizards' screeching mating call and felt real meaning in the lost words. Maybe she'd be more agreeable when Eugene wasn't around.

There were things to consider, but there were too many unanswered questions, too much I still didn't know. Maybe the father could help with that. The timer sounded, and I twisted under the jet and rinsed the soap from my body. I dried off and climbed into baggy shorts and a TCPD academy shirt.

The foyer was dark save a single spotlight above James's desk. The coffee remained in the carafe and would be good over ice in the morning.

I opened the cabinet beneath the coffee maker. The tiny fridge hosted drinks and snacks. Including bottles of beer I kept for such occasions. I pulled one out, popped the top, and walked to my room.

My reconstructed string chart hung on the wall, Rick its centerpiece. I stared hard at his picture as if he would speak from beyond the grave and cast light on this mystery. I remembered Prissy's words. *"Loonies ain't the only friends T-Van had, you know. Might've been someone else, someone he trusted a whole lot."* I weighed that and thought of something else. I stood and wrote it on a sticky note. *What was Ken Scholar doing at Prissy Vanderwal's?*

I stood back and studied the question, waiting for an answer. Was Scholar part of cuff 'em or cut 'em? I hesitated on the next question. Was he somehow partnered up with Rick? If so, what was the scheme? Debbie's words came back to me. *"He went down there two or three times a week."*

What did that mean for Rick? And, what could Scholar's connection be to all this? Those questions led me to some dark places, and meant I'd have to look for skeletons in closets I didn't want to. I drank a healthy swig of beer and remembered the letters.

I pulled them out and put them on the end table. I reread Mattie's letter and felt the scabs on my broken heart tear open. I fought back tears and pulled out a paper.

Mattie,

Reading your letter has brought me such joy. I have to admit, I like helping these people, but what gives me the strength to go on is the knowledge that each person I help brings me closer to the day I can be with you again.

I'm on a new case this week, a missing boy, and it makes me think of you, missing from my life in a very different way. I have a big hearing next week and I'll know more about the direction of our lives after that.

In the meantime, know I love and miss you in a way that words can't do justice to.

All My Love!

Dad

I read the letter and felt the distance between us. This had to end soon, or I would go crazy. I took a deep breath and sat back, staring at the ceiling.

Chapter Seven

I woke up with the beer still on the end table. I'd been having a dream. Mattie and I were having dinner at Jake's coffee shop. She was eating spaghetti, and I was eating yellow rice and beans. We had been talking and laughing and sharing our lives in the way most people take for granted. It warmed parts of my soul that had been empty for months. Waking up and realizing none of it was real killed a piece of me. I looked at the letter, still laying on the couch where I'd fallen asleep. It was inadequate, but it would also have to do. I folded it and placed it in an envelope.

I changed into dungarees and a grey crew neck under a sleek charcoal jacket. I slipped the envelope in my pocket and passed into the hallway. The foyer was as I'd left it five hours ago—dark with a spotlight over James's desk. I looked over the quiet office, lamented that I couldn't sleep in a little more, and stepped out into the early morning.

* * *

AJ's Lounge is as far from the glitz and glam of the downtown district as you can get and as close as the Upper City comes to the Lower. I stepped inside and remembered the Mine Shaft. Nothing about *this* bar's hole-in-the-wall motif was faked. It was a legit dive, complete with dirty floors, sour smell, and rough crowd.

A couple of tough-looking bruisers gave me double takes, but none seemed to want trouble. Izquierda was crooning away in some Spanglish hybrid that assaulted the ears. It was a vast improvement on the Dead Lizards, though that wasn't a high bar. I remembered Maggie's tale of his dream to sing before sold out crowds and felt a pang of pity. He'd clung to his ambition with the determination of a drowning man, but I couldn't say he'd been rewarded for his resolve.

I grabbed a corner booth at the back and watched the man belt away, sweat pouring down his golden-brown face. His expression was pure intensity, a concentrated attempt to infuse his song with emotion. But his abused, weary voice only managed desperation.

"Get you something, hun?"

I looked at a waitress as weary and tired as Carlo's voice. It was probably the house specialty. "Whatever you have in a bottle."

"Sure."

I watched her leave and tried to imagine a time when she had been youthful and energetic, but only saw the hard life she must be pushing though to look like that.

She brought me the beer, and I handed her a pair of twenties. "Keep one for yourself and give the other to Carlo. Tell him I need a few minutes of his time before he leaves." She looked at the notes with suspicion. "I can go talk to him myself, but I'm looking for someone to vouch for me. Understand?" She nodded, but I didn't see comprehension in her tiny eyes. "And bring me one of whatever he drinks. I'll pay for that with the beer."

Carlo broke into a painful version of "Tycho City," a repurposed song from Earth about New York, New York.

The waitress returned with his drink. "Carlo's winding down, now." I nodded and paid the thirteen-bill tab with a twenty and waved away the change. The wonder in the waitress's eyes was mixed with distrust. Maybe she thought I was gonna kill him.

I thought of Prissy Vanderwal and wondered. No one even pretended to care when he finished, and his crooning was replaced by the low murmur of bar conversation.

The waitress walked up and spoke to Carlo. I watched her hand him the note. He looked at it and then at me. His face was more honest and open than I'd expected from a man jumping from bar gig to bar gig. I raised my beer and gestured toward his drink on the table.

Carlo nodded and came straight over. Packing up could wait. "Do I know you?"

I looked at his full, round face and dark eyes, trying to see a sign of the boy I was looking for. It wasn't a total failure, but I would never have picked him out of a lineup. I gestured to the seat across from me. "No, but I'd like to borrow your memory for a few minutes, if that's all right."

"Gotta be at work in a couple of hours." Carlo worked as a maintenance tech in the Aces High Casino, downtown.

"This won't take long. Besides, every second means another layer of ice melts, and I doubt the drinks at this place can tolerate that for long."

He offered that open-faced joy, and I hated the world for treating Carlo Izquierda as it had. "All right. Have it your way." He squeezed his girth into the booth across from me and held out his hands in query.

"It's about Bertrand."

That good-natured openness was replaced by twenty years' hard living in the bars of Tycho City. "Maggie sent you?" I nodded. "He in trouble?"

"I'm not sure, yet. I thought you might be able to help me." Carlo eased back into his seat. I took that as an invitation to ask my questions. "You have much contact with Bertrand?"

I saw some of my sadness in his grin. "Some."

"His mom said you didn't have much of a relationship, at all."

"'That was what she wanted. It wasn't a class thing, not with her—I blew it." I nodded my understanding, and he gestured at his rotund form. "I didn't always look so old and fat or sound so—rough." His expression said the latter hurt worse than the former. "A young man singing away on a stage faces certain temptations he's not prepared to resist."

I thought of Rick. Some men were never prepared to resist those temptations.

"I was always gone. We'd been cut off by her family. Maggie was raising Bernie by herself. They told her if she wanted to cavort with a deadbeat musician, she could do it on her own." I offered a commiserating smile. "By the time I realized what I doing to our marriage, her mom showed up at our flat, a pReC full of holos." He smiled in teasing outrage. "Had hired one of you bastards to follow me around. Maggie was devastated.

"Anytime I ever get to feeling sorry for myself, I remember that look and all I did to earn it." His eyes teared, he cleared his throat, and moved on. "Anyhow, her family offered to bring her back into the fold if she would swear to never see me again."

I thought of the cold, composed woman and could see the path the reckless youth Carlo described. "But she didn't block you from his life."

"For a while, but Maggie's a good woman—and fair. Bertrand needed his papa." We shared the grief of estranged dads. "He was slow to come around, was angry over his mother. Said she'd never gotten over the way I did her, never let another man into her life."

And then she chose Dick. I marveled at how such a thing was possible but turned my thoughts toward the church brochure and steamy letters. "So, is he any good at keeping things from his mother?"

Carlo laughed at that. "What kid isn't?"

"When is the last time you talked to him?"

"Me? Oh, four or five weeks ago."

"That unusual?"

"It's the longest since the trouble with his mother started. I wasn't worried. He's at the age, right?"

"Trouble with his mom?"

"More like mom's boyfriend. That guy's a real asshole." He looked at me with sincere anger. "You know, Maggie deserves better, especially after what I put her through."

"He ever hit Bertrand?"

Anger clouded Carlo's expression. "You know something?"

"No. Just covering all the bases."

The anger ebbed, and I thought Dick owed me a life debt. "Dick is a good name for him. That's all."

"You know how he gets along with Maggie?"

"Dick? The way Bertrand tells it, they don't have much to do with each other, at all."

"Marriage of convenience?"

"For Dick, maybe, but I can't imagine what Maggie gets out of it."

I thought about all those years just her and Bertrand and imagined what him coming of age would do Maggie. "I think I understand." I changed the subject. "Tell me about the Sunrise Tabernacle."

His confusion was unmistakable. "The what?"

"The fancy temple in the west borough. I found a pamphlet in his desk."

Carlo shook his head. "That's news to me. His mother never had any use for the church and I"—he gestured at the lounge—"This isn't exactly God's country."

"So, who introduced him to the church?"

Carlo shrugged and looked out at the bar. I could hear the guesswork in his voice. "A girl?"

"Any ideas on which girl?"

"They're all the same at that age, aren't they?"

I laughed. I could see how he'd been a lady-killer in his youth. "I think the boys are all the same at that age, too."

This time Carlo laughed. "You have a point there. I'm part of his life but not those parts, if you know what I mean?"

"So, nothing about his friends?"

"We usually talked music and culture streams, but I did get the impression his friends were...never the same for very long." He slammed the drink and set the glass on the table. His words were bogged down by a moroseness I knew too well. "My son is a stranger to me, mister."

"Frank," I said.

"Frank." I saw years of regret fill those open, honest features. "He's his own person with his own life, and I'm barely a footnote."

I thought of Mattie and the letter in my pocket. "I understand."

He excused himself, and I offered a card, but there was no more laughing, no more good-natured smiles.

* * *

The Ink Garden Chapter of New Sunrise Outreach was on the Third Level of the Lower City. It was a well-painted, well-maintained storefront in the middle of the dusty, dirty block. The face had been recently painted a pleasing pale blue. The windows were clean and welcoming. Someone had painted a giant sun breaking the low horizon of the window; orange-yellow streaks reached toward the top frame. "God Loves a Second Chance" was painted in red letters. I could see the suggestion of a rec room beyond the glass, kids playing some sort of table game.

A blue and white awning reached out into the walkway, running the face of the center. A sign had been stenciled into the canvas: SUNRISE TABERNACLE OUTREACH CENTER. The crisp, white letters stood out in this narrow ravine of dusty, dirty poverty, a beacon in the dark. I glanced up the ravine toward the Fourth Level walkway. Strands of clothesline bridging the gap. Glum faces looked down from open windows, resigned despondency in every line.

I stepped under the awning toward the center's doors. They parted without a touch, and I felt the unmistakable presence of the Sunrise AI. "God loves when you accept His Grace," Petrovich's silky, voice drawled into my brain.

There was an unsettling scraping sensation in the base of my skull fostered the image of a beetle burrowing. A cresting wave of paranoia filled my soul, but I cast it aside. Nothing could be done about that, now. I drew the kerchief from my mouth and nose and looked the place over.

The inside of the building was as clean and neat as the outside. The piney, antiseptic smell of industrial cleaner filled my nostrils. The gloss of cobalt and white floor tiles reflected the overhead lights. The walls hadn't been painted in the last couple of days, but they were clean, with a soft blue color reminiscent of the outside decor.

The space to my right was a rec room with electronic and tabletop games. A pair of boys played foosball with youthful energy. They each wore a sky-blue jump suit and were too busy playing to even spare me a second glance. I watched them for several rounds; one a brown face with close-cropped hair and a great nose, the other scrawny and pale with long hair that hung low enough in the gravity to obscure his face.

Neither looked up once. Something about that bothered me, but I continued my journey. I approached a desk and was greeted by a holographic AI. It wore Petrovich's face and smiled as if it had been daydreaming about my visit for weeks. "Hello, Detective Frank Parker. Welcome to New Sunrise. Are you here for counseling services?" He blinked at me and the silence stretched, filled only by the rattling and scrape of foosball being played in silence.

"No," I said. "I came to ask you about a young lady who attended here a few years back."

The cordial expression never left the avatar's face, but its words became iron hard. "I'm afraid we do not supply that kind of information to outsiders."

"I understand. Perhaps there is a person I could talk to?"

The smile fell from the avatar's face. "I have told you all you are going to hear."

"But surely you have someone who—"

A door behind the counter opened, and two large men in embroidered shirts with counselor written on the left breast stepped out. They were tall. They were wide. And, they were grim-faced.

"I told you, Mr. Parker," the AI said. "We don't provide that here. Please do not return or I'll be forced to call the police."

The two men strode to the back of the counter and stared. Neither spoke, and I figured I'd better leave before they decided I did need counseling. "Take it easy," I said, and turned toward the door.

I paused and watched the kids for several long seconds. They kept playing with sullen intent as if on some kind of job, as if there was nothing else in the whole world but getting that ball into their opponent's goal, as if their lives depended on it.

I heard the shudder of the swinging counter door behind me and stepped through the automatic doors and onto the street. I waited until I was a full block away before looking over my shoulder. No one stood under the awning, but there seemed to be less sky-blue through the window than I would've expected.

Chapter Eight

I decided to press my luck while I was in the Lower City and descended toward the Floor and all its dangers, rather than rise toward the Train Level and its relative safety. I strode down dusty treads, keeping away from the nasty handrails. I pulled my microfiber kerchief as high on my nose as I dared and tried to act as if I belonged there. It was easy enough for a lifelong native, but lifelong natives met tragedy down here every day.

The Floor was several hundred lumens darker than the rest of the Lower City. It also never ceased to seem darker than the last time I was there. Foot traffic was sparser on the Floor. People only moved about when they had to, and then in groups. A lone wolf like me was liable to be a tempting target. But I was here to do something about that.

Harold's Sporting Goods was a dirty, grimy store in a long line of dirty, grimy stores. The gloom in either direction was palpable with shadows as thick as the unrelenting dust. But the streetlamp in front of the door shined like the sun, casting its harsh white spotlight on everyone coming and going.

I felt naked reaching for the door handle and felt a couple thousand prying eyes staring as I pushed my way inside. I waited for the doors to close behind me and let my eyes adjust to their new surroundings.

The tiny shop would have been cluttered under normal circumstances, but the low ceiling that bent my head forward made the place claustrophobic. The smell of vinyl and leather mingled with a sour funk somewhere between old sweat and mold. No patrons were here, but he did very little business over the counter.

The ringing bell drew a ghost of a man from the back room. I couldn't see apprehension in his demeanor, but hiding apprehension was the first lesson you learned on the Floor. He pulled his brown military surplus coat a little tighter and scowled. "I thought I told you to never come back."

I forced a smile. "You made it a frustrating experience, but I don't remember you saying that."

"Get out, before someone burns down my business."

"I would have thought you'd be happy to see me alive after all the trouble your job offer has gotten me."

"I've got my own problems. Like the price on your head."

I nodded. "Sure, but I'm still a cop. Cop killers don't walk."

"Tell that to your partner."

I managed not to reach across the counter. "I have money, this time."

"Oh? And, what does that mean to a dead man?"

"Ain't no one here but you and me."

Don glanced over my shoulder at the door. "You come to threaten me again with your authority, Mr. Policeman? 'Cause the way I hear it, you ain't got no friends in the PD these days."

"I told you; I have an expense account. Now, are you interested, or do I take my business elsewhere?"

Don licked his lips, the wheels behind his dark eyes churning. "What kind of expense account?"

"The big kind."

"I need ten thousand."

That got a laugh. "Yours isn't the lone palm I gotta grease, Don."

"Okay, five." That was quite a drop and would have been very telling had cost been my main concern.

"I'll give you two. Five hundred for a decent gun and rounds. Fifteen for a reference."

"A thousand for the gun. The reference depends on who it is."

I stared for several long seconds. "Okay." I plopped ten hundred-bill notes onto the counter. Don picked them up, fanned them, and stashed them into his pocket with such speed, I assumed he counted them via osmosis. The Kholar ten-mil appeared from beneath his counter with the same alacrity. I hefted the gun and looked it over. "Clean?"

"Would I sell anything less?"

I grunted a subtle disagreement and studied the blue steel at arm's length. "And the rounds?"

He placed a box of one hundred caseless rounds on the counter.

I raised an eyebrow. "One box for a thousand bills?" He frowned and put a second box on the counter. I nodded my approval.

"Now," he said with a note of urgency. "What is this reference you need?"

"Mickey Khatri used to...authenticate your products. You still using her?" Michelle "Mickey" Khatri is one of the finest electronic forgers and hackers in the city. She was also a wanted criminal.

"Yeah, that's not gonna happen."

"What was it you told me the last time I was here? You're not labor pool? Well, I'm not expecting you to be my recruiter, either. Tell her I have work for her. It's challenging. It's big. And I'm happy to compensate her for it."

Don studied me. "That's it?"

I slid a thousand bills across the table. "That's it."

He glared at the money. "I thought you offered two grand."

"I did, but I'm giving half now and half when she recs me." I smiled.

"I thought I wasn't labor pool."

"Consider it an incentive."

Don glared at the money as if it had betrayed him, but he swiped it off the table and stowed it in a pocket. "I'll do what I can."

"I knew you would." I stood to my full height, stooping at the neck, and was struck by a thought. "You have any countersurveillance packages?"

Don grinned at me. "Someone following you, Officer Parker?"

"More than one, Don. More than one."

* * *

I stood in the shadow of the Timmons Park apartment building, as if the Lower City was bright enough for there to be anything but gloom. Sparse foot traffic shuffled in both directions, kerchiefs pulled tight against the relentless dust.

I'd spent a lot of years knocking on doors, but I'd seldom dreaded knocking like I did with this one. There was time for one last, deep breath, then I pushed inside, the familiar smells of human fluids and trash assaulting my nose through my dust-crusted face cover.

The sounds of mundane conversation, anger, and ecstasy echoed at random doors up and down the hallways. I climbed past the second sublevel that hosted David Carson's apartment. *"Rick used to go down there to see him—once, twice a week."*

I closed my eyes against the knowledge my investigation had brought. Rick knew David Carson, a close associate of Giovanni Rocamora; the same David Carson who'd ended up murdered by Rocamora; the same David Carson who'd been Rick's super, whose murder case Rick had traded for without a word to me. *"Rick used to go down there to see him—once, twice a week."*

He knew this guy. Had spent time with him, once or twice a week. So, what was the connection? Was Rick providing protection on the side? Was David his paymaster? Were they killed when their operation was discovered? I thought of Tsaris and the Professional Standards investigation of the Three-three. That would fit. It would also explain why he was looking at me so hard. I was Rick's partner, even if I was oblivious to it all.

But could it be the other way around? Was Carson an informer and Rick his contact? The murders still go down the same way, but with different motives. What was it Prissy said? *"Loonies ain't the only friends T-Van had, you know. Might've been someone else, someone he trusted a whole lot."*

What if Rick had uncovered dirty cops? What if he was investigating—Tsaris could have been his handler! The cops found out and killed him! There was nothing comforting in the thought, but it would exonerate Rick. *"We gotta be careful on this one, partner...Someone's watching."*

The words hit me in the face, stopping me where I stood. Who was watching? I'd always thought he'd been talking about the way we'd been pushing the envelope, how we'd gone to that Sixth Level to hustle "Fast Eddie" Perkins. But what if he was afraid of giving Tsaris leverage on him? Or, maybe he was worried the cuff 'em or cut 'em crew was onto him. I shook off the thought. There was no way to know.

The door before me opened. I hadn't even realized I'd knocked. Debbie Sanchez glared with hard sapphires. Her short hair was unbrushed. I tried not to notice her nipples pushing against the T-shirt hanging to her knees and glimpsed the room over her shoulder. It looked different, neater. A man's grey coat had been neatly folded on the arm of the burgundy couch.

"It's you." She managed not to vomit, but her expression said it hadn't been easy.

"Yeah. I came to see how you're doing."

A voice called from inside. "Deb?" It was a man's, thick with sleep.

My face twisted in disgust, but she wasn't having it. "Don't you dare look at me like that, Frank Parker. At least I waited until he was dead to fuck around. Did he?" She turned her head into the apartment. "Hang on—it's someone from my ex-husband's work."

Debbie stepped outside, and I got a better look of the interior. A pair of men's shoes were on the floor, black and dressy, but built for walking. The door closed, leaving the two of us alone in the gloomy hallway. "What?"

I wondered where the kids were but knew better than to ask. She was hostile enough as it was. "I came to ask a few questions about Rick."

"Oh? You still looking to clear his good name?"

I considered that. "I'm trying to find the truth."

Her steely eyes studied me for several moments. Then she said, "What do you wanna know?"

"David Carson, you said he went down to see him two or three times a week. He ever say *anything* about why he was going down there?"

She sighed, her eyes staring into some far away thoughts. "No. Honestly, I—Yeah! One time he came back really late, and I was waiting for him. I told him I was tired of him going down to hang out with DC."

"DC?"

She frowned and flinched. "That's what he called him, David Carson, right?" I nodded. "Well, he comes back, and I let him have it. I accused him of banging some girl down there, Carter's sister, maybe. He laughed at me and said he was down there playing cards."

"Cards?"

"Yeah, he tells me he's been cleaning Carson's clock at poker. Even showed me the money."

It took me seconds to find my voice. "Why didn't you tell me?"

She shrugged and glanced down the hallway. "I didn't believe him, for one thing."

"Oh?"

"I know you worship him, Frank, but take it from the person who knew him best in the world. Rick was a lying piece of shit. I took it for granted he was lying and called him on his bullshit."

"You said he showed you money."

Her head nodded in sweeping, exaggerated motions. "I'll say! Ten thousand—cash." I cleared my throat, but she pressed the point. "Ten thousand, *exactly*." A bitter chuckle rose from her throat. "Who wins *exactly* ten thousand bills? I'm schlepping drinks and shaking my ass at the Vargus for a couple hundred in tips, and this guy pulls down ten grand in a card game? Right."

I wanted to cry. The image I'd had of Rick uncovering a bunch of dirty cops turned to dust in my mind. "How about a cop named Scholar, Ken Scholar. Any of that sound familiar?"

"Why are you asking about him?"

I shrugged and hedged the truth out of habit. "They worked together once during my suspension. I thought maybe..."

"You think he was dirty." Her voice was cold and certain. I nodded. "And you think this—Scholar could be in on it?"

I thought of him standing in the mouth of that alley. "I'm just looking for a place to start."

"Well, I don't know that name. Sorry."

I didn't think she was, but I'd gotten what I came for, and decided this was a good chance to end our conversation. "Thanks, Deb." We were turning in opposite directions, but I stopped. "And, Deb?"

She turned back, the door cracked. "I'm getting closer, and I'm going to find who did this."

Her tiny Adam's Apple bobbed in time to a hard swallow. Her smile looked forced and her eyes filled with tears. "I know."

* * *

I left Debbie and got back to the Upper City as fast as my feet would carry me. By the time I stood in the light of the neon skyscrapers, I was hungry. It had been a while since I'd had Joe's eggs and potatoes, and I decided his coffee would be good after the morning I'd had.

Joe's was still being renovated after a guy named JD Waters and I got into a gun battle with a Loonie hit squad. Waters had saved my life by holing the head of a Loonie named Rico at twenty paces. One and done. I stared at the booth. It had been roped off with faux police tape that forbade entry. Pair of life-sized holograms sat across from each other. I recognized the attire I'd been wearing on that fateful night on one. The other wore JD's outfit. It was us!

My hologram looked up at me. "I don't want no trouble, Otto. You stay back."

Waters smirked. "Yeah, we just wanna cup 'o coffee."

"You like it?" Joe leaned on the counter, a towel over his left shoulder.

"It's different, Joe."

He laughed. "Changed the name to go with the new motif: the Landmark Café! What do you think?"

I noted the crowd. "It seems to be popular."

"Popular? It's crazy! I can't cook the food fast enough. Hired five people in three weeks and—"

"Hey, Joe!"

He looked toward the voice. A teen behind the counter looked at him with a lost expression. "Be right there." He looked back to me. "Gotta go. Sit where you want.".

I took a seat in the corner by the window, my back to the wall and my eyes on the walkway beyond. "They aren't all out to kill you, you know." Joe put a cup of coffee on the table in front of me.

"Special blend?"

"Would anything else do for you?"

I smiled and drew a sip. "The Landmark Café, huh?"

A bright smile creased Joe's fleshy face. "I can't seat them all. It's crazy, but your shootout has turned me into the hottest spot in the city!"

"That make me a partner?"

Joe laughed. "I saved your ass that night. Cost me my 'bot, too." Mandy had been his robot servant that distracted the Loonies long enough for Waters and me to turn the table on them—literally. They'd tried to ventilate Joe for his efforts, but I was finding Joe to be a resourceful fella.

I made a show of looking at the holograms. "Very lifelike."

"You think so?" He bent down and hushed his voice. "Pulled your images off the media streams. Had the whole thing customized."

"Sounds expensive."

Joe waved the concern away. "Already made my investment back and then some."

"Shrewd." I glanced behind the counter. "All the work you've done, and you still have the bullet holes in the wall."

"All part of the attraction," said Joe. "Management wanted it covered up. Had to fight with 'em for a week about leaving them. People are still coming from all over the city, just to see where those Loonies bought it."

I noticed the "chalk" outline on the floor where Rico had fallen. "Charming."

He must've heard the disdain in my voice. "It's ghoulish, but what are you gonna do?"

"Run an ad in the tourist streams."

Joe chuckled. "I like the way you think, but I'm way ahead of yo—" Another employee called him. "Be back."

I pulled the love letters from my pocket and read all the pledges of love and promises of sexual fulfilment, the crafted love scenes and carnal memories that read like a brothel menu. I smiled and resisted a pang of jealousy. There was something here, something in the writing and structure. I considered Camilla's middle name, Cate, and savored her name, Ca-milla. Something about that felt right.

"Soup's up!" Joe was putting a plate of potatoes and eggs on the table in front of me.

"You never even took my order."

"On the house. You gonna complain?"

"How could I? It's my favorite."

Joe glanced at the outline on the floor, and I saw some of the horror from that night reflected in his small, dark eyes. He swept the emotion away, and looked at me with that warm, cocksure smile of his. "Consider it compensation for the man who made the Landmark a landmark."

"Well, in that case, what else is on the menu?"

"Don't go being ungrateful." The stack of letters caught his eye. "You back to work?"

I smiled and put the top one face down. "Yeah."

"Big secret?"

I shrugged. "Chasing a rich kid who's taken a vacation from reality."

"Sounds boring."

I held up the papers. "Reading his love letters."

He leaned forward and rolled his eyes to look down his upturned face. "Sexy?"

"Very."

He chuckled and leaned back. "Boring." The word grew two syllables in his mouth. "Teenagers may want sex all the time, but what the hell do they know about it? Right?"

And that was the feeling I'd been having. There was a note of real expertise here! "These letters were written by his—girlfriend."

"Student?"

"Not sure, yet, but she sounds experienced."

Joe feigned renewed interest. "Is that so?"

"Stop it, you perv. You've got a diner to run." He grinned and was gone.

I watched him leave and considered where to go now. Something kept coming back to me; the connection to New Sunrise Tabernacle might be thin, but it was there. What if I dug and found a deeper connection? I thought of the church AI and frowned. Sometimes you just had to take a chance.

Chapter Nine

The New Sunrise Tabernacle was a stone-and-glass manifestation of all I considered wrong with religion. The slate grey moonrock had been treated to take on a marble appearance. Its stained-glass windows featured generic symbols of religion: a bright sun on a pale blue background, angels looking down, and men bowing in worship.

New Sunrise was the latest iteration in a religious movement called Unity Worship. It purported to unite all of humanity's religions under one roof for the purpose of bringing people together. I wasn't sure how many people were being brought together, but, if the tabernacle was any indicator, lots of money was. I climbed the steps and passed into a magnificent foyer of immaculate faux marble.

The columns were all done in tiles that combined to form full color displays of religious scenes tied to many faiths, though the Abrahamic religions seemed to be the most represented. The same was true of the stained-glass scenes, paintings, and statues.

The church AI told me there were three directions I could go: left toward the outreach center and pantry for the poor, forward into the sanctuary, or right towards the business office. I turned right down a long corridor that curved along the massive sanctuary. More paintings and ornate statues went by as I walked. Golden chandeliers hung from high, arched ceilings, and I tried not to think of what the pantry for the poor or its outreach centers could do with the wealth on display.

"We try to make our place of worship pleasing to the eye in order to attract those who might be most in need of our help," the AI said with the soft southern twang of Wayne Petrovich, pastor and swindler-in-chief. *"Tycho City is well-known for its bright lights and ostentatious design. We have attempted to create a temple that will both conform to this environment while also standing out as a place of worship."*

I realized the AI was probing my mind and adjusting its monologue to change my perceptions. I tried to suppress my conscious thoughts and hoped it wouldn't ID me from the outreach center. Infiltrating AIs were forbidden in Tycho City Municipal Code because of all the implications associated with mind-bending AI and the damage they could do.

Moguls like Katsaros were always pushing the boundaries of these "suggestive AIs," but they had to be careful. Penalties were stiff. Tycho relied on an unearned reputation for being fair and just. If they let the casinos leave every tourist who passed through the town broke and dejected, it wouldn't take long for the market to dry up.

Religious institutions were a different matter. They were given more latitude, on the theory that God could better connect with His followers when guided by the benevolent hand of a computer. Church attorneys had called the experience spiritual and argued connecting with blessed programs was tantamount to a religious right and denying the opportunity suppressed religious freedom. Preachers and attorneys: a match made in Heaven.

"Remember," said AI Petrovich's velvet voice. *"Give a thousand bills and join the Lord's Legion. Get a visit with Pastor Wayne and a behind-the-scenes look at all the great works your gift is doing..."*

I pushed the voice from my head and hoped the familiar scraping sensation at the base of my skull was paranoia. Petrovich's main office stood behind a pair of heavy, dark-stained oak doors with gold lever handles. The right handle turned, and I stepped into an office that made the rest of the church look modest by comparison.

It was huge; bigger than Janet Foxx's expanse of an office, but that was where the similarities ended. Where Janet's office was stylish but simple in its décor, this place was crammed full of dark wood furniture and busts. The maroon carpet had the thickness of uncured concrete but was infinitely softer. The moonboard walls were painted an oak brown that would have made a lesser room seem claustrophobic, but not this monstrosity.

Instead, it provided a perfect contrast for the gold-framed paintings I assumed were commissioned for this very room. There were scenes from many religions, but these were more specific and seemed more Christian in their influence: the parting of the Red Sea, the struggle between David and Goliath, and the crucifixion of Jesus Christ stood out from my cultural studies classes as a boy.

But the object that drew the eye was the massive portrait hanging behind his assistant's desk. A gold-framed, full-bodied portrait of Reverend Wayne Petrovich took up most of the four and a half meters of the wall's height, the top frame resting half a meter short of the gold crown molding. He was dressed in the raiment of his church and smiling that broad smile, looking out with hard emeralds that punched though the soul. I held its gaze and felt the scraping in the base of my skull intensify.

"May I help you?" A pretty, heart-shaped face smiled from beneath a drape of dark hair.

"Yes, I'm here to see Pastor Wayne."

Her smile never faltered. "You have an appointment?"

"I'm afraid not."

Her smile grew wider, the sickly sweetness in her voice intensifying. "Pastor Wayne is a very busy man."

I handed her a Fillamayum card. "I understand, but it's a matter of grave importance."

She read the name, and her smile broke for a moment. "I'll tell him." Her eyes moved and lips quivered in a way that suggested she was accessing her pReC. The girl looked at me, her smile returning to its full brightness. "Pastor Wayne will be out to see you in a moment."

I offered a dim smile in return. "Thank you."

I took in the museum pieces around the room. Dark wood bookshelves with pictures of the pastor graduating seminary school. A blonde-haired woman who must be his wife smiled in pride over his shoulder. A collection of leather-bound books sat side by side: the Bible, Quran, and Torah. A few Hindi statues and at least one Buddha marked the shelves.

There were models, too, dioramas of the old church Petrovich had founded on the Third Level of the Lower City. The various versions of the church I was standing in, showing its incredible growth in the dozen or so years the man had been in the Upper City. The tabernacle had blossomed from a simple corner building in the southeastern section of the city, to a massive operation that spanned the entire block. An impressive collection of restaurants and cafés surrounded New Sunrise, attracted to the worship center's immense crowds. It was rumored the church owned several of these businesses. I didn't doubt that for a moment.

I turned from the tabernacle to the biggest and most impressive piece in the collection—the palatial home Petrovich had built for himself on the surface. The massive moonrock manse had been constructed in the classical Greco-Roman style with a collection of tall columns supporting the massive stone structure. Lesser structures were in evidence among the trees and brush and grass spanning the domed biosphere.

"Quite the homestead the pastor has for himself."

The first real frown crossed the girl's face. "God's Prophet should want for nothing."

Prophet? I'd never heard that parable before. "Well, He's certainly rewarded Pastor Petrovich."

A voice of warm honey drawled in answer. "The Sabbatical affords me a place to bring our most at-risk parishioners out, to get them away from the stresses of this hustle and bustle world. It gives them a chance to focus on themselves and their Godly relationship." I dismissed the level of the tithing required to purchase such solitude and offered my hand to the flesh and blood Wayne Petrovich. His grip was warm and strong. That faux smile stretched across his bronze face, dimpling smooth, clean-shaven cheeks. "What can I do for you, Detective?"

"I was hoping to ask you a few questions about a parishioner."

Pastor Petrovich nodded as if he'd expected nothing less. "Stacy, I'll be in the sanctuary, if you need me."

She beamed that smile of hers, and Petrovich waited until we were in the hallway, his voice and our footfalls echoing between the moonwalk floors and high ceilings. "Frank Parker, Private Detective." There was a pensive quality to his voice, as if he was sampling my name, trying to decide what to make of it. "You're the one who got Garrett Latham off death row." It wasn't a question.

"I was part of that."

Petrovich smiled. "The Lord loves a modest man. You worship, Detective Parker?" He turned right, through a set of double doors, and led me into a sanctuary that could host a sporting event. Three levels of balcony seating looked down on an altar that reminded me of a theater stage. "Twenty-five thousand, six hundred and seventy-two," he said into my musings.

I thought of that scratching in the base of my skull and wondered what his invasive AI could read. "That's a lot of people."

He grinned. "We host two services on Friday and Saturday and three on Sunday." He paused. "You've caught us in an afternoon lull."

Coming between services on a Saturday was the only way I would catch him. "How big is your parish?"

He smiled as if the notion was the furthest thing from his mind. "Whatever the Lord provides for the week." The "aw-shucks" routine didn't suit him. "But you didn't answer my question. Do you worship?"

I glanced at the altar and tried not to see the flag-draped coffin that had been there on my last visit. "I worship at the altar of justice."

Petrovich laughed. "As a lawman, I'd think you would." We took several more steps before he spoke again. "A man needs more than an occupation to make him whole."

I thought of Mattie. "He does."

He gave me a sidelong glance that made me think I was being appraised. "You said you had questions?"

I looked back at the altar. *"This is Tycho City Dispatch Operations issuing a final call out for Detective Richard Sanchez, faithful servant, dedicated father, loving husband, and loyal brother."* I pushed the memory away. "I'm looking into a disappearance. He might've been a parishioner of yours."

"Oh?"

"Bertrand Mellenburg."

Petrovich's brow furled; his mouth puffed into a thoughtful frown. "Disappeared, you say?"

"Yes."

He waited, as if giving me the chance to say more. When I didn't, he offered me my card. "I'm sorry, but you know we can't speak of members of the church."

I turned my head and narrowed my eyes. "Can't comment on members of the church? And if he's in danger?"

He shrugged. "We put our faith in the Lord."

"Surely a Christian man such as yourself would understand the needs of his parents—"

"The boy is an adult. I'm afraid I can't help you, Detective. Sorry.

And, this isn't a Christian church. All faiths are welcome."

I smirked. "Get more tithes that way."

Petrovich's smile said he'd heard it all before, and I couldn't hurt him, but the anger smoldering in those emeralds told a different tale. "More power to do His good works, Mr. Parker."

Mister Parker! I stopped midturn and looked back at the man. "Oh, I hope no harm comes to Bertrand, Mister Petrovich."

Some of the air came out of his smile. "Excuse me?"

"You knew Bertrand Mellenburg was of age. That tells me you know him, by name. And, I find that most curious. If anything unfortunate were to befall him and it was revealed you could have helped him...I'd hate to be you."

His deflated smile became a full-fledged frown, and the smoldering anger in his green eyes flared into dark rage.

I left him standing in the center aisle, glaring at my departure. I was outside and on the street when my pReC chimed with an address. Farah's Fantasyland, 46232 Beaudale Ct., in forty-five minutes.

Chapter Ten

Farah's was nestled in the ground-level floor of a high-rise, much like Joe's Landmark Café, but this place had a very different veneer. The doors were frosted glass with the head of an elephant etched into the face of each. Pulsing indigo light from the opposite side gave the salon a nightclub feel, though there was no booming music to complete the effect.

They parted, allowing cold air to roll over me, and I pressed into the chilly embrace. The floor was covered in soft black tiles. A pair of yellow theater light strips marked the walkway. They contrasted with the indigo lighting, providing a guide for guests.

A soothing voice filled my head. *"Welcome, Mr. Parker. Please follow the red line to your booth."* The line appeared in my second sight and led me through the dark blue salon. The clean, sterile smell and open emptiness of the floor gave the place a medical feel. Black curtains were drawn across individual berths along both walls, providing its users with privacy. One berth was empty, and I glanced at one of the "benches." It was padded, but had the feel of a gurney, with elongated arms reaching out at horizontal angles. It brought to mind a morgue, and I shuddered.

A faceless robot with a barrel-shaped head waited at the head of the bench. It gestured with long, sleek arms that glowed white in the dark light. I paused, an irrational, claustrophobic fear tugging at me.

"Please," the soothing voice said into my head, *"lie down. It is quite safe."*

I've never been a fan of letting people run around in my head. Now, we were gonna deep dive into my well of consciousness. But I didn't see another choice. It was either lay here or walk away from Bertrand. I glanced at the robot as if it could feel this awkward moment, its featureless, barrel face staring back.

"Please remove your shirt and lie on the couch." I did as it asked. The robot loomed over me, thin, mechanical fingers placing sticker probes on my chest and head. A pair of beams shot from a thick, black lens in the bot's chest, bisecting my face with measuring lasers.

"Please slip your head inside the helmet."

I cleared my throat, cursed my nervousness, and slid into the stationary helm mounted into the top of the bench. There was the sensation of movement in the helmet, metal cold on my skin, the whirring of servos filling its hollowness.

The robot helped the bench snare me in its grip; cold, heavy bands engulfed my chest and arms. Each leg was snared high and low. A sharp pain pierced my arm, followed by a cold sensation racing up from the site. My heart slowed, and my mind relaxed.

It found the range on the probes mounted on my head and linked to my pReC with a jolt. My body jerked in surprise, tensing against the restraints. A tingle rippled through me, and a strange detachment pulled my mind into a black shaft of emptiness. I grunted against the weight pressing down on my body as my speed built. My stomach twisted against the fall, forcing acidic vomit to the back of my throat.

The fall stopped without an impact. I opened my eyes. I was in a police interrogation room. Dana Cooper stood before me, but her expression and body language were wrong. "You're not Dana."

The woman smiled. "I'm not." I didn't like that and tried to block off my mind. "I can't read your mind. Well, I'm choosing not to. Don gave me some background, and I tried to choose an avatar that would prompt a positive response without appearing—manipulative."

"Great job." I motioned at the setting. "Was that why you chose an interrogation room?"

"It has the benefit of being familiar. You don't feel threatened, do you?"

I considered it. "It's fine."

"I was told you have a job."

"I do." She gestured for me to continue. "I need an avatar, maybe two."

"For?"

"AI breach, the Sunrise Tabernacle."

Tension filled the simulation, transmitting a ripple of nervous energy into my soul. "Petrovich has his own software people—good people."

"I never said it would be easy."

Dana grimaced. "Are you looking to penetrate their database?"

I thought about that. "I'm not sure what I'm gonna need."

"Then you should tell me what you have in mind." I did, and that tension intensified. "What you ask is not so simple. The designer's signature is hard to hide from forensic analysis."

"Meaning you could be at risk?"

Dana offered an alien smile. "Without question."

"Can you do it or not?"

"I can get you onto the premises without setting off the AI's security protocols, especially if you're going to be one of thousands, but breaking into the database is a very different thing."

That wasn't what I wanted to hear. "What would that take?"

"Some gadgets, some technique on your part, and lots of intense software, but I'll need to work on that." Several seconds ticked by. "I'll be sending you a package by courier... the moment you send me payment." She sent a link to my pReC, and I sent five grand to her account. "Okay, you'll get your package tonight. Go over it with care."

She waved her hand and the world around us fell into darkness.

* * *

I woke up on the couch. The helmet had been pulled from my head. The restraints had been removed, leaving my bare skin to shiver in the cold air.

A featureless barrel face looked down at me. "Thank you for visiting Farah's Fantasyland. Please come back soon!" I sat up, and almost rolled onto the floor. "You might feel a sensation of detachment for the next couple of hours."

I looked back at the bot. "You don't say."

It didn't seem to find me funny.

My feet found the floor, and I supported my body with outstretched arms. My pReC chronometer said it was after sixteen hundred. Mickey had kept me under while she slipped away, but she had been here. Direct-wire connection was the best way to prevent eavesdropping.

I took my first tenuous steps and managed to get first to the aisle, then to the empty front desk, and last onto the walkway outside. Even the muted light so far removed from the downtown glitz hurt my eyes. I considered my options but saw only one course of action. "Have you found him already?" Maggie's grey eyes gazed into my brain.

The hope I saw in her face made me feel terrible. "Not yet, but I am making some progress."

"That's great!"

"It is, but success breeds challenges. Can I come by to see you?"

Her eyes narrowed. "Sure."

"I'll be there in twenty minutes or so."

Chapter Eleven

Maggie saw me to the comfort of her balcony, the one that looked down on the city and up at the Earth in the same glorious moment. She added to the hospitality by offering me a drink. I accepted, and she poured two fingers from a crystal decanter into matching tumblers. I leaned on the railing and took the glass she offered me.

"I don't assume you came to pass the time."

"I didn't." We shared a smile, and I looked back at the sea of neons filling the canyon. "Is Dick here?"

"He's at the club." There was a note of defiant sadness, and I wondered if she was telling me or trying to convince me.

"Good. He was kind of in the way the last time."

"He's my husband." The outrage in her voice sounded hollow, or maybe I didn't care.

"I've got a few leads on Bertrand." She waited, all pretense of anger gone. "My initial interviews say he was heavy into a club called Student Union Against Repressive Treatment. That sound familiar to you?"

"Repressive Treatment?" She tasted the words and wrinkled her nose in disgust. "Doesn't sound like anything we've ever been a part of."

"No. It's a club at school."

"Really?"

"Yeah, the faculty sponsor of the club is a Camilla Zimmerman. That ring any bells?"

She shook her head. "You think she wrote those letters? That she's M?"

"It's a possibility," I said. "Still no idea who might've introduced him to the New Sunrise Tabernacle?"

"No. Do they have a presence on campus?"

"Not that I've established." I stood upright and leaned backward on the corner of the bannister, stretching both of my arms out so I could grip the top of the rails. I met her sharp gaze and chose my next words carefully. "It may be nothing, but I've had some conversations with the church that have been unproductive."

I told her about my conversation with Petrovich, his powerful AI, and the connection between Zimmerman and New Sunrise. I laid out my thoughts and told her about Khatri and the avatar.

When I finished, she said, "Isn't that illegal?"

"That's why it's so expensive."

I watched her weigh my words, but she surprised me when she spoke. "You would do that for my son?"

"Yes."

"Why?"

I thought of Mattie and the gulf separating us. "I'd want someone to do it for me."

Maggie studied me for several long moments. "You're a good man, Frank Parker."

I felt the self-deprecation in my smile. "I can think of a few hundred who'd disagree."

"Let them." She let the words hang between us. "You're here because you don't want Angelo to know about this."

My lips twisted. "My relationship with Mr. Katsaros is not entirely symbiotic."

"You don't need him knowing you're breaking the law in such a big way."

"You'd have made a great cop, Maggie."

She laughed at that. "No, thanks, property development and construction are far more profitable, thank you." My stomach growled, and her eyes grew wide. "I'm a terrible host! Would you like dinner?"

I gave a weak smile. "I'll have to pass. Tomorrow's a big day and I have lots to do before bed."

Maggie didn't argue, but she did follow me to the door.

I paused and looked at her. "This may get very expensive. I know Katsaros told you a five thousand-bill expense account would be enough but be prepared to spend more."

I tried to see suspicion in her face but saw none. "How much more?"

"Ten. To start. Khatri's expensive, and, if I do go head-to-head with the church, I'm gonna be using her a lot."

She nodded. "I'll get it set up."

"Thanks, Maggie."

* * *

I pushed through the front door of the office with bags in my hand. "Chinese!"

Janet had been lounging on the plush leather chair in her office. She looked up and grinned. "Yum!"

I strode past her and placed the bags on her massive, tidy desk. She jumped from the couch and grabbed a container of fried rice with algae chicken or pork. Her chopsticks found a huge portion of rice and crammed it into her mouth. The woman made sounds more suited for the bedroom than the dining room, and she offered me the container, her mouth still stuffed full of rice. "Want some?"

I forked orange chicken and chomped down on it, drawing a scowl.

"Barbarian."

I smiled. "Been a day."

She perked up. "Oh! I almost forgot. For you." She fetched a package from the corner of her desk. "Arrived by courier twenty minutes ago."

I gave it a curious look. A simple box, no labels, no identifying marks. "Sure it's not a bomb?"

"Frank! Don't say things like that."

I wasn't entirely joking, but I had a guess about who'd sent this. "I think it's my Sunday best for church tomorrow." I opened it, saw more boxes swathed in packing material including one with sleek black gloves on the label, and a tiny pill bottle.

"Church?"

"For Bertrand. I think I'm moving in the right direction." I took another bite, chewed, and swallowed. "But I might've taken a big step toward Rick's killer."

She turned her head and stopped chewing. I shared my thoughts on Prissy Vanderwal's words and described my conversation with Debbie.

"Ten grand?" Her voice was incredulous.

"Cash," I confirmed.

She sat back and stared through the walls into faraway thoughts. "Damn!"

"Yeah."

"Frank, I'm sorry."

"It doesn't matter. I'm still gonna find his killer." I looked into her discolored face. "We all deserve a little justice." She gave a solemn nod, and I swallowed the chicken. "You still have the files the city has on me?"

"Of course. We still have to go through our strategy."

"I know," I said. "But I'd prefer to go over that file while it's still fresh on my mind."

She recced it to me, and I retired to my room. I spent the next two hours reading about how I had wrecked a surveillance op and what a bad cop I was. Captain Rodson had filed an evaluation that characterized me as in need of "frequent and close supervision." His comments lashed me for following my "own investigation in contravention to direct orders."

But it was all stuff I'd read before. It was all stuff I'd been told. I closed the folder and stared at my string chart. I read the latest note. *What was Ken Scholar doing at Prissy Vanderwal's?*

Were you his partner, Ken? I'd never considered Ken a great cop. Was that an act? Was he actually just corrupt? I thought about how tired he always looked. Every cop looked that way, but maybe he was serving two masters. The possibility was enticing.

My pReC flashed. I'd received a static message from an anonymous source. It read: Good for one use only. I smiled and opened the file.

Chapter Twelve

"God loves forgiveness!" Unrestrained joy played across Reverend Wayne Petrovich's sweat-glistened face; his perfect white smile visible from the third row of the mezzanine without the benefit of the pReC stream flooding the auditorium. I'd considered sitting closer, but I was taking a big enough chance with the AI and its facial recognition. The last thing I needed was Petrovich's gaze falling on me in the front row.

I came in with the rush and engaged a nice family from uptown, gesturing and stooping to talk to their young children at the right times. It had been a weak effort at avoiding the facial recognition software but strolling in with a hoodie and mirrored glasses seemed a good way to end up having a mano a mano conversation with an usher.

"He is waiting for you to accept His Grace." Petrovich's voice was single malt Scotch. His tanned face contorted in the sweet pain of a truth he was desperate for his audience to accept. "It doesn't matter by what name you call him: Mohammed, Jesus, Yahweh, or Buddha. We are all brothers and sisters. We are all beset by demons, by urges. Our darker natures haunt us and bring us misery, only to blame it on others." The cadence was the perfect mix of wise father and concerned friend.

He waved his hands in dismissal. "That's not the way. Because, in the end, you are left with you and your demons." He paused for some well-placed amens and offered the crowd a broad, knowing grin. The gentle presence of the AI cautioned me. "Because that's how their master works, snuggling up to those darker natures we find acceptable, driving people from our lives one"—the look on his face said *wait for it*—"enemy at a time. And once you're alone and have no one in your life, where do you turn?"

The crowd shouted, "Demons!"

I thought Petrovich was gonna cry from unrestrained joy, his message received, his life's work complete. "Hallelujah!" Real tears rolled down his cheeks, and I was in awe at the show I was witnessing. "Please, let us reach out and forgive one another."

The man to my right turned and offered his hand. I returned the gesture and repeated left, rear, and center. The AI rejoiced at our fraternal display. A beautiful soprano filled the great hall. I didn't recognize the song, but I saw the deployment of the ushers and felt the AI press harder against my consciousness.

A casino comic's joke reached out from my memory. "I entered New Sunrise a filthy sinner with an expensive gambling habit and left a purified saint with an expensive church habit."

I accessed my pReC and fed a thousand Lunar bills into the virtual collection plate. The AI was delighted by this, and a warm blessing passed through my soul. I felt the whisper of a voice. *"God loves a generous man!"* My pReC flashed, and an icon hovered in my second sight: a pass to the Lord's Legion.

The singing came to a halt, and Petrovich stood on the pulpit, his hands clasped in joy, a broad smile with too much sincerity to be real spread across his face. "Thank you all for giving of your time. God loves the dedicated."

The crowd responded, "Amen!"

"Let us pray." He closed his eyes. "Lord, we come to you as servants." The crowd joined him in perfect unison. "Take from us our sins, lead us to wisdom, and heal us in our spirits!"

He grinned out at the congregation, a broad white smile of paternal approval on his face. "Go forth and live a righteous life."

The crowd responded, "God loves a righteous man!" A murmur consumed the hall, and the crowd began to break up. I decided not to touch the icon in my pReC. That could be problematic with my projected avatar. I turned toward the exit, hoping the things I'd heard about this church were accurate. A pair of ushers in funeral attire smiled and nodded as the congregation passed between them. The dusky one on my left stuck out a hand at my approach. "Mr. Lee?"

My avatar was named Charles Lee. "Yes?"

"The Lord loves a generous man!"

I smiled. "Just doing my part."

His smile grew brighter. "And humble!"

I was overtaken by the feeling that New Sunrise ushers weren't picked at random. "Why would I keep for myself that which could help others?"

The usher radiated joy, and I thought he might cry at the profundity of my words. "Amen! I'm Brother Toll, Rudy Toll."

"Good to meet you, Mr. Toll."

"Brother Toll."

"Brother Toll," I said.

"Pastor Wayne is always looking for folks for the Lord's Legion. People who are out to make a difference. People like you."

He left off people with money, but I didn't point it out. "I would be honored."

"Come!" he said, and led me through the thinning tide of departing worshippers. He seemed careful to smile and greet people as he went, calling most by name and offering his wishes and salutations to others not present. His words were so precise and accurate I wondered how much was coming from his mind and how much was being influenced by the AI. "How long have you come to church here?" I asked.

"Seven years," he said with an easy, unconcerned air. If the AI was picking up on any latent suspicion, it wasn't telling Toll. "I was touched by the spirit in Pandrom."

"Really?"

"Yep! I was up for drugs and grand theft. Pastor Rachael came out, spreading the word. She reached out in spirit and touched my very soul. That was it for me."

I managed not to shiver at the man's precise choice of words. "Amen!" I said, with less conviction than I should. Something nearing a scowl crossed his face, and I found a sheepish smile to hide behind. "Sorry, Brother Toll. I just can't imagine what that must be like, prison life."

His expression softened. "It was no joy ride, that's for sure, but it was nothing like the hell that awaits humanity's sinners. That's for sure."

We reached the front of the sanctuary and passed through a door to the left of the massive altar/stage that had hosted Petrovich, down a corridor, and through a pair of doors cast open where it T-ed off with another corridor. The greeting room was large and almost as luxurious as Petrovich's office. A linen-covered buffet table was laid out in the middle of the room. It was covered in bowls of fresh fruit and other luxurious foods that weren't often seen this side of a casino restaurant. Beautiful people in elegant dress gathered around, chatting and eating. There was no sign of usher escorts, and I concluded they must've come on their own, policed by faith or the AI.

"This is magnificent!" I said, without having to put exaggeration into my voice.

"It is," Brother Toll agreed. "Pastor Wayne believes the blessings of God are bestowed with greatest zeal on those who serve him best."

I bet he did. Aloud I said, "This is a great spread! Where does he get it?"

"Pandrom Prison has quite a hydroponic setup." Toll's voice held the pride of a man with insider knowledge. "It's one of the many benefits of ministering there."

I nodded, wondering what other benefits he enjoyed. "Pastor Wayne isn't here?"

"No, he's seeing the flock off. He'll be back as soon as the crowd clears."

A lean man with skin of coal and the eyes of an eagle stood in the center of the room. His heavy lips frowned in disapproval at me, and I was sure he'd seen through my cover.

"Ah, Deacon Frey!" said Toll, taking the man's hand. "This is Charles Lee, newest member of the Lord's Legion."

Something about the look that passed between them said *I'll be the judge of that.* But Frey turned with a broad, white smile that contrasted with his dark face and took my offered hand. "It's a pleasure to meet you, Brother Lee. I'm Deacon Remy Frey." He spoke with the same southern lilt Petrovich did, but the deep baritone was rich where Petrovich's speech was higher and thinner. "I heard of your generous tithe to the church. Magnificent!"

"I have more than I could spend. Why not give God the extra?"

"Indeed. God loves a generous man!" I was beginning to see a pattern. I commented again on the amazing spread, but Frey demurred. "God provides."

"Indeed." I cleared my throat and leaned close. "Is there a place I can use the restroom? The morning's coffee is catching up to me."

Frey's voice took on a patronizing tone. "Weakness of the flesh and the demons that take ahold of us." I forced a smile and waited.

He directed me down the leg of the T that ran behind the altar. I followed his directions, but, despite my bulging bladder, I didn't dare relieve myself. I gazed at the membrane glove I'd slipped over my hand. My pReC whirred to life, and the avatar spread tentacles that reached my fingers and toes. It was reading the data off Frey's shed skin cells through nanofibers to my nerves. The avatar grew within my consciousness, consuming all the space and pushing me aside. It was unsettling and sent me into a claustrophobic panic.

I dropped the pill Khatri had couriered to Foxx's office under my tongue. I felt a little better, and pushed back at the constricted feeling, willing myself to take slow, deep breaths. The hallway down which I'd traveled stood empty.

I turned from the way I'd come and walked on a thick burgundy carpet. Framed pictures featuring Petrovich in a myriad of church functions stared from the golden-brown walls on either side; christenings, holiday celebrations, weddings, and at least one funeral looked over the wide, impressive hallway.

I reached another T and turned left toward a door I knew would take me to the restricted offices in the back. The extravagances fell away as I approached the guts of the church; plush carpet became moonwalk tiles, high-quality paint turned into washable vinyl, the picture frames lost their fanciness, but not their frequency. Petrovich, it seemed, really liked himself.

There was a door at the end of the hallway, heavy metal under a dark wood facade. A tiny screen and visor were built into the wall to its right. The avatar's tentacles reached deep into my pReC and out to my eyes. I was wearing interactive contact lenses that had come in Khatri's care package.

I pressed my membrane-covered right hand against the screen and my eyes to the visor. If the avatar misread Frey's biometric data, or the information had become corrupted, I would be busted. If Frey didn't have clearance to be back here, I was busted. If a real person was watching their cameras, I was busted.

A red glow filled my eyes, scanning them from top to bottom. I wasn't sure how a surface contact lens was going to change the appearance of my retina, even with Frey's data, but the light faded, and the heavy door clacked.

I pulled on it and passed into the cool darkness. The glass face of an empty security station stared from my right. I cast a glance at empty chairs and dark electronics; they'd gotten complacent, relying on the scanner instead of having real guards. God loves a fickle man!

A long row of offices lined the left side of the corridor that lay before me. Cubicles spread out to my right, quiet and empty. I had a generic floor plan, but no description of what this room was or where I could find access to the church files I needed to find out about Bertrand Mellenburg. The pressure pushed in the base of my brain. The AI was taking a special interest in me.

I scanned the shadows. A lonely white light in the center of the room broke up what would have been pitch darkness in the office. I walked across grey carpet, the rustle of my clothes filling the silence.

I tried to access the network via my pReC, but even being in the office space wasn't enough. I would have to get to the mainframe. Frosted glass betraying the glow of blue and yellow lights drew my eye. This was going to be the place.

Another screen waited for my hand. Sweat was building under the membrane, and I wondered if it would botch the reading. I pressed hard and glanced over my shoulder. I could see the edge of the door past the security booth. Nothing.

The panel under my hand chirped, and the frosted glass panel slid aside. I pushed into the room before it had cleared my path. A black machine stood before me, whirring with blinking blue, yellow, and reds. A black tabletop lay across its face, where a new visor beckoned.

I took one last glance over my shoulder and sat on the tiny stool placed before the visor. I pressed my eyes to the visor and let the avatar do its work. Nothing happened for several long, tense moments, but then I felt as if I was falling and falling. The sickening motion left my stomach behind and cast me into a dark room filled with a blue glow.

Ribbons of brightly colored data streamed by in superhighways of information. I caught glimpses of images, pictures of people and events. Videos moved past my right. Text files passed my left. Others streamed at all heights and angles. Vids, pics, text, but nothing I could process. Jumbled, indistinguishable voices chattered, filling the space around me with a low buzz. I looked up. The scene was repeated for as far as the eye could see. It was too much.

I called into the streams, "I'm looking for Bertrand Mellenburg!"

The ribbons continued to stream, and the voices continued to chatter. I reached out and touched the nearest stream. The room bloomed with vivid colors and images. I was in the stream, living the information. It was a sunlit room of yellows and whites with a rich wood floor. A family stood with a baby, smiling at me. The warm, caring voice of a woman filled the air. "Here at New Sunrise Outreach, we know life can go from this..."

The world around me changed. On a Lower City street, dark, dingy, a dying light flickered, dancing over the youth's pallid face. A world-weary depression etched her features, a needle in her right hand. I knew without being told this was the baby who'd been held with such affection in the parents' arms.

"...to this, without understanding where we went wrong."

The scene flashed again, a clean bunk in the New Sunrise Outreach center. The girl was lying on the bed, staring up at the ceiling. Then a series of scenes; a classroom, a worship service, and the girl sweeping, mopping, and washing dishes. "God sees the path that we can't and sets us on it. All we have to do is let him show us the way."

We were back in the sunroom. Mom and dad were older but smiling. The daughter was wedged between them in an embrace of family love. I tried not to think of Suzanne and Mattie, but the hole in my heart wailed in pain.

I pushed out of the stream, heaving, tears trying to break through my façade. Now was not the time for this. The ribbons of data were still calling to me. Sensory overload. I looked around, called names, reached out with my pReC, and found a single door hidden in the blue dimness.

The door did nothing to call the eye to it, a dull spot in a dull background, hiding behind the bright contrasts of data streams. No voices called from its jamb. No lights showed from the cracks. No placard labeled its purpose. I looked over the ribbons of information. Bertrand was here, somewhere, but the cop in me said something interesting was behind that door.

I stepped through the streams and reached for the door. It wouldn't open. I closed my eyes and reached out through my pReC. The avatar reinforced me, and the door gave way, opening beneath Frey's authorization. Pressure in the base of my skull built. The AI was taking a closer look, probing me. The room was a bank of old-fashioned mailboxes, each tiny, burnished metal door denying access to all who didn't have the key. Would Frey, a simple deacon, have access to intense security files? Or, was he more than a deacon?

Most of the mailboxes had people's names. Dennis Calloway, Walter Ginson, Emily Harris. Others had legal or military-sounding code words. Operation Dinah, Lex Talionis, and Sword of Damocles. I tried one box after another—nothing, nothing, more nothing. I frowned.

I was back on the stool, turning my head to stare through the frosted glass. The lights had come on in the office. I turned off the computer and looked for places to hide. A one-meter by one-meter maintenance access panel was the sole option. I looked back, heart racing. I could try to play it straight, tell him I was lost. But that would never work, not in the nerve center to the church's greatest secrets. I crept with as little noise as I could to the back of the room and slid the panel off with the barest squeak. God loves a sneaky man.

A dark shape moved across the frosted glass, his silhouette backlit by the lonely light in the office. I crouched inside and gripped the vent cover's louvers and eased the cover onto its seating grooves. I waited until I heard the chimes of access before lowering it into place, hoping the beeps would cover the squeak.

"Hello!" It was Frey's voice. I didn't dare look out. Sweat poured in the suffocating heat, but I dare not approach the panel. "I know you're here, Lee. If that's your real name."

I heard nothing to lead me to believe he was getting closer, but the fans that whirred in near silence outside, roared in here. I stared at the slots on the panel, waiting for a mahogany face to appear, to see a big brown hand reaching for the louvers. But nothing came.

The sound of the door closing created a moment of decision. Was he standing there, waiting me out? Had he left, looking for me elsewhere? I didn't take long to decide; if he was still in the room, it was because he was creeping up to look inside this compartment and would find me anyway. If he was gone, I was roasting for no reason.

I gave him a sixty count before sliding the panel from its seat and easing into the cool air of the isolation room. I replaced the panel, waited, and listened. Nothing. I hadn't heard him leave, but if he'd left while I was in hell's wind tunnel, I'd have never heard him. I waited another sixty count and took a longing look at the visor. Truth was there, but I'd overstayed my welcome. I pressed my sweaty hand against the screen and held an anxious breath. It chimed and opened to an empty office.

I strode across the barren space and through the front door like I owned it. I pulled the membrane from my hand and stuffed it into my pocket. The corridor was empty, and cool on my roasted skin. I pulled my coat off and draped it over my shoulder in a carefree gesture of faux innocence. I passed the hallway from which I'd launched my subversive operation and took the next left along the back of the altar. It was restricted, of course, part of Petrovich's private sanctum, but that was the most innocuous transgression I'd committed in the last ten minutes.

The gold-handled double door to the private green room where Petrovich was supposed to hang out before his shows passed to my left as the backstage entrance to the altar passed on my right. The T-intersection loomed ahead. A closed door stood in my way, and a ripple of panic passed through me. Did I need authorization to get through the door? But there was no sign of a sensor panel.

I blew out a breath, opened the door, and came face-to-face with Petrovich. His plastic smile was gone. Dour, pursed lips took its place, accusing green embers glared from a face tight with anger. "Detective... Parker. Isn't it?"

I held his gaze, trying to avoid the bruiser companions flanking him. "I'm honored you remember."

"Don't be. Have we done something to wrong you, Detective?"

"I'm just going where the case takes me."

A frosty smile tugged at the corners of his mouth. "Religious worship is the last bastion of privacy, Detective. I would think a *former* police officer would understand that."

"Asking questions isn't illegal."

"But breaking into my database is very illegal. As is projecting a false electronic ID."

I nodded. "So, call the cops. Turn over your data records, grant them access to your database. Maybe you can explain to them what Lex Talionis is or explain the Sword of Damocles to them."

His bronze face reddened. "I won't have to explain anything, Detective. This is a place of worship, immune from prying eyes."

"Until you invite them," I lied. Tycho law was very clear; all they would have to show is that I had broken into their files using a false eID and outlawed software. The contents of those files were irrelevant and usually redacted from court records, if their content was exposed at all.

"If a sworn officer comes across felonious activity in the course of his duties..." I shrugged for emphasis.

He glared for several long moments, but Wayne Petrovich was a preacher, not a lawyer. He stepped close, his cinnamon breath caressing my nose. "I'm going to have to ask you to leave and not come back, Detective."

I grinned. "God loves the resolute."

He made no gestures and made no sounds, but the ushers stepped forward as one. If I stayed any longer, I'd get that police visit and maybe some broken bones for my trouble.

I pushed between them and moved up the corridor, toward the front of the church. Petrovich's joyous, inspired voice turned into iron. "Make sure he leaves. If he tries to come back, make him regret it."

"Yes, Prophet." There was something about a big, stormtrooper type calling a man Prophet that sent shivers down my spine. The big men followed me to the door and stood at the top of the steps until I was out of sight.

* * *

I waited until I could no longer feel the AI scratching at the base of my skull and recced Cyndi. "Do the names Dennis Calloway, Walter Ginson, or Emily Harris mean anything to you?"

She got a pensive look on her face. "Yeah—their names came up during my research."

"And?"

"And, what? I told you I was doing a surface dig. I stayed away from bitter feuds."

"Well, the church has files on these people."

"Church files? What kind of church files?"

"The secret kind." I glanced over my shoulder. No one seemed to be there, but this wouldn't be the first time my senses lied to me.

"You got a look at the church's files?"

"It took some doing and culminated in a very uncomfortable confrontation with Petrovich, but, yeah. I saw some titles."

"Be careful, Frank. Petrovich is a ruthless bastard."

"Yeah. His people actually call him Prophet."

"It's a lot easier to get into his little cult than it is to get out."

"Cult?"

"I don't know what else you'd call it. Remember Degrass and Palmer last year?"

"The sex traffickers?" Tommy Henson had done a few articles on them. I'd come across them doing research on the Marquez case. "I remember."

"It wasn't widely reported, but they had been members of the Lord's Legion."

"They were part of the Legion?"

"What do you know about the Legion?"

I shrugged. "They made me a member."

"You?"

"Don't you laugh. I had all the credentials necessary."

"Money?"

I couldn't hold back the laugh. "And lots of it."

"Well, being in the Legion didn't do Degrass and Palmer any good. They took a plea deal of twenty-five to life in Pandrom."

I recalled the mountain of charges facing the pair. "Twenty-five to life? That has a chance at parole! What leverage did the defense have to pull that off?"

"Wouldn't you like to know? The records were sealed by court order to 'protect the victims.'"

"You don't sound like you buy the official story."

"Of course, I don't," Cyndi confirmed. "You're a cop. How many times have you seen the victim's identity redacted, but the file left as a matter of public record? The only time they pull the whole thing is when the victim is well-known and easily identified."

"And, these vics were never IDed?"

"Not during my coverage."

"So, it wasn't to protect them." I remembered Allyssa Ramacci telling me how Petrovich was one of her patrons. I wondered if he wasn't underwriting the carnal bliss to make his subjects more malleable if things went sideways. He wouldn't be the first to utilize that kind of tactic. "This guy's supposed to be a preacher, not a mafioso."

"Like I said, you know how to pick 'em."

I took another paranoid look over my shoulder. It's not paranoia if it's true. The pReC interrupted my philosophizing. The face looked familiar to me, but the name jumped out. Winnie Odili!

"I gotta take this one, Cyndi. Thanks for everything!" I broke the connection. And looked into bloodshot eyes. They pleaded through the data stream connecting us. "Parker?"

"Yeah."

"I need to meet you."

Chapter Thirteen

I stood outside in the foot traffic, staring at the coffee shop with its burnished metal siding and clean windows. One of the last times I saw my baby girl was right here. Mattie! I heaved a sigh and stepped through the door. I placed my hand on the upper doorframe as I passed through, sticking the fisheye cam from Don's countersurveillance package to watch my back. I hoped I looked smooth and natural doing it, but the motion felt as graceful as falling downstairs. The magnetic switch triggered the device, and it began to communicate with my pReC, filling my second sight with a view of the walkway outside. I gave the crowd a careful look, but nothing jumped out at me.

Winnie had already arrived, drinking coffee with shaky hands. Her dark face was pale in the cheeks. Her full lips were pressed together in streetwise apprehension.

"Doesn't look like you need that stuff," I said, motioning at the riptides in her coffee cup.

"Prissy's dead. Pulled her off the damned machines this morning."

"I'm sorr—"

"Spare us both, cop. You don't give a shit about some Lower City girl any more than them doctors at the hospital."

I looked around the room. A few people glanced at the loudness of her voice, but no one seemed too interested. My second sight said foot traffic was light outside with nothing threatening or suspicious.

"I loved T, you know." I hadn't known, but I nodded. "He was gonna be a made man after setting that cop up."

"He killed him? The cop?"

She shook her head. "Nah."

"Who did?"

"No idea."

"Why'd they kill him?"

She shrugged. "Some big gang secret needed protectin'."

My heart raced. "What secret?"

"T never said."

Outside, a familiar form walked by the front of the shop. He kept walking, and I held my attention on the conversation at hand. "You know anyone else involved in this?"

She shrugged and shook her head. "I do know it was a big deal to the Rock."

I'd been glancing at my shadow, but her words perked me up. "Rocamora? What was his interest?"

"Don't know, but T said he gave him his orders hisself—very specific." Bitterness stained her pretty face. "That made T so happy."

"So, why say something now?"

She broke down and started to blubber. I glanced around the room and saw more than annoyed glances. Winnie was drawing attention. Her voice came out low and hard. "They killed him. Killed Prissy. All to protect that fuck Rocamora and his crew."

I cringed. Talking like that in the Lower City was tantamount to drinking poison. "Protect him from what? From who?"

"Wish I knew. I'd tell you everything, right here."

I believed her. "Did he ever say anything to you about David Carson?"

Winnie looked like I'd struck her. "Wachu know about DC?"

"I know he worked Rocamora's club. That he was supposed to have been very close to the Rock's girlfriend."

She blew out a disgusted laugh. "Yeah, that was DC. Couldn't keep his damn pants on."

"Were you... close?"

"No!" Her evasive eyes and taut face told a different tale, but I didn't push it. "He was always working an angle. T couldn't stand him." I nodded and prodded her. "DC wasn't no damned good as a DJ, but he considered hisself a real T-Town Killa."

T-Town was a big Lower City DJ and composer of what passed for music in some circles. "So, what was he doing at the Revolution?"

"He was the Rock's boy. You didn't tell the Rock's boy no."

"What do you mean the Rock's boy?"

She shrugged. "Just that. Wasn't no damned secret. Everyone knew."

I tried to remember the intel sheets on Carson. They had all given him loose ties to the Lunatics and Rocamora but nothing direct. "Were he and Rocamora friends from the old days?"

Winnie's laugh was harsh. "You're funny, cop. DC was a poser, a fake. He was about as gangster as you."

I thought of "Fast Eddie" Perkins and Kelly Gordon, and I wondered how gangster I really was. "So, what was his story?"

Winnie shook her head. "No one knew."

"But they talked about it?"

"Yeah, everyone talked."

"And?"

"And, nothin'. Just a bunch of rumors."

"Like?"

"You name it. He had dirt on the Rock. Others said the Rock was soft on DC because he'd done him a solid once. Shit like that. Ain't no one know for sure."

"No word on the favor?"

"Supposed to be some super street spy bullshit—real DL stuff."

"What do you think?"

"Me?" Winnie's eyes moved across the coffeehouse. "I try not to."

"But, if you were..."

She seemed to choose her words with care. "I think the Rock don't care nothing about no one but the Rock. That bullshit about him being soft on DC because of somethin' he did in the old days? Bullshit. And, DC having dirt on the Rock don't feel right, either. The Rock'd just kill him and leave him for everyone to see." She paused and seemed to think hard on something. "Nah, DC was still useful, else the Rock'd have killed him years ago. Simple as that."

That was my read, too. "And DC never told you anything about any of this when you were together?"

Her face spasmed. "What?"

"Come on, Winnie, I've been lied to too many times to not see it when you told me you hadn't slept with him."

She scowled, and I thought she might storm out, but she said, "I didn't know him then. You know? He talked all badass, like he was somethin'. I was just a young gir—"

"I'm not judging you, Winn, just tell me what he said."

She stopped and looked like she'd bitten into a lemon. "He used to say he made the Rock who he was, that without him, Rocamora would still be a hustling street punk slinging K or Plant."

"He say why?"

"Nah," Winnie chuckled. "One time—afterwards, he bragged to me that the Rock paid him to bang bitches. Just braggin' away."

"Brave talk."

"Not so brave. Later, he begged me not to say nothin'. Told me the Rock would kill him, if it got out."

"Did you?"

"Say something?" I nodded, and she gave me a smile. "I didn't get this far being stupid, cop. Other girls, though..."

I nodded. "Aren't you afraid they'll kill you for talking to me?"

"So, what if they do? Just another Lower City whore to add to the rest, right?"

I tried to look at her but failed. "Well, I think enough people have died. I—"

"I told you, don't give me that concerned cop bullshit, just 'cause I can help you. They think they can intimidate me by killing everyone I care about. Well, they've just given me nothing to lose." She rolled her eyes. "I just as soon not help the likes of you, but, if that's the only way"—she gathered her things and stood—"then I guess that's the only way, but that don't mean I gotta be happy about it."

"One more thing." She stopped and waited. "Cuff 'em or cut 'em, that mean anything to you?" She shook her head. "How about dirty cops? You ever hear about dirty cops linked to the Rock or DC?"

She snorted a laugh. "Everybody knows if you're gonna get to the top of the game, you gotta pay the toll."

"Pay the toll? What the hell does that mean?"

"Police always gonna get their cut. You wanna get to the top, you gotta cut 'em in."

"And, these cops, you don't know who they are?"

She snorted again. "What the hell makes you think I wanna know something like that? It gets a lot harder to breathe when you know shit like that."

I watched Winnie go and started to connect some ugly dots. There wasn't much new there, but it helped confirm some things. Rock was definitely working with or for a cabal of dirty cops. Was Rick one of them? What other conclusion was there to draw? *"Rick used to go down there to see him—once, twice a week."* I thought of Tsaris's investigation. Had he cornered Rick and tried to turn him? *"We gotta be careful on this one, partner... Someone's watching."*

Things were starting to come together, but I didn't like the picture it was painting. "What were you working on, Rick?" I stood and walked into the street. My tail turned and stepped into a souvenir shop, but I didn't even look his way. I turned left and strode past him on my way to the Lower City. I watched him follow me in the fisheye for as long as it stayed in range.

* * *

I walked past the Third Region checkpoint. A moose of a man stood at the intake line in body armor, sporting hardware rarely seen this side of the military. "Virg!" Virgil's massive head turned my way. His dark face scowled at me, but I thought I could detect a note of camaraderie in those big features. I grinned. "Admit it; you're starting to like me."

Virgil's scowl deepened, but something of the smile he was suppressing broke through, a display of white teeth on his dark face. My smile broadened and I made my way to a locker. The pistol I'd bought at Harold's waited there. I pulled it from its hiding place and tucked it into my waistband.

I covered my face with the kerchief, taking care not to glance back at my tail. The crowd was heavy this time of day, and I had to weave in and out through the throng. I didn't look. If he was following, he had to be close, and eye contact at this range could prove awkward. Besides, I was willing to bet he wouldn't do me right here. Though he might have, if he knew where I was going.

Fernando's was a restaurant on the Third Level, a cop favorite for its fast, portable food and good prices and quality, considering its limitations. I stepped inside and took a seat at the back of the restaurant, next to the hallway leading to the bathrooms and emergency exit.

A pair of lean, golden-brown legs came into my peripheral vision. I looked up into a face that had been the subject of male fantasies. She wore the tiny shorts and tied off button-down shirt for which she was famous... maybe her face wasn't the only subject of the fantasies, after all.

"Frank! How are you?"

"Alive, Carmen. How are you?"

"Still working here." There was a resigned quality to her voice, but we both knew plenty of people didn't have the benefit of any job. She leaned close, her smile becoming conspiratorial. "You working a job?"

I grinned. "A good cop never tells."

She nodded as if we were having a secret conversation no one else could understand. Maybe we were.

"Cuban sandwich and *plantanos.*"

"Tea?"

"Please."

She smiled and turned to the counter. I watched her shorts struggle to keep ahold of her ass cheeks and pulled up my pReC. "This is Dana Cooper of the Thirty-third Precinct. If you..." I broke the connection and turned back to the feed from the second fisheye. I'd placed it on Fernando's door, same as at Jake's.

My tail was out there, watching the door from across the walkway. I pulled the case files up on my pReC and compared them to the conversation with Winnie; swimming upstream against the idea that Rick had been on the take, wanting to see something else in the tea leaves.

"He used to say he made the Rock who he was, that without him, Rocamora would still be a hustling street punk slinging K or Plant." Rocamora had been a lowly dealer five short years ago. He'd been the beneficiary of some fortuitous arrests by the TCPD and some well-timed violence on his part.

I thought of the rumors Rocamora had provided dirt on his superiors in return for selective enforcement of Tycho City law and weighed that against Tsaris's investigation and this David Carson story. I remembered how Dana had called him a player. I remember rejecting the notion he'd been stupid enough to bed Monique Benson, but had he been dumb enough to spill Rocamora's secrets to pry her out of her underwear? *"I've seen men do some stupid shit for pussy."*

Again, I was inclined to agree with Dana's wisdom. So, had Carson been his connection to TCPD? Had he—I raged against the pain to put it together—had he been the go-between for Rick and Rocamora? Had he been the link?

"He went down there two or three times a week."

"...Carson's maintenance job? Timmons Park. Rick didn't mention that to a single person... Scholar thinks that Rick was Giovanni's Hook."

Scholar! I remember that shitbird skulking around while I was interviewing Pricilla, hours before she did her rounds with a Lunatic hit squad. Was he a good cop, following up on his case, or was he in league with Rick? They'd worked together. *"Last time they stuck me with that asshat, Scholar. Working next to him is like a goddamned prison sentence."*

I thought again of Rick's warning. *"Someone's watching."* Was Scholar one of the watchers? Were they working together? *"Loonies ain't the only friends T-Van had, you know."* Too many unanswered questions. My head swirled with paranoid vertigo.

Carmen brought my food; I watched her leave and ate. My shadow hovered two doors down across the walkway and around the corner. His view was blurry, smudged by the collection of dust in the air. He would have some answers. I bit into the Cuban sandwich. The bread was flaky and crispy, but those who'd had the real thing said it was a poor stand-in. Us locals loved it.

Three-quarters of the first half had disappeared in three bites. I washed it with gritty tea and finished the first half before Carmen had set her next plate. Cops eat fast under normal circumstances, but my masticating was keeping up with my churning mind. I wanted to finish, so I could get on to my next objective. I accessed the restaurant AI with my pReC and paid, leaving Carmen a generous tip.

I headed down the restroom corridor, passed it, and hit the back door. The alarm jangled, and I upped my pace. My shadow perked up, staring into the grimy glass face of the restaurant. I reached the end of the alley that emptied onto Twelfth Ave and turned south, crossed Dover Street and turned east, keeping close to the building faces. He'd moved from his perch and was trying to glimpse into Fernando's.

I entered the frame in my pReC, meters away and closing. I waited until I was a meter from the man before drawing the pistol from my waistband and pushing it into his back.

"That's enough." The man stiffened but didn't move or speak. "You've tried to kill me twice, now, and even you might get lucky, if I give you enough Mulligans. Wanna tell me what that was all about?"

"Go fuck yourself." His voice was hoarse, and I got the impression he was disguising it.

I stood closer than I would've liked, but it was the only way with so many people around. "Get on your knees and cross your legs." The man knelt in a slow, deliberate motion, his hands out to his sides, but he tumbled forward on all fours. I leaned forward and gripped a handful of hoodie. "Up! On your knee—"

My shadow turned, throwing a handful of moon dust into my face. The dust went into my eyes, my nose, and worst of all my big, open mouth. It hit the back of my throat and cascaded into my windpipe. My lungs recoiled from the insult, racking my body with spasms that almost made me forget about being in a blind fight for my life.

I think it was the back of his head that smashed my nose. He slapped the gun from my hand and pushed me hard in the light gravity. I kept my feet, coughing and hacking. I was able to clear my right eye enough to see him reaching for his gun. I stepped forward, gripped the pistol, and caught the man over the eye with an elbow. I bent the man's arm hard, breaking the gun from his grasp. I chopped at his face, catching his throat with my forearm. A short, underhanded punch found its way into his solar plexus and my knee found his testicles.

He lashed out with an elbow, catching me above my closed left eye, and I met his lunging face with a headbutt. I caught a cheekbone or the corner of his forehead, because nothing crunched or broke, but an explosion of pain erupted where the hard bone hit my face.

The man toppled backward, kicking up a plume of dust. He rolled into the fall and rose on the backside, running the other way. He punched a hole through the crowd gathered to watch our struggle. I made sure he was gone, but I was coughing and wheezing too much pursue.

I took a knee. Dirty rivulets of tears soon ran down a face white with moon dust. It was several minutes before I looked down on a Tycon Industries caseless. I reached into my pocket, pulled out the napkin I'd pilfered from Fernando's, and used it to pick up the gun. I stared at its blue steel, wrapped it in the napkin, and put it in my pocket. I could almost see straight and glanced around. A crowd had gathered to watch, but none spoke. "Any of you seen my gun?"

The crowd responded by breaking up and fading into the larger flow, still moving past. Great! I was still watching them go when Dana Cooper's image filled my second sight. "Dana! I thought you'd forgotten I existed!"

"No, as much as I've tried."

"I was hoping for your help with a missing persons case I've picked up."

"Looking to bring another runaway sex worker to justice, Frank?"

Ouch. "Fuck you, Dana! I need your help. You gonna help me or not?"

There was a long pause. "What do you need, Frank?"

"Someone just tried to kill me. I think it's the same guy who burned down my apartment."

"I thought we decided that was the Loonies."

"I've had a change of heart on that one. I'm

starting to think he's related to Rick's murder. Maybe even the trigger man."

She was quiet for several long seconds. "You really think that?"

I thought about it. "Yeah, I think I do."

"Where are you?"

"Fernando's."

"I'll be there in thirty."

Chapter Fourteen

I slid the gun across the table, still wrapped in the napkin. "Thanks for coming down, Dana. I need to know who this douche bag is and who's paying him to take shots at me."

"Whoever it is, they're not getting their money's worth."

"You could at least pretend to give a shit that someone's trying to kill me." She grinned and dropped the gun in a bag sans napkin, folded the package carefully, and put the whole thing into her purse. "Besides," I continued. "He's proving slippery enough."

"How'd he get away, if you had the drop on him?"

"Bastard dusted my face. I was too close. Too many people around, and I was trying to take him down easy. Lucky he didn't plug me."

"Sounds like you're both slippery."

I laughed. "Maybe so, Dana. Maybe so."

"You're still looking for Rick's killer?"

"Someone has to."

She frowned and looked out the window. "You may find shit you don't want to, Frank."

"Like?"

"Like Rick being dirty. Like the fact that you're throwing your career and family away for a crooked cop."

I thought about what Winnie told me. *"Some big gang secret needed protectin'."*

"I'm willing to go where the case takes me."

Dana looked across the restaurant and nodded. "I'll see what I can find out." She stood and was gone.

* * *

I turned back to my gritty tea, but I could still see the view of the fisheye through my second sight. Dana turned up the walkway past a pair of clown-faced figures bumming close to the spot I'd had my run-in with the shadow. I frowned, cursing my stupidity. I should've known better than to linger after the fight, but I'd been so eager to meet up with Dana it hadn't occurred to me.

A deep green face looked out from beneath a shock of neon green hair. Coincidence? I didn't have much use for coincidences. I thought about the alley, but these guys hadn't come alone. Another pair of Loonies lounged at the east end of the block, hemming me in. Surely, they'd been smart enough to put someone on the back door. I should've put a fisheye there, but it had seemed so inconsequential at the time.

I mulled over my problem and found one advantage; they didn't know they'd been spotted. It wasn't much of a hand, but what choice did I have? An inspiration struck me, and I decided to use a page from my shadow's book. I waved at Carmen. "Yes, Frank?"

"Can you bring me a to-go cup?" I held up my glass. It was almost full. "I only need the cup."

She smiled and brought me an empty cellulose cup. I thanked her and stood, leaving the remnants of my iced tea sweating on the table. The walkway was congested, its occupants kicking up a choking cloud of moon dust. I slipped a kerchief over my face and knelt to adjust the cuff of my pants.

The Loonies stood in the view of the fisheye, straining to find me, bodies turned into coiled springs. I scooped a healthy dose of dust from the walkway gutter into my empty cup and rose. I never even glanced at the men but kept my attention on the transmission from the fisheye. Mr. Green relaxed and shared a glance with the man next to him. It was the thug with the pale blue face and silver hair. Another Loonie appeared on my side of the street, apparently from his position at the end of the alley onto Twelfth. The expansive view of the fisheye let me see his partner emerge at the opposite end of the block.

I was glad I'd chosen this tack. The alley would have been a death trap. I shifted my focus back on the three Lunatics closest to me and slipped through the crowd, allowing it to take me toward the middle of the street, a casual attempt to thread the needle that was doomed to fail. Fortunately, I wasn't counting on it to succeed.

The fisheye looked on as Mr. Green shared a smirk with Silver Hair. He motioned, and the pair sauntered into the crowd, malicious glee on their faces. My grip on the cup tightened. Laugh it up, assholes.

I was steps from Twelfth when Mr. Green put a hand on my shoulder. "We meet agai—"

His mouth was open all the way when the dust hit him in the face, turning his green face clown-white. It was an improvement. A croaking cough escaped his crusted lips, and he clutched at his throat. I'd tried to swipe the cup to catch both of them in the dust plume, but Silver Hair turned and only received a glancing blow from what was left over.

There was no time to relish the moment. The clown from the alley was approaching my six. If he didn't know something was up, he would soon. The foot traffic parted as he closed, giving me the chance I was hoping for. I stepped back with my right foot and put all my weight into the retrograde movement of my elbow.

I caught the Lunatic in his grinning mouth, and the feeling of his lips shredding between my elbow and his teeth gave me great joy. I spun, reached down, grabbed a handful of groin and shirt, and lifted him in the low G. Silver Hair was recovering from his brush with the dust. I heaved his friend into his chest and sent the pair bowling across the dusty walkway.

I was running before the cloud had time to blossom. The stairs were crowded, and I tried not to trample people in my flight. I had never been the one to chase the rabbit, and a glance over my shoulder told me I didn't make a good rabbit, either.

Inky faces and bright hair were already reaching the foot of the stairs. "Move! Coming through. Watch out!" I called from burning lungs. "Step aside, police matter!"

I hit the Fourth Mezzanine and made the turn on the landing, climbing the narrow chasm of the Lower City, through the dust and the grime, past the dirty, disheveled masses. My breath was hot in my kerchief and sour with fear. The indignant shouts of civilians and angry threats of the Loonies filled my ears.

I took two steps at a time, then three, then four. My legs protested and lungs burned. I made the Fifth Mezzanine and turned. I only needed to make the Sixth Level and the safety of the sanctuary of the TRS. A train rattled on the elevated trestle, urging me on. I was going to make it.

That's when they stepped into my path. A big, red-faced man with bright yellow hair and a thin, lithe woman with shorn head and metal studs circling her jet black crown. An ash grey stripe covered her eyes and ran down her nose and mouth. It hugged the contours of the features, forming a misshapen hourglass. She smiled with black lips and teeth that had been filed into points.

She used the terrain of the stairs to catapult down at me, catching me in the chest and sending me careening backward down the stairs. I bowled through my pursuers and landed hard on the landing below.

I tried to rise, but the impact had taken my last bit of strength. The woman landed on my chest with both feet. I felt a pop, but couldn't muster a proper scream, leaving me to cough and hack and wheeze. Another blow found my ribs. Someone's foot found my crotch. I tried to cover myself, putting my arms over my head. The first baton strike hit me in the forearm, and another landed hard on my leg, just missing my knee. A fist slipped past my drawn arms, catching me in the temple. Another found my ear. Another the point of my cheek. They were coming too fast and furious to count, but the explosion ended them all.

Someone shouted, in a deep baritone, "That's enough! Get out of here, or the next blast will turn half of you into a pink spray."

Several long moments passed before a Goliath loomed over me. I gazed up into a familiar face. I hadn't thought Virgil could look any bigger, but I was wrong. He seemed twice his normal size from the walkway. "Aw, shit!" he said. "If I'd have known it was you, I'd have stayed up on the platform."

Chapter Fifteen

"Coffee?" The mug looked like a child's teacup in Virgil's massive paw.

I pulled the compress from my head and smiled. "Thanks." It was fresh-brewed and soothed my sand-blasted throat. I grunted and nodded my head in satisfaction. "Damn fine."

Virgil grinned. "Dog shit should be damn fine as close as those Loonies had been to punching your ticket."

I grinned. "Who said this isn't dog shit?"

The big man suppressed a smile and turned serious. "You're quite the hit with these Lunatics, Parker. Sooner or later one of them is gonna kill you."

I offered Virgil a bloody grin. This was the second time he'd saved me from Loonies chasing me from the Lower City. "Not as long as I have you around, Virg."

Virgil grunted. "Shit! Ain't gonna be around all the time. Don't wanna be. Got enough problems of my own."

The Third Region medic poked my tender rib cage, jerking me back to reality. He was my second in two days. I was either living very right or very wrong. "Ouch!"

"You say you heard a crack?"

"Pop. Crack. Something."

The medic nodded. "No way to be sure, but probably cracked a rib."

I took a deep breath, and my body recoiled from the pain. The medic nodded as if this confirmed some inner diagnosis. "Yep. Probably cracked a rib. No tellin' what else could be busted up in there. Doc'd probably do a full body scan to rule out occult—hidden injuries."

"I'm fine, gonna be sore a couple of days."

The medic shrugged and reached into his bag. "Allergies?" I shook my head, and he tossed me a packet of pills. "These'll keep the edge off as long as you don't run around getting into more fights."

"I'll be careful."

"Shit!" Virgil said, and let go a hearty laugh.

The medic shrugged and put a tablet in my face. "No law against being stupid."

I signed with his stylet and scowled at his words. He didn't seem impressed and returned the implement to the breast pocket of his blue jumpsuit. "Have a good day, Mr. Parker."

I waited until the door closed before looking at Virgil. "So, I'm free to go?"

Virgil grinned back. "'Fraid not." I plopped a pair of the pills into my mouth and washed them down with cooling coffee. "We've been asked to hold on to you until a TCPD rep can get here."

I thought of my encounter at the hospital with Hammond. "You can't hold me forever, you know."

"Listen, Parker, I can hold you for twenty hours as a witness, longer if actual interviewing is involved. If I decide I wanna suspect you of an actual crime, that time limit goes to seventy-two. But you know that. So, unless you want a lesson in the limits of your civil rights, I say you keep it to yourself."

Virgil was right. He was just doing his job. "Yeah, sorry." Virgil nodded, and I said, "It's Frank."

Virgil turned back to me. "What's that?"

"Call me Frank. You've earned it. Twice."

Virgil's big brown eyes studied me and nodded. "Okay, Frank. You need anything else?"

"Nah, I'll just wait here for Hammond."

Virgil nodded and left. Hammond didn't show up. Willis Rodson did. "Holy shit, Frank! You look like hell."

"I've been worse."

Rodson smiled. He turned and nodded at Virgil in the doorway. Virgil glanced at me and was gone. Rodson waited until he was outside before turning on his Concerned Supervisor face. "Word on the street is someone tried to take a swipe at you."

"The street, huh?"

Rodson smiled. "Seriously, you doin' okay?"

"Like I said, been worse."

Rodson shrugged out of his grey jacket and folded it and placed it on a convenient chair. He propped a black shod foot on the seat and leaned close. "How long am I supposed to let Cooper be your errand girl before putting a stop to it?" So, he wasn't a complete stooge. I shrugged and looked at the wall. He pressed his point. "TCPD is a municipal agency. We're not an extension of the Frank Parker Detective Agency."

I stared through the cuffed grey slacks and well-worn shoes at a life I was no longer part of. "If it makes you feel better, she's not been much help, lately."

"And why do you think that is?"

I rolled that thought through my brain and nodded. "Shouldn't my lawyer be here for this?"

"She's here." Janet Foxx stood in the doorway. "Sergeant Milloy was generous enough to call me on your behalf, Frank."

"Sergeant Milloy?"

"Virgil Milloy."

I glanced at the big man in the doorway behind her. He smiled. Rodson frowned. "I wasn't interrogating him, counselor. I was just advising him—"

"I heard. Consider him advised. Are you filing any charges?"

He chuckled, the concerned supervisor a distant memory. "As if I need them."

"So, no, then."

Rodson held her haughty stare with an angry scowl of his own. "No."

Foxx's face lit up. "Excellent! Now, get out."

He frowned at her, glared at me, and grabbed his coat. I wondered what Captain Rod might have to say to Virgil, but I recalled Virgil's size and decided Rodson didn't have the balls.

Foxx waited until he was gone and turned on me. "You've been busy." She reached into her briefcase and tossed a pulp document on the desk next to me.

I read the bold letters: Second District Court of Tycho and... "Motion for Protective Order?"

"It's already been granted ex parte by Judge Harven. You can't go anywhere near Petrovich or his churches—including the outreach centers. Apparently, you've been making quite the impression everywhere you go."

"Yeah, I'm a regular party favor."

"Well, don't take this lightly. He got it processed in four hours on a Sunday. That's no mean feat."

Even my murder warrants took longer on Sundays.

She looked at the door and frowned. "How about Rodson? What did he have to say?"

"Nothing. He'd just gotten here." I scooted my butt from the desktop and started toward the door. "I think my last bridge to the TCPD is burned."

"I'm sorry to hear that, Frank."

I paused at the door and thought of all I'd learned this morning. "Me, too. I think."

* * *

Foxx and I rode to the surface. "Listen, Frank, we need to go over the strategy we're going with for the hearing next week."

I nodded, only half listening. "Let me run something by you, Janet."

Her long glance said she didn't appreciate the forthcoming change of subject. "Yes?"

I told her about my week, from Pricilla to Winnie. I told her about Rick's paranoid behavior and what Debbie had said about him going to Carson's two or three times a week.

She listened, her irritation forgotten. "And you want what from me? To look into my crystal ball and tell you Rick was clean?"

I laughed at my own desperation. "Yeah, I guess I do."

A smile creased her tiny mouth, but it was a sad one. "You're the trained investigator. I don't have to tell you he could have been undercover or recruited to turn state's evidence."

"But he took the Carson case—traded for it. I busted his balls over that, asked him if he was trying to get into the gang unit."

"And you're wondering why he would just trade for the case instead of telling the investigators what he knew?" I nodded. "Maybe he did. Scholar, Rodson, and Tsaris are all superiors, right?"

I considered that. Had he gone to someone else? If so, who? "That's something else. Scholar was there."

"Where?"

"I ran into him after interviewing Pricilla, outside her apartment."

"Was he following you or her?"

I shrugged. "No way to know for sure, but him turning up there seems suspicious."

Foxx nodded. "Or, he's conducting an investigation of his own."

"Without his partner?"

"Rick did it." She turned a knowing smile at me. "So, did you, as I recall." I grinned. Her car was on a pad outside the tram station. The yawning door opened to a plush, ruby red interior. My pReC pinged.

"It's Cyndi," I told her. "I have to take this." I turned my attention to the pReC. "Talk to me, Cyndi!"

"Got the rundown on those names for you."

"Awesome!" I gave Foxx a thumbs up and turned away from the car. "Lay it on me."

"Dennis Calloway was once an assistant minister and very public face of the church. No one knows what went wrong, but he was disgraced after being caught stealing hundreds of thousands from church coffers."

I chuckled. "Stupid Dennis! Didn't he know that was Petrovich's hard-stolen money?"

"If he stole it at all."

"Excuse me?"

"He's protested his innocence the whole time, saying the church set him up."

I thought about Petrovich and considered the balls it would take to steal from him. "What kind of case did they have?"

"Solid. Money had been flowing from church holdings to Calloway's accounts in increments for almost a year before he was caught."

"So, Calloway's full of shit."

"Maybe. There is evidence to suggest Calloway's relationship with the church had been in decline for years. It's possible he started building a nest egg for his pending departure."

"But?"

"But he contended Petrovich saw the threat coming and put his toadies up to framing the embezzlement scheme on him as an insurance policy."

"So, the big bad preacher set him up?" I didn't like Petrovich, but that seemed a step too far.

"It gets better. A common allegation of former members is that Petrovich expected church allegiance to supersede loyalty to the family."

"Turning your own family into church spies." It was a common tactic in cults.

Cyndi nodded. "Calloway's own wife, Jillian, and daughter Nadia have publicly shunned him, calling him a thief and a heretic. Court records imply that he had every intention of fighting the charges but settled after a private meeting with church attorneys."

I looked over the files she sent me. "The prosecutor wasn't even there?"

"Not according to court records, though the events of the meeting are off the record. His official conviction is for petty theft with a public sentence and full restitution. He also was sentenced to a hundred hours community service—at New Sunrise Outreach centers. He's now divorced and broken, living in the Lower City. He signed an NDA and can't discuss the events as part of the criminal plea. So, I wouldn't expect much from him."

Nondisclosure agreements were binding with clearly defined and harsh penalties for violating their terms.

"Wow!"

"Wow, indeed."

"Ginson?"

"Walter Ginson was an elder, the Lord's Legion's Legate, innermost circle, but his story is very different. He actually left the church after an 'unspecified disagreement' with the leadership. Apparently, it came up fast and he literally stormed out of a meeting, never to return."

"Any indication of what it was about?"

"Nothing firm, but Ginson seems to believe Petrovich was carrying on with his wife."

"His wife?"

"Don't sound so surprised. Most cult leaders claim sexual rights over the entire congregation. It establishes their dominance."

I considered that and remembered the way the church officers called him Prophet. "And Ginson got tired of sharing?"

"Or wanted cut in. What I do know is that he was accused and convicted of carrying on inappropriate relationships with minor children."

"What?"

"Yep. Gonna be in Pandrom until he's old and grey."

I remembered my brief stay at Pandrom. "If the prisoners don't kill him first. Who made the accusation?"

"Several children in the church. The transcripts are redacted to protect the accusers."

I pondered this and thought again of coincidence. "Lawsuits from the family?"

"Against the church? No. Didn't even leave."

"And, no one gets suspicious?"

"You're the cop. You tell me what they could do without someone from the inside coming forward?"

I remembered how hard it was to penetrate the gangs, and we had legislation on our side. Churches were shielded by religious freedom laws, and this was the largest, most powerful church in the city. "Harris?"

"She might've been the smart one. Left the church and went straight to the city attorney. Retaining the services of a private lawyer was challenging. Apparently, every litigator worth having has done work for the church or its affiliates, creating a conflict of interest for them."

"Attorney ethics." I turned the oxymoron into profanity.

Cyndy chuckled her agreement. "Well, she found a small firm to take her case, but I'm not sure how that's going."

"So, she's not under a gag order?"

"Other than one her attorney might have advised? No."

I nodded at this. "I'll start with her. You have the address?"

Cyndi sent it to me. "Good luck, Frank. You're tangling with a gorilla."

"Thanks, Cyndi. Tell Brenda I said hey."

Chapter Sixteen

The address Cyndi gave me wasn't far from Drane Street and the apartment where Simon Frost and his crew caught up with Lenny Marquez and Tommy Henson. I stood in the walkway outside the entrance to Emily Harris's building. Traffic was always light in this part of town and a middle-aged couple sitting on a bench at the end of the block stood out to me.

Their posture seemed stiff and contrived, and I caught the woman's gaze lingering on the front door to Harris's building as they talked. I made note of her plain brown features before glancing in the other direction. No one lounged on that corner, but there was a greasy spoon with windows that reflected more light than they let in. I'd done plenty of surveilling and figured that was a pretty good place for a stakeout.

I stepped onto the vestibule platform, activating the security AI. The holographic avatar had a peachy coloration with a salt-and-pepper mustache over a dour frown. He spoke with the stiff formality of a butler. "May I help you?"

"Yes," I said. "I'm here for Miss Harris's flat, room twelve fifteen."

"Please wait while I ring her."

A woman's face replaced the avatar. The lines on her wary face spoke of yearlong stress. "Who are you? Reporter? I already told you people, I—"

"I'm not a reporter."

"A cop?"

"Of sorts."

"Private cop." It wasn't a question. "Who're you working for?"

"I'm looking for a missing person." I tried not to think about the last time I'd been in this neighborhood looking for a missing person.

"Well, whoever you're looking for isn't here."

"That doesn't mean you can't help me find him."

"I don't talk to strangers."

"I'm Frank."

"Seriously, what do you want, Frank?"

"I'm searching for a young man who may have disappeared into the New Sunrise Tabernacle."

Her laugh was mirthless. "Then say goodbye."

"I'm serious. I want to find him before it's too late."

"If he's in the church, then it's already too late." Her posture shifted in a way that suggested she was turning away.

I stepped closer to the camera. "Please. There aren't a lot of options, and I need something."

She frowned, and her eyes darted over my shoulder. "And how do I know the church didn't send you?"

I wanted to ask if she thought a church would do such a thing, but I remembered Cyndi's report and the couple outside. "You'll have to trust me."

Resigned softness tempered her world-weary features, and the door slid aside.

I passed through a no-frills foyer and rode the elevator to the twelfth floor. I knocked on a white door in a narrow corridor of clean carpet and old paint. The door opened to the same haggard face on a scrawny body. I had seen pics from Cyndi's story. The change made me wonder if she didn't have a drug or health problem.

The tired smile she flashed me said the unspoken concern wasn't foreign to her. She held her arms up and out, twisting her body in display. "Not what you expected? Stress is a killer."

"Stress?" I asked from behind my smile.

Her face soured. "Let's just say no good deed goes unpunished."

I nodded as if I'd never heard truer words and obeyed her unspoken offer to enter. Her apartment was simple and tidy, like the rest of the building.

"I hope you're a better detective than a salesman, Frank."

I shrugged. "I win some. I lose some."

Her smile felt genuine but was still weary. "You're in for a hell of a fight, if you're looking to get this kid back from the church."

"Tell me about that."

"Coffee?" I nodded and she moved to the tiny kitchenette to pour. The fresh smell suggested she'd brewed it recently.

"You make this for me?"

She was pouring the coffee, her back to me. "You look like you need it."

That was quite a statement coming from this haggard husk. "I do."

"Dairy? Sweetener?"

"And take up room for the coffee?" She turned, nodding in approval. I took a drink. It was okay for homemade. "So, you were telling me about the uphill battle I'm about to fight?"

She took a sip and made a face I took to be dissatisfaction. "What's to tell? They find people who are directionless and lost. They offer answers, belonging, and a little human interaction. That's all it takes."

"You make it sound so simple."

She frowned and averted her gaze. There were no windows, nothing to offer a view beyond the confines of this austere flat. "People aren't complicated, Mr. Parker. Most of us are just looking for somewhere to belong. When we don't find that in our normal lives..." She shrugged. "It's not so hard to draw us into a new one."

"Is that how they got you?"

Her smile was sad. "This conversation isn't about me."

I nodded at that and drew one of the letters from Bertrand's room. "You think this could be part of the scheme?"

She read the letter. "Sure, see how she talks about no one caring. The flippant comment about his mother and the world being against him? It could be just the talk of a rebellious lover, but I see signs of recruitment."

"Recruitment?"

"Yeah, we had people who would go out into the world and find parishioners, usually through a profession like bartender or mental health counselors or even sex workers."

"Sex workers?"

"Sure. Anything that brings you in contact with people who are desperate or lonely."

"College professor?"

"I don't know of any, but I don't see why not. Lots of college kids drifting around rudderless." I thought of the crew in the Mine Shaft and nodded. She continued. "And the sex? Wraps them around the finger."

"Around something." We shared a grin. "Were you a recruiter?"

Her smile fell, and she moved her gaze to the wall. "I told you; I don't wanna talk about me."

I nodded and went back to the matter at hand. "Does the name Camilla Zimmerman mean anything to you?"

She thought for several long moments. "No."

"Mary Hauser?"

"No."

"What do you know about Walter Ginson?"

Blue-grey terror met my gaze. "Why do you want to know about Walt?"

"Just curious. His name was on the same list as yours."

It was the wrong thing to say. "What? What list?"

I tried to sound nonchalant. "A list I found in a New Sunrise database."

Harris looked as if she'd taken a right cross from the champ, her terror muted by shock. Her voice was softened by distance, but there was no mistaking the iron in it. "You have to leave."

"But I— "

"Now! I can't—if they—you have to go."

I frowned and paused at the door. "If I— "

"Now, Frank."

I left. The man and woman from the corner were gone, but another man stood across the walk, interacting with a pReC. I frowned. It wasn't paranoia, if it was true.

* * *

I was hungry and decided to head to the Ferguson and Joe's place. The crowd pushed out into the lobby of the high-rise, and I wondered if anyone from the building could even eat here in the hour they got for lunch. I doubted Joe much cared where the money came from when there was this much of it.

A new presence I'd never noticed touched my pReC. A cartoon avatar that looked nothing like Joe gazed into my brain. He had long bangs that swept over his left eye and eyes too blue to belong to a real person. "Welcome to the Landmark! How many?"

"One, Parker."

The avatar's eyes widened in excitement. "Yes, Mr. Parker! You are most welcome here!" A red line like the one from the surfing parlor guided me through the crowd. I caught a few looks of indignation as I strode past, but no one said anything.

A young woman met me at the hostess podium and offered me a smile. "Mr. Parker!" she said. "It's great to have you here at the Landmark."

I thanked her, amazed by the transformation this place was going through. Conversations competed with each other to fill the space, hurting my ears and making it hard to hear the hostess two steps in front of me. "Quite the crowd."

She leaned in and shouted back. "Mr. Obradovich has been adding staff and business hours. There's talk of expanding to accommodate more guests."

I considered the layout, renting an occupancy on the ground floor of a high-rise office building. There didn't seem much opportunity.

The hostess led me to my booth, and I slipped into it. A plain-faced brown woman strode by outside. She wore a different outfit and lacked her partner, but I'd taken enough notice of her at Emily Harris's home to recognize her from the bench.

Pros. Had they followed me to Emily's? Or, had they been watching her for someone else and picked me up there? Both were distinct possibilities, but my instincts said the latter. Now they were following me, too. Great. I'd add them to the list.

Harris hadn't been the help I'd hoped, but I should never have brought Ginson into the conversation. Her terrified eyes stared out from my memory, a testimony to the power of Petrovich. I tried to escape the contagion of her fear, but it crept around the edge of my consciousness and tugged at my resolve.

I didn't have to do this. I could tell Maggie there was no way to know if he'd slipped into the grasp of the church. Let her take on this monster herself. I had my own problems, after all. That's when I saw the male component of the duo.

He'd lost his designer button-down and exchanged it for a black T-shirt under a brown sport coat, his sandy hair covered by a black beret. His eyes lingered, but not for long. I worried he might know he'd been made. Then, I wasn't.

These predators were stalking people who'd done nothing more than decide they didn't want to be a part of Petrovich's circle, or, worse, were deemed a threat to his power. The fear was flushed in a flood of rage. Who knew if Ginson was innocent or not? But it was clear it wasn't justice that had motivated Petrovich in his takedown. Dennis Calloway might've been blameless of everything but bad judgment. Yet, his life lay in ruins.

And, Harris! I remembered the terror in her eyes. The haunted look on her face. The eroded remains of her body. *"Stress is a killer."* What were they doing to poor, misguided Bertrand, hypnotized by belonging and at-will sex? I didn't know, but I was going to find out. Bertrand wasn't going to be another Lenny Marquez.

"Frank!" I looked up to see Joe coming across the floor.

"Joe."

"I thought that was you. Why didn't you say something?"

I tried to smile. "You were busy."

Joe stopped short of my table and studied me with streetwise eyes. "Who should I be worried about?"

"What are you talking about, Joe?"

"Only seen that look on you once," he said. "When you lit out of here after your shootout with those Loonies."

"Had some developments in my case. That's all."

"Bad developments?"

"Let's just say I know what I'm up against, now."

"Useful information."

"Some of those people are floating around, right now."

Joe's face grew taut. "There gonna be problems?"

I glanced out the window. "Nah. They're just tailing me. I might need a back way out of here, though."

"Sure." He placed a hand on my table and went back toward the front of the diner.

I watched him pass behind the counter and enter the chaos of the kitchen. I thought about Bertrand, and recalled Camilla describing her class as misfits and malcontents. I compared that to what Harris said about recruitment *"...most of us are just looking for somewhere to belong. When we don't find that in our normal lives..."* Was it that simple?

I pulled the letter from my pocket and read it again. Don't worry about a world where no one cares or parents who don't understand. What we have is right, and we have our own truth. I stared at the M. Milla, Millie. There was no way to be sure. A plate of faux potatoes and sausage dropped onto my table. Joe smiled down from behind his apron. "You look deep in thought."

"A detective is never off duty."

"Now that you know what you're up against, you any closer to solving this one?"

"A little."

Joe looked over my face. "I suggest you hurry. A man your age can only handle so much pressure, you know."

"Are the jokes free?"

He laughed. "You can compensate me in the gratuity."

"Don't count on it." I drew a sip of the tea and stared in amazement. "Is this a special blend, too?" He nodded. "What other expensive commodities do you have back there?"

"Wouldn't you like to know?" He left me to my food. I gulped at it, washing mouthfuls down with the tea, my mind racing, pondering my next move and searching for a path to the answers I needed.

I glimpsed the couple in the lobby. Back together? Amateurish behavior for pros, but they probably weren't used to tailing experienced police officers, either.

Joe returned as I was swallowing the last of his culinary delight. "How was it?"

I offered a soft belch. "Those people floating around?" His face became serious, his undivided attention on me. "They're here, in your queue."

I didn't look in their direction and was happy to see Joe's eyes stay on mine. "Definitely gonna need that back door."

"This is becoming a habit with you."

I forced a smile. "I take that as a sign I'm doing something right."

"Hey, I'm grateful for the notoriety and all, but I don't need another shootout here."

"Like I said, these people are just following me around. They're not looking to kill me. Yet."

"Well, when they reach that level, can you take them to some other diner? There is such thing as overexposure, you know."

"That's gratitude for you."

"Hey, who took those Loonies out and saved your sorry ass?"

"JD Waters?"

Joe looked at me with dead eyes. "That's not funny."

"I think it's hilarious, Joe. Thanks." I stood and left via the back door. I turned up the street and made the corner. No one seemed to be following.

My pReC chimed. It was a message from Dana. *Gun's stolen from a shop on the floor. No DNA no prints.* I sent back a single word: *Thanks.*

Chapter Seventeen

I walked uptown. It took a little longer to get there, but the exercise worked the body, and I needed to do something since I'd fallen out of my workout routine. It also added to the workload of any would-be followers and gave me more time to think. I was liking Camilla for being the mysterious M, but banging the kid's brains out and kidnapping him were two very different things.

A new perspective was in order, or that's what I told myself. I walked into a familiar building, rode a familiar elevator to the thirty-third floor, and strode up to a familiar room. I knocked.

Allyssa Ramacci opened the door and gazed out at me. Her lovely face was a yellow-green mess. Her once dainty nose was listing and swollen. The derma-glues had helped with the cuts, but there was no sign of the expensive cosmetic procedures a woman of her status and occupation would require. A ghoulish road map stitched across her forehead and wrapped around her left eye and nose. She offered a tight-lipped smile, swollen and cut, and I wondered what the inside of her mouth looked like. She turned her head to speak. "I wondered if you would come."

"I wondered if you'd want me to." She offered another closed-mouthed smile and turned back into her suite. I struggled to keep my gaze from her red silk kimono.

"I could lie and say it's always a pleasure, but the cop in you would see through it." She led me through the foyer. I stopped in the doorway to the living room. Something was very different. She told me before I could put the question to words. “I’m moving.”

“What?”

“I’m moving. Katsaros has given me a week to get out. The notice papers were sitting on my bedside table when I came out of the—when I woke up.”

She read the outrage on my face and made a halfhearted effort at humor. “Come on, Frank. You don’t expect Katsaros to leave a battered hag like me to meet-and-greet with his most select clients? Do you?” She poured from a decanter on a convenient drink cart and took a long draught. “Drink?”

I shook my head. She took another long gulp and added to the tumbler. I caught a glimpse of her open mouth and the missing front teeth. “Rachael Meyhew is taking over.” The name meant nothing to me, but the animosity in Allyssa’s voice said they weren’t friends.

“What are you gonna do?”

She shrugged. “Run one of the resorts, if I’m lucky. If not...” We both knew she could never make it as a proper whore. The business was too unforgiving. “They’re already calling me Scarface. Maybe I can use that to my advantage.” Her voice cracked, and I thought I could see unshed tears in her eyes, but she turned away and cleared her throat. “It’s Karma. Gets us all, someday.” Suddenly, I didn’t want that perspective I’d come for. “So, what brings you by, Frank?”

I pushed a smile onto my face. “Can’t a guy come by to see how you’re doing?”

“Some guys. Not you. Frank Parker on your doorstep means he needs a favor.”

I’d been hearing that a lot, lately. “Maybe I don’t want a favor.”

She sighed. “Don’t get all sentimental on me, now, Frank. What’s the problem?” She stood by the serving cart, drink in hand, staring through swollen eyes.

I looked away, trying not to think of the inequity of the situation. *"If you tell her, I'll kill your family."*

"What is it, Frank?"

"I need a female perspective on something. These were found by my client. They belong to her missing son." I handed her the letters and let her read.

She finished and looked up at me. "Sounds like typical fantasies to me. What's the problem?"

I wanted to tell her that this calamity that had befallen her was temporary, that she would bounce back, get back into her stride. "I know this happened because—"

"If you're going to do something like take blame for this or admit to prior knowledge, save it. We both knew what helping you meant for me."

She turned her face again, but this time there were shed tears running down her cheeks. She handed me the letters without looking at me. "I haven't always done right by these girls. You don't get to the top by doing that. But then along came Lenny. Something about the way trying to help her made me feel has broken me." She sniffed and wiped her eyes. "I don't know how much longer I could live with myself, now. Isn't that silly?" She looked at me with wet, dark eyes. "Fucked and sucked my way to the top of a business like this, selling my soul one piece at a time for another foothold, usually on some other girl's face. But after Lenny, all I can think about is the destruction I've brought to people's lives, how much I've exploited them, so I could live in a nice suite on the thirty-third floor of a chic hotel. Isn't that crazy?"

I thought of the first time I met her, just weeks ago, how I'd taken a chance that the way she talked about "my girls" hadn't been bullshit. I smiled and touched her shoulder. "I never saw you that way." It was probably less than the total truth, but there was enough of it to leave the rest unspoken. "That's why I came to you in the first place. It's why you were waiting for me on the balcony."

She smiled at that, remembering. "That was quite a visit."

"It was." It was also in the past, and we both knew it. "I didn't come here for your opinion on the letter. Not really. I came to see if you were okay."

She shrugged. "I'll be okay."

I nodded at the lie, wondering what she would do with her life, wondering if there was something I could do to help, not that I'd done much to help to this point. "You deserve better than this."

Her smile was still closed but less muted. "That's nice of you to say, Frank. Maybe we'll both get what we deserve."

I wasn't sure I was comfortable with that idea. "Maybe."

"I hope you don't mind," she said, "but I really have to get packed. An old friend is helping me move, and I want to be ready when he gets here."

I folded the letters and put them in my pocket. "Yeah. Yeah, sure. I have things to do, anyway."

She smiled, and her lips parted just enough to reveal the gap in her teeth.

I turned from the suite, strode back to the elevator, and pushed the recall button.

"Frank!" Allyssa ran to me, still barefoot, still in her silky red kimono. She threw her arms around me and pressed her lips to mine. There was nothing erotic about it, no passion, only sincere, platonic affection. She pulled her arms from around my neck, tugged on the lapels of my jacket, and smoothed it with her palms.

Her voice was a whisper, desperate and hoarse. "You have to do something for me, Frank." I tried to step away, to create space, but she held tight to me. "I'm serious. We both know you owe me, and I need you to do something, something only you can do."

I didn't want to ask. "What is it?"

"Take these fuckers down. Katsaros, Frost, all of them. Make them pay for Lenny, for all the Lennies they've wronged."

Was that all she wanted? Sure, Allyssa, let me jump right on that, as soon as I heal the sick, and make the blind see. But I'd made similar promises to myself and didn't have the heart to make her mood worse. "You know I want nothing more."

She pecked my lips and stumbled back up the corridor.

* * *

Janet was packing up for the day when I got back to the office. "It's after four on a Sunday. I thought you lawyer-types kept cushy business hours."

"I've been drawing up a counter to the protective motion Petrovich filed on you. You're welcome." The smile trying to break through her lawyer scowl was my clue she wasn't pissed. "Besides, I'm going home to a big, lonely penthouse. Why not work in a big, lonely office?"

"If only I could have your problems."

"Laugh it up, mister. Being married to a rich and powerful shithead may seem like a party, but it has all kinds of burdens."

"Like more to take in the divorce?"

"Depends on how much the lawyers leave." We shared a grin. "But it carries a whole new set of worries like the media, friends, and associations we share, and, mostly, how do I work in a city like this, if they side with him?"

I thought about that. I was having a helluva time with my divorce. How would I feel about the media following my every step, digging into my past, posting them on the twenty-four hour feeds? What if our shared associates were the most powerful in the city? What would that do to the stakes? "Your friends in Not Guilty wouldn't help after Latham?"

Not Guilty was the nonprofit for whom Janet volunteered. They were the likely benefactor of her Sunday afternoon marathon and had, at Janet's behest, utilized my services to find exonerating evidence for the man convicted of one of Tycho City's most notorious murders. It made a splash in the media and gave them weeks of good press.

She laughed. "I might've given them a bombshell, but who spread the word?" She read the frown on my face. "Exactly. Besides, this is all old news. And, if there's one truism in Tycho society, it's what have you done for me lately?" I had no response. She drew a deep breath. "How's the Mellenburg Case coming?"

I shrugged. "I think he's disappeared into New Sunrise, and I'm beginning to suspect the letters are from one of their recruiters."

"You have an idea on who that is?"

"Some."

"Well, while I was preparing your response, I did some research, and I think I might have something for you."

"For me?"

"Yep!" My pReC dinged and a file appeared in the corner of my vision. The case wasn't quite ten years old. "Most of it's been sealed, but plenty of files were made public after discovery."

"Darlene Hurt?"

"Yeah, the first defector from Petrovich's inner sanctum. Speaks of brainwashing and physical, mental, and sexual abuse, real cult stuff."

"What happened to her?"

"Typical smear campaign. She's crazy, nothing to see here but us righteous warriors for God. Sister Hurt lost some of her influence and wants us to pay. The typical." I nodded and read. Janet kept talking. "Until she took her own life."

"What?"

"That was the official conclusion, anyway. They found a suicide note and the pills she took."

"But?"

Janet shrugged. "You know how those cases are. The note seemed legit, but some will never believe a woman in that kind o struggle killed herself."

"What do you think?"

"Hard to say. Seen plenty of people do it during epic stress like that; your whole world turned against you, family shunning you, spreading lies—or exposing ugly truths. You never know."

I nodded.

"Anyway, I'm out of here. Rec me if you need me."

"Will do." I hesitated. "And, Janet?" She turned and waited. "If you ever want to just go get a cup of coffee, I know some great places."

The way she smiled made me feel good about myself. "I think I'd like that, Frank."

"Me, too."

I watched her leave, promising myself someday wouldn't turn into never. I showered, walked back down the plush corridor, past the silent busts and paintings, and stood in my room, wrapped in a towel hitched at my waist.

There was nothing special in the file. The court sealed it after Hurt's death. I looked up and through my string chart on the wall. Wasn't that odd? To seal a case after someone's death? Her privacy wasn't a factor anymore. Right?

I thought of reccing Janet, but let it go. It could wait.

Chapter Eighteen

I was in the middle of a dream, but it faded before I was fully awake and was a distant memory by the time I spoke into my pReC. "Hello." I must've sounded like a pirate at the end of a six-day bender.

"Mr. Parker? Detective Parker?"

I cleared my throat. "That's right."

"I'm Carrie DiPompo. You remember me?"

That woke me up. I sniffed again and tried to rub life into my tired face. "The club secretary. I remember."

"I hope it's not too late to rec you, but I've been thinking about the day you talked to me at the Mine Shaft." She paused. I remained quiet. She'd come this far on her own. I didn't want to blow it with my big mouth. "Did you mean what you said about him being in trouble?"

"There's no way to know for sure, but that's my mission; find him, make sure he's not in trouble, and try to help him if he is."

She weighed those words for a long time. "And if he's just off doing his own thing, even if it's something his mom doesn't approve of?"

"That'll be between them. I'm not looking to kidnap or hurt him, if that's what you mean."

"And his folks?"

I thought about that. "I've worked for people who've lied to me before. I think they're being straight when they say they want to make sure he's okay and want to help him."

There was another long pause. "There's a concrete park not far from the Mine Shaft."

"On campus?" I asked, not wanting another run-in with the campus police.

"No, it's on Fairview and Sumpter."

That would be easy enough to find. I told her to sit tight. I'd be there soon.

* * *

Carrie DiPompo sat on a bench with the posture of a wash rag. She was garbed in the same expensive labels, looking rebel-chic and wearing the morose depression of her generation like a cloak. Her dark eyes almost met mine as I walked up. "You came."

"You thought I wouldn't?"

"I could tell you were sleeping and—"

"You thought I'd sleep in rather than come out here."

She looked into the distance and smiled. It was a pretty smile, even if I did only get a glancing view. "You wanna walk?" She didn't say it was because she didn't want to be seen talking with me, but she led me from campus toward the glass and steel mid-rises of midtown. "You were serious about helping Bernie? That you think he's in trouble?"

"I do."

She looked into some inner thoughts and seemed to come to a decision. "What do you need to know about him?"

"What's he like? Who does he hang out with?" I paused. "Does he have a girlfriend?"

Carrie thought about that, midnight hair hanging loose in the Lunar gravity. She spoke with hesitation. "Not a regular girlfriend, at least he didn't. He did have a few special friends." I noted the intimate worry in Carrie's demeanor and wondered what Eugene would think about that. "He hates being a rich kid. Says it makes him feel guilty and dirty to have so much when life is so unfair to the rest of the world."

I contrasted the nice house and the grungy look he liked to sport and doubted it was the money he had the problem with. "How about his parents? He ever talk about them?"

Carrie was staring into a dark storefront where a mannequin in a stylish coat proffered a simple leather clutch. It was a Sarsoon design and worth more than I made as a TCPD detective in a quarter. She frowned and looked at me for the first time. "Mostly his mom." I waited for her to continue. "She was always on him about his grades, talking shit about his friends. That woman was a devil! She was terrified he would embarrass her, telling him to remember what it meant to be a Mellenburg in this town, and was always threatening to cut him off."

I thought of Maggie and tried to reconcile the concerned mom I'd met with the domineering bitch Carrie was describing.

"And, her husband!" said Carrie. "Apparently, he was doing all he could to push Bernie out. Said he was a leech and that his mom was coddling him too much. Wanted him to get out and be a man."

"So, he was possessive of the mother?"

Her lips twitched. "Not the mother. Bernie thinks he's just after her money."

I thought of the pretty boy with his tennis tan, and manicured good looks. That piece seemed a very good fit. "And, dad?"

"Don't know much about him. Just that he's poor."

"What did Bertrand think about all that? Do you think he'd up and leave over that kind of thing?"

"You mean run away?"

I swept the dark streets, looking for signs of tagalongs. I didn't see any, but that meant exactly nothing. "Yeah, do you think he'd get out on his own and forge a new life away from all this?"

We walked several paces in silence, and Carrie shook her head. "I don't think so. The—it's expensive to live out here, you know."

Especially when you're sporting designer labels and running up two-hundred-bill-a-night bar tabs. I left the thought unspoken. "And, if he found someone with money?"

Her voice got quiet. "I don't know. Eugene—Eugene and I—"

"He's not the sharing type."

"Yeah."

"So, how did Eugene come into the picture?"

Her face grew pale, and she looked at me with terror. "You're not gonna talk to Eugene? Are you? H-he wouldn't like this."

"Nope. Not unless he did something to Bertrand, and I don't think actual violence is his thing. At least, not against other men."

She averted her eyes, and I didn't press. "It was the M-plant."

"M-plant?"

"Yeah, it's a—"

"I know what it is. Are you saying he has a drug problem?"

"I wouldn't call it a 'problem.' We liked a little bump when we partied together and it's intense during sex."

I didn't want this barely legal child going on about her sex life. "So, his mom cut the purse strings?"

She laughed. "You kidding? That woman's answer to her son's problems was to spend money on him."

Wasn't this the same girl who was just telling me what a domineering bitch Maggie Mellenburg had been? "So, what happened?"

"His dealer cut him off. Wouldn't take his money. I had to buy our last couple scores. That got so old. Quality interface shit is expensive, and my folks ain't rollin' like his. You know?"

I was beginning to. "So, once he couldn't provide the M-plant, you moved on?"

Carrie turned on me, offering the first sign of an emotion that wasn't blue. Her voice echoed off the sleeping storefronts. "Hey! It's not like that! I-I cared. We were just friends, enjoying each other's company for a while. That's all."

"I wasn't judging," I lied with the ease of a decades-long professional. "I'm trying to figure out why a drug dealer would turn away someone like Bertrand, if his account was current."

She studied me with sulky anger, as if trying to decide whether I was calling her a whore. "You'd have to ask Missy."

"Missy?"

"Missy Two-fingers. She's a college kid with a side hustle slinging Plant."

"That's a heavy-duty side hustle."

She shrugged. "Tuition ain't cheap. You know?"

I nodded. "So, what's the deal? If mama Mellenburg didn't cut the purse strings, and Missy didn't go straight, what happened?"

She shrugged. "She has this gorilla working for her named Carl. He told Bernie his money was no good anymore. He was cut off."

Dealers weren't what you'd call selective about their clientele. They sold to six-year-olds with the same zeal they did twenty-somethings. And, they kept selling until they were put out of business or the buyer couldn't pay. But, in all my twenty years, I couldn't remember a single time when one had refused service for personal reasons. "He say why?"

"Nope. He just told us Missy wouldn't serve him anymore."

"What did Bernie say about it?"

She shrugged. "What the hell was he gonna say? When a guy like Carl tells you to get lost, you get lost."

"But he had no idea why he was excluded?"

"No, but that's when he started sending me by myself."

"And Carl—he knew you."

"Sure."

"And sold to you anyway?"

"At first."

"At first?"

"Yeah, Bernie would give me the cash and up I'd go."

"I thought you said you were buying."

Carrie became indignant. "Only the first two! I told him I couldn't afford it, paying *and* going up there by myself while he cowered in the lobby. Missy may be a college student, but she's still a drug dealer, and there was Carl. He started paying after that. Still almost wasn't worth the extra fifty to go up there."

"Wait, he was paying you?"

"Yeah. But Missy found out, somehow. Wouldn't sell to me. Put the word out on us both. The college drug scene is pretty tight. I wasn't going to the Lower City to get my score, so..."

You ditched him. "You got this Missy's address?"

"I don't know— "

"Like you said, the college drug scene is small. It won't take much for me to find out." I pulled a fifty from my pocket. "But you could save me a lot of time and energy."

She gave me the address, and I gave her the money. "When's the last time you two hung out?"

She pocketed the cash. "Been a couple of weeks."

"Where you gettin' your scores?"

She looked into the shadowy storefronts. "Eugene."

"Do you know if Bertrand ever found another source?"

"It's possible. He'd looked terrible for a while, but the last time I saw him, he looked good, almost happy."

"When was that?"

"Student Union. Two weeks or so. He was at a club meeting."

"Was he with anyone?"

"You mean like a girl?"

"Yeah, like a girl."

"Not that I can remember."

"Did you ever know of any girlfriends, real girlfriends. Maybe with a name starting with 'M'?"

She took several seconds to answer. "Not that I know of." There was an awkward pause. "Bernie was a nice kid, but not particularly charismatic. You know? He got a lot of acceptance through his ability to pay for things."

Like your M-plant. Again, I left the comment unspoken. "What about Mary Hauser or Camilla Zimmerman?"

"The profs?"

I nodded.

"I don't know anything about Hauser, but Doctor Zimmerman? She's very close to Bernie."

"Close? What kind of close?"

"You know. He was in her club and hung out with her after class and did stuff with her."

"Are they involved?"

"You mean fucking?"

"Yeah."

She thought about that. "Sure, they could be, but he's never said so."

I pulled another fifty from my pocket. I didn't want to pay her again, but I might need something from her later. And, this girl didn't strike me as one to do charity work. "Take care of yourself, Carrie, and let me know if anything else comes up."

I stepped away, still scanning for tails. I considered Carrie's story. *"Doctor Zimmerman? She's very close to Bernie...You know. He was in her club and hung out with her after class and did stuff with her."* This meant one of two things. Carrie, with no apparent motive, was lying about Camilla Zimmerman's relationship with Bertrand, or Zimmerman was lying about her relationship Bertrand; the same Camilla Zimmerman who taught his favorite class Wednesdays and Fridays, the same Camilla

Zimmerman who was the faculty sponsor for his most treasured club, and the same Camilla Zimmerman who had loose ties to the New Sunrise Outreach center, the same New Sunrise Tabernacle that had a flier in his bedroom. That was a lot of coincidence or a lot of motive to lie. I sighed and walked on through the darkness.

Chapter Nineteen

I sat in an uppity doughnut house on the bottom floor of Maggie Mellenburg's building, drinking passable coffee and eating ten bill apiece doughnuts. I was hoping to catch Maggie on her way to work, but another stepped out of the elevator first.

Dick Chandler wore an athletic outfit similar to the one he'd sported the day I met him. He carried a gym bag in his left hand and turned toward the bathrooms next to the concierge desk.

I paid my tab and considered moving over to the elevator but thought better of it. The point of coming here this way was to speak to Maggie alone. If he came out of the bathroom while I was still waiting for the elevator, that plan might have to keep for another day.

Besides, something about his behavior made me curious. I touched the waitress's sleeve as she strode by. "This building have a gym?"

"Sure, second floor." She leaned forward and whispered as if delivering bad news. "Residents only."

I nodded, thanked her, and watched the bathroom door. When Chandler reappeared, he wore clothes more suited for the nightclub than working out. His button-down had no tie and hung open at the top, revealing the bulk of two powerful, shorn pecs. The sleeves had been rolled up to reveal a big-faced gold watch that matched his necklace. He still carried the gym bag I assumed held the clothes he'd worn in the elevator.

He strode across the polished grey tile, over the maroon rug, and through the gold-barred glass where he turned left and disappeared. I was halfway to the elevators, laughing at the man's brazenness, when Carrie DiPompo's words came back to me. *"Bernie thinks he's just after her money."*

I stopped and looked at the door through which he'd just passed. The elevatored dinged open behind me, offering transport to the Mellenburg suite. But I moved toward the front door, the street beyond, and Dick Chandler's destination.

* * *

I ended up chasing Maggie Mellenburg to her office. It was afternoon by the time I sat in her chair, watching her register the scene before her. She sat up behind her immense desk, the pics I'd provided her splayed across its tidy surface.

I didn't see how this could be a surprise, but there was genuine shock and pain in her expression as she thumbed through the twenty-by-twelve pics I'd printed from the hotel security feeds. The images of Dick having an intimate breakfast with a dark-haired twenty-something with a sleek, curvy body might've been explicable if not for his change of clothes and story about being at the gym. But feeding each other and walking hand in hand to the hotel elevators were irrefutably adulterous. The pics of their make out session in the elevator and the way they groped each other all the way to the room was overkill.

"This was at the Devonshire?"

I nodded. Katsaros owned the Devonshire. Getting high quality pics from the security system was easy for a paid consultant like me.

Maggie glared across the table. "How dare you snoop into the privacy of my marriage?" I hadn't expected that response. "Did it ever occur to you we had an open relationship?"

I held her gaze and saw pain blended with the anger. "No." The blunt response took her by surprise and shaved the edge off her rage. "He walked out of the elevator, went to the bathroom—still in your building—and changed out of gym clothes into slut gear. You'd already told me he was supposed to be at the gym. Even if that was your story to keep me from knowing your business, why the Houdini trick in the bathroom?"

She stared for several long moments and averted her gaze.

I cleared my throat and continued. "Look, I was on my way to your apartment to discuss some revelations in the case, revelations that involved your husband."

Maggie wiped her eyes and looked at me. "About Dick?" I nodded. "What about him?"

I told her Carrie DiPompo's story, holding back the stuff about the drug dealer and Zimmerman. "So, he was driving Bertrand away?"

"That's her story."

"And, this girl, she's a girlfriend?"

"Casually intimate seems more accurate."

Her slender mouth worked as she mulled that over. "And you think I'm choosing Dick over Bertrand?"

"I don't think a smart, talented woman like you needs me to tell you anything." I stood. "I'm here to get Bertrand back. But, when I do, the home he comes back to will have a lot to do with how long he stays."

"I see."

I hovered for a moment. "I'm sorry about this. But for what it's worth, uncomplicate what's standing between you and Bertrand before it's too late."

She smiled and showed no sign of being annoyed at my presumptiveness. "Thank you, Detective Parker. You've given me a lot to think about."

I frowned and left.

* * *

Missy "Two-fingers" Castellano lived on two floors of the Harpex Building, a residential tower just off campus. It sold itself as an "affordable" alternative to student housing, offering freedom and independence from campus scrutiny. I wasn't sure what affordable meant to them, but I could almost get a monthly rate at the Olympian for the rent this place charged.

The building had a distinguished, elite atmosphere, save for the laughter and boisterous noise from the bar that mingled with the deep bass of the dance club. Both were going strong, and it wasn't even two in the afternoon.

I stepped onto the elevator car and felt the AI touch my pReC. *"Floor please?"*

"Fifty."

The car hesitated, then carried me up to the fiftieth floor. It opened, and I stepped into a foyer. I rang the bell and a behemoth in a charcoal tank top glared down at me. His left hand held the door. His right was hidden by the jamb. The suspicion on his face said he didn't know me and didn't like the unknown. Carl, I presumed. "What?"

"I'm here to see Missy 'Two-fingers.'"

His smile said he bet I wanted a lot of things I didn't get. "Well, she ain't seein' visitors. You here to buy, buy. If not..." He gestured toward the elevator behind me.

I smiled and leaned forward, tucking my hands behind my back. "I didn't come here to start trouble. I just need a few minutes of her time, and I'll never come back again."

He finished opening the door and stepped forward to fill it, exposing the Kholar ten-mil in his right hand. "I think you're—"

The click of Jupiter's hammer being pulled stopped the man mid-sentence. I'd placed its mouth into the bulge of his crotch. "The gun,"

I said. "On the floor."

It fell with a soft *thunk* onto the thick carpet.

"Kick it to me." He hesitated. "Kick it to me or the rats in this place will be playing soccer with your nuts." He kicked it. I passed it to the corner of the foyer with an outside kick.

"Any more like you in there?"

He shook his head. "Good, turn your ass around and lead me inside. And don't forget; I have a shotgun in this thing."

We stepped inside the suite to a second antechamber. Shelves of bagged drugs lined both sides of the door. A pretty schoolgirl-looking woman stood before a table stacked high with cash. She was pointing a shotgun toward me and my human shield. It was bigger than she was, but the look on her face said she was willing to use it.

I tried to sound blasé, but you can only sound so blasé when staring into the black death of a shotgun barrel. "What the hell are you gonna do with that thing?"

"Blow your fucking head off, if you so much as wiggle."

I tried to wet my parched vocal cords so I didn't sound like a prepubescent teen. "That's no precision instrument you're wielding. You might get enough to take me out, but Tiny Tim here will be peppered too.

"And, what are you gonna tell the cops about these two bleeding fellas on the floor, and your little distribution center here?" I motioned toward the racks of drugs against the wall. "I don't think the manager you're paying off will cover for a gunfight with injuries, especially when the cops come sniffing around." Her eyes flicked to Carl and back to me. I took heart when she didn't blast me into the Netherworld. "All I need is five minutes of your time. No violence, no cops, no trouble with the landlord."

"And, if I push you out that door and tell you to go fuck yourself?"

I shrugged. "I can make life hard for you."

"I told you," said Carl. "As soon as you give into one, they're all gonna come around wanting a piece."

"It wasn't like that, Carl," the girl said, and turned her eyes at me. "I ain't cutting you in on shit, mister. So, if that's your plan, go ahead. I'll be gone before you get back with the writ."

"And be completely cut off from your customers." I held her walnut gaze. "Or, I can move among your customers and ferret out your new location. But let's save us all the trouble and hear me out."

She studied me for several long moments, then she let the shotgun barrel sag toward the floor. "Carl, give us a few minutes, huh?"

"Miss Castellano, I don't think this is a good idea."

I jammed Jupiter harder into his back. "You aren't being paid to do the thinking, Carl. Your boss is making a sound decision. Stay out of her way and let her make it."

He glared over his shoulder but made no move against me. I gestured at Missy. "Put it on the table, nice and easy."

She did what I asked, and I stepped away from Carl but within Missy's line of sight. I pointed Jupiter toward the floor, but he could be up and sited in a moment. "I don't care if Carl hears this or not, but I won't have him causing trouble."

"Carl, go down to the bar and get a drink."

"But I—"

"I'm not asking, Carl." Her tone offered no compromise. He stood and slunk away, like a giant child being sent to his room.

I watched him go and eyed him on the security monitor once he entered the elevator foyer. He passed through the door and turned to retrieve the gun I'd kicked into the corner. I suffered a few tense moments as he stared through the moonboard wall, knowing what he was thinking. But any shots fired blindly into that rock would be just as likely to hit her as me and would draw all kinds of attention. He frowned at the camera, turned to the elevator, and went to the lobby.

"He's a good man," Missy said when the doors closed.

"Protective."

"That's his job." I smiled but offered no response. "You wanna come inside and talk over drinks?"

I glanced at the monitor over the door. "I kinda like the view from here."

"There's a whole bank of them inside," she said. "Come on."

I followed her into an ultramodern suite with a glass face that looked out in all directions. My shoes *clacked* on the polished grey moonwalk tiles. A black and gold living room set with beige cushions sat on a black carpet. It looked down on the school campus.

I could make out the social sciences building, admin, the student union, and the promenade where I'd been attacked. "Quite the view."

"Yes, it is." She poured us each a couple of fingers from the decanter on the bar and brought mine. It was a single malt, as smooth as Katsaros's stock. I gave her a complimenting nod and she returned the gesture with a weak smile.

She took a sip and gazed through the glass. Her brown eyes glittered in the reflection, and I could see the brazen schoolgirl who watched a side hustle turn into an empire she could scarcely imagine. I also saw the end: lots of blood or lots of prison. Maybe both. Either way, this girl had months to enjoy this, a year if she was lucky.

The smile faded, and she turned her tough-girl routine on me. "So, what do you want?"

I made a show of swirling the drink in my hand. "I want to know why you stopped selling M-plant to Bertrand Mellenburg."

She was a gifted amateur, but she couldn't fool someone with my background. The question caught her off guard. "I—he wasn't paying his bill."

I glanced at the monitor behind the bar. The foyer was still empty. I made a buzzing sound. "*Eeen!* My source tells me ole Bertrand paid cash, every time. Mamma was footin' the bill, and she's my paymaster. So, try again."

Missy let out a sigh and shook her head, her dark curls bouncing with her hoop earrings. "Am I ever going to be rid of this fucking kid?" She let out another sigh and looked long and hard look out the window. "It was the cop."

"What cop?"

She looked up from her view. "What do ya mean what cop? You think I ask these fuckers their names? They show up with a badge, I gotta listen. Right?"

I shrugged. "So, this cop. What did he want?"

"What do you think?" She turned back to the window. "Told me to stop serving your boy. Says he'll make it hard if I don't. You know, the same routine that got you in here."

"That's all he wanted was for you to stop serving the kid?"

She blew out another sigh. "That was supposed to be the deal."

"But?"

"He recced me a week or so later, said the kid's girl was coming up here, buying for both of them. Told me she was off-limits, too." I flashed a pic to her pReC. Her posture shifted to betray her attention. "Yeah, DiPompo, that was her."

I glanced at the monitor. "This cop, he tell you why he was so interested in this one particular kid?"

"Said his grades were slipping." Missy chuckled and looked at me. "Can you believe that shit? His grades."

I offered a weak smile and took a long shot. "This cop, he TCPD?"

"Nah, campus fuzz."

Her words poured over me like ice water. "Describe him for me."

She looked from the window, as if taking me in for the first time. "Little shorter than you, bald head, thick eyebrows." She appraised my clothes in a way that made me feel self-conscious. "Snappier dresser."

I knew a campus cop who matched that description.

I glanced at the monitor. The coast was still clear. "All right. You think of anything else, you let me know."

"You think of something else, you'd better ask."

I smiled and paused at the doorway. "You mind if I say something?"

"What?"

I gestured at the room around me. "This, all this, isn't worth the rest of your life."

She threw her drink back, gulped it, and said, "If you say so."

I shrugged and left the queen to her realm.

* * *

The desk officer for the Harper Ellis Campus Police said Detective Sergeant Jorge Gomez had just gotten off duty. I flashed him an old badge I'd reported lost and asked if I could get his pReC address. He shook his head.

I grinned. "Okay, have it your way. You can deliver a message for him?" He shrugged. I don't think he liked me very much. "Tell him Frank Parker wants to meet him at the Blue Knight on Prestone. Tell him Missy Two-fingers sent me."

The message didn't seem to improve my standing. "That's it?"

"That's it."

He looked at me with flat eyes "I'll tell him."

* * *

The Blue Knight had an old-fashioned painted sign, hung on an old-fashioned awning. It featured a knight in blue armor on a destrier. His shield was a great oval police badge. The windows were blackened with blue strobes flashing over the door.

I stepped inside. A long bar ran along the back of the building. A pair of cops played billiards on a table to my left. The imitation stained glass hanging above the table provided the bar with its dingy light. I nodded at the players, and they nodded back, but I could feel the suspicion at a stranger entering their domain.

"The hell is this bullshit about?"

I turned to the voice. Jorge Gomez stood in the hallway leading to the bathrooms. His sharp, brown eyes studied me with wary focus.

I forced a smile. "Just a little chat, Jorge."

He grunted in a way that suggested he had nothing to say. "Well, what do you want?" I motioned to a booth in the corner. He glanced that way. "Whatever."

I stepped over to the bartender, ordered a pair of lagers in bottles. He frowned and handed them off. Apparently, he knew Jorge and didn't seem to like the look of our exchange. I took them over to our table and sat. "I come in peace."

He took the beer, but I knew this didn't make us friends. "What do you want?"

I drew a swig and glanced over my shoulder. We were alone. I leaned close and said, "You know, I just figured it was the size of the campus that brought you so fast—a detective sergeant. But then I had new information come my way that put all that on its head. Wanna tell me about it?"

Gomez stared across the table with flat eyes. He might be a campus cop, but there was no reason to think he'd be a pushover. "I don't know what there is to tell."

"Look, Jorge—"

"Sergeant Gomez."

I stopped, stared hard into his unwavering dark orbs, and cleared my throat. "Look, you don't want to do this, and I don't either. I'm working for a high-octane go-getter. She wants to find her missing boy—you know—Bertrand Mellenburg." I couldn't say what changed about Gomez's face, but he flinched. "You recognize that name. Right?"

Gomez's eyes moved to the bar and back.

"We both know you do. We both know you went up to Missy Castellano's. We both know you told her to stop providing M-plant to Bertrand. And, we both know you were following me the day I was assaulted near the ice cream shop. So, the only thing I need to know is who and why?"

Rowdy bar noise filled the void between us for several seconds. The pool players broke a fresh rack. A bar fly walked some lucky patron outside. "I wasn't doing anything shady, if that's what you're asking."

"Help me understand."

He blew out a resigned sigh, glanced around the bar, and leaned forward, elbows on the table. The light hanging above reflected on his head. "I have this special friend. She's faculty." All roads lead to Zimmerman. "She told me she was worried about one of her pet projects."

"Bertrand."

He offered a sideways nod. "Yeah."

I watched a big-bellied specimen push into the men's room. "And how did you find Castellano?"

He took a swig of beer. "My professor friend gave me her address."

"And, this friend, she's Camilla Zimmerman." I didn't phrase it as a question.

He stared at me for a handful of heartbeats and frowned. "Cami, yeah." Cami. "Said he was a teacher's pet, struggling to get by. Told me he was in danger of getting tossed if something didn't change. Wanted me to go to Castellano and put the fear of the law in her."

"And you agreed."

Jorge shrugged. "What was the big deal? I suppose someone could create ethics issues for me, but there's nothing illegal about it."

"And Castellano folded?"

"Like a broken lounge chair."

He grinned across the table, and I found myself liking this campus cop. "You ever know her to sleep with her students?"

"Know? Nah. Wonder?" He shrugged. "I don't know a lot about her, but not much would surprise me, either. She gives me a very worldly feel, ya know?"

I nodded. "You ever know her to go by names other than Camilla or Cami? Something with an M—Milly?"

Gomez shook his head. "She's kinda wild in the sack, though. Fantasy and role-playing is something I could definitely see her being into."

"Tell me about the day she had you follow me around campus."

Gomez sighed and took another swig. "She recced me. Said some suspicious 'creep' was sniffing around asking questions. Told me I should keep an eye on you while you were on campus."

I considered that. "She tell you I was looking for Bertrand? Or that she lied to me about knowing him?"

"No." He leaned across the table. "This Bertrand, how long has he been missing?"

I considered not answering, but he'd been straight with me, and I didn't think he'd been trying to do anything but help his professor lover keep an eye on her students. "Going on two weeks."

His face tightened with worry. Both of us knew a minor ethics issue could become a major problem or even a criminal offense, if it turned out his rule-bending helped Zimmerman commit a major crime, especially on a high-profile student. I did the best I could to allay his fears. "Thanks for not being a dick about this, Jorge. I'll keep this out of the report."

Jorge smiled, but he couldn't afford to be relieved. He'd just been told Camilla Zimmerman had been putting his good faith to nefarious use. If this blew up, my report would be the least of his worries.

I checked the time on my pReC. "You've been to her place?"

"Sure."

"Think you could help a brother out?"

There was strain in his smile. "As long as you put in a good word for me when the time comes."

I didn't have the heart to tell him what a character reference from me was worth. "You got it, bro."

Chapter Twenty

Camilla Zimmerman's flat was in a mid-rise on not far from campus. It didn't wear the party atmosphere of the Harpex nor the rundown feel of the Lower City. It was a simple place with modest carpet that seemed mostly maintained. The plain walls were unadorned by fancy trim or ostentatious implements, but they had been painted in the last half-decade. This season was a crisp blue, but I wouldn't have been surprised if they used surplus stock on the whole building.

There was no security AI, either. Some people liked that. It helped maintain the illusion of privacy. As if practically every move we made wasn't already under some all-seeing eye. I glanced up at the camera in the elevator car.

The doors parted, and I stepped out onto the twenty-third floor. It was a wide, spacious corridor with chocolate brown carpet. I turned right and positioned myself in front of apartment twenty-five thirty and rang the buzzer. No one answered. I rang again. Nothing.

I checked the time. Past twenty-one hundred. Doctor Zimmerman was out late. How interesting. I glanced in both directions again, trying not to think of the cameras taking footage from at least two vantage points on each end of the hallway. Most of the time, they ran for the purpose of providing a record of the goings-on, so it could be referenced later. Other times, there were human guards or AIs programmed to spot suspicious activity. This would have to be quick.

I sprayed DexDan200 on the lens of her thumb sensor to bring out old fingerprints and DNA, and pressed a NanoSheen gloved finger to mold to those prints and provide human warmth for the sensor. I pressed firmly but not hard and waited. A few tense moments passed and the sensor pad chimed, lit up green, and released the lock.

I pushed the door open and stepped into a clean-smelling apartment full of purples and blues. The furniture was faux, silver-grey leather over simulated wood. A glass top table with a digital picture frame was aimed at me. The pictures were of the same mocha-skinned woman in various poses with various backgrounds. A much younger Camilla appeared in some of them, and they seemed close, even familial.

The floors were flat moonwalk tile. A rug covered most of it. I left the light off and drew a handlight from my pocket. It turned night into day, but blackness was a thumb push away if I heard sounds of someone opening the door.

The living room offered nothing in the way of storage space and nothing seemed to be in plain view. I got down on the floor and swept the beam under the couch and matching chairs. It was a little dustier under there. A castaway pair of lace-up flats and a lone sock stared back, but no bins, no ream of paper.

I rose on popping knees and passed a neat kitchen with a serving bar. It was quaint, and bigger than the one I had shared with Suzanne and Mattie. I sighed and felt their absence. Had it only been a couple of months since this chaos began? Would it be another couple before it was over? Longer? Forever?

I filled the silence with a long forlorn sigh and turned from the fancy computerized refrigerator and prep island with its pots and pans suspended overhead and opened the bathroom. It had been cleaned in the last week or so, though the trash was getting full. I glanced through the wire lattice of the can but saw nothing that justified sorting through bathroom refuse of a woman I barely knew.

The cabinet over the toilet was full of towels, a box of sanitary napkins, and pretty-smelling soaps. The sink had a toothbrush and nothing else. I tugged on the mirror. It opened, exposing some makeup-looking cream and powders to dust on her face.

I moved them about, looking for anything hiding, but it was all labels promising vibrant colors and long-lasting finish. I closed the door and looked at the tired face in the mirror. Pale, with haggard, bloodshot eyes and a three-days' growth. I ran my hands over the jowls and listened to the *scratch, scratch, scratch* of my rough hands on my whiskery face.

I moved to the bedroom. It was a little less kempt that the rest of the home. The covers on the bed were still askew, the bedspread spilling onto the soft grey carpet. A few clothes were scattered on the floor and one big pile had collected in the corner.

I opened the folding doors to the closet and started moving through the clothes one at a time. I pushed my hands into pockets with the deft precision of experience, searching one article after another.

A woman's voice passed through the closed front door. I turned the light off and held my breath. I stared through the open bedroom door and had a good look at the front. The low-pitched voice of a man was followed by high-pitched laughter. The sounds moved down the corridor, toward the elevators.

No one opened the door. The woman's voice returned, more distant. *Ding.* The elevator doors opening. The talking resumed but became indistinct and was gone. I waited several more seconds, listening for anything, but there was nothing.

I turned the light back on and resumed my search. The clothes were clean. Nothing on the overhead shelf. I closed the doors as I'd found them. I did the same for the clothes on the floor, the bureau, and the bed. Nothing. I moved to the second bedroom. It had been fashioned as an office. A tiny desk lived in the corner by a digital window frame.

The picture was relayed in real time from cameras on the outside of the building.

The bright lights of the downtown district danced in the darkness. You could lean forward and gaze down at the hectic pedestrian walks seventy meters below. You could look up and watch the air cars stream along between the buildings at a hundred meters.

I shrugged off the view, turned my attention to the desk, and found what I was looking for laying in plain view: a pad of multicolored stationery with gold leaf trim laying right on top. I set it aside and searched the rest of the desk, top to bottom, and found a stack of New Sunrise Outreach pamphlets like the one from Bertrand's room and one graphite pencil.

I picked up the pencil and ran it over the top paper in the pad, taking care not to use too much pressure. A familiar script came to life:

My Dearest Harry,

I hope this letter finds you well and as hungry for me as I am for you. Not being with you is killing me. I ache to have you inside me, to feel your tongue on my body, to taste your body with my tongue!

I'm sorry you're finding things so difficult at home, but I think I can show you a thing or two about the world and the path to Truth. Meet me at the Randy's tonight, and we can talk about it.

Then we can go to my place and raise our love to a new level.

M.

M. I pulled the top copy, folded it, and placed it onto my jacket. The rest of the office was empty save a hard drive on the floor I wasn't likely to get into and a bean bag chair in the corner.

I glanced into the closet; empty save a hand-operated vacuum and an empty clothes basket. I slipped through the corridor and past the kitchen only to realize I was hungry. The Blue Knight's beer was all I'd had by mouth in the last twelve hours.

I found some bread-like product on her counter and laid it open to make room for a nice spreadable meat substance or vegi-compound. There were tomatoes and lettuce from a container labeled Third Region Farms. I remembered Wendy Jenkins and the operation she had at Pandrom. It was almost enough to kill my appetite. I added some cheese product and a bean spread to my sandwich and closed everything back up. I opened the door again, stooped to place it all on the same shelf and stopped in mid-act.

My eyes fell upon a clear bag with tiny, paper-thin tabs. I couldn't say where I set the sandwich ingredients. I needed my hands free to reach for the bag of pale green pills with straight-edged veins of yellow-beige computer board running through them. I'd never spent any time in narcotics, but plenty of people had been killed over this drug, M-plant.

It was supposed to be kept cool and dry, but only distributors bothered with the cool part. I pulled the insulated case designed to keep out moisture and set it on the table, next to my sandwich. I laid it out and counted. This was almost ten k in M-plant. More than enough to send Zimmerman to tend the Pandrom Farms for decades.

Things were really coming together, now.

* * *

I was dreaming about Mattie again, and of the false promise I'd been forced to make to her, when the *beep* of Camilla Zimmerman's door reached into my slumber. I jerked awake on her couch and was greeted by the silhouette of a man and woman in the doorway. They were melded together, mouths searching each other, clothes coming off.

I almost felt a pang of pity for the young man. His plans for the evening were about to take a drastic turn. I pressed the handlight switch with my thumb and bathed them in brightness.

It had the same effect as pouring icy water on humping dogs. Camilla turned in my direction, one hand shielding her eyes, the other moving toward her purse. Her ride for the evening was a teenager, younger than Bertrand. He was skinny, with dark brown skin and thick black hair that hung in a coarse drape over his forehead. He guarded his eyes from the light as his body language shifted from surprised to angry.

"What's up, Camilla? Or should I call you M?"

The kid glared against the bright white beam of my handlight. He looked at Camilla. "What's all this about, Milly?"

So, it was Milly. "You must be Harry!"

"It's Harrison. Who the fuck are you? And how do you know my name?"

I held the graphite copy up. "I got it off this." I drew Bertrand's letter from the other pocket. "It reminds me a lot of this one, written a few short weeks ago to another student." I glanced at Zimmerman. "Isn't that right, Milly?" She looked as if there might've been a frog swimming in her soup. "Some pretty racy literature for a church recruiter, wouldn't you say, Milly?"

"Harrison, I want you to leave. Mr. Parker and I have some things to clear up."

"No way!" Harry took a step toward me. "I'm not scared of this guy."

"Be smart, Harry. What do you think the cops'll say about this bag of M-plant with Milly's prints and DNA all over it?" I gestured at the bag next to me. "And, these letters? When they find out they're in her hand—what do you think'll happen to her, then?"

Harry didn't back down. "There's nothing illegal about our letters. We're in love!"

"Sure you are, but what about Bertrand?"

"Bertrand?" He looked at Camilla.

"I have to talk to this man, Harry. I'll rec you later. K?" She looked at me. "There's no law against what we're doing."

I shrugged and held her gaze. "Maybe, but if you or any of your affiliates profited, this would become fraud. And, you're forgetting the drugs. That's distribution level shit. That alone gets you to Pandrom for a long, long time."

Camilla paled and spoke in her best professor voice. "Go, Harrison. I'll rec you later."

Harry gave a last frustrated glance to each of us and left. Camilla waited until the elevator took him from the floor before speaking. "Who do you think you are—"

"We're past that, Milly. Tell me what I need to know, or my next conversation is with a campus detective."

She glared for several long moments and then sighed. "What?"

"Tell me everything, from the beginning. The whole scam, the indoctrination, how you came to be a member, everything. Leave nothing out."

"There's no group. I—"

"I know all about New Sunrise Outreach and how it operates. I know about recruitment and how drugs and sex are major components of that process. I know you were pinched as a minor for stealing from a Lower City New Sunrise temple and did community service there. I found literature from that same New Sunrise in Bertrand's room. The same room his mother found these." I held up the letters. "I can drop all of this in your lap and let the police do their work, but I suspect there's no time for that. Shoot straight with me, save me some time, and I'll try to help a sister out. Lie to me, and I'll turn you over to someone you don't want to lie to."

She sighed again and stared through the wall behind me. "I was hungry, doing what I had to to survive in the Lower City. Got caught stealing from a collection plate like I'd done a hundred times." She paused, and I waited. "It wasn't simple extortion. One of the deacons... actually took an interest. She took me under her wing and protected me, offered me a better life than panhandling and stealing for my next meal. She convinced the Prophet to give me a chance."

Prophet. "So, they spoke on your behalf and cut a deal for you to do community service."

She looked at the picture on the end table and nodded. "Outreach was better than jail."

"How much better?"

She hesitated. "There's an initiation process... once you get past that, it's a pretty good life, better than the Lower City."

"Initiation? You mean indoctrination?" She wouldn't meet my gaze. "All that bullshit about belonging and finding a better life was a prybar to manipulate your victims into going along with this. Right?"

Her head snapped up, bringing her gaze to mine. "Bertrand wasn't a vic—"

"That's all you wanted, to get this kid to trust you, so you could send him off to indoctrination. Right? Is that where Bertrand is right now?"

She took several guilty moments to answer. "He left last Friday for sabbatical."

"Left? This is Tycho City. Where the hell—"

I remembered Petrovich's diorama from the office. "Holy shit! He's in the compound?" Zimmerman nodded. Rage overtook me. "And that was fine by you. Right?" This woman disgusted me, but I needed her help and tongue-lashing her wouldn't do Bertrand any good. "How long is he gonna be there?"

"As long as it takes."

"As long as it takes?"

Her eyes found the floor again. "Initiation can be intense."

A cold fire burned inside me, and I nodded for her to continue. "Intense."

We shared a long, tense silence, and Zimmerman said, "They are well-versed in reaching people on a spiritual level."

I remembered my visit from the church and the outreach center. "They use the AI."

She glanced at the pic on the end table and back to the floor. "It accelerates the progression through direct interface and eases the candidate's inhibitions."

Candidate! I was seething. "You mean it makes bending their mind to your will easier." She didn't respond. "And that's where the M-plant comes in?" She nodded. M-plant accentuated the impact of the AI and would further segregate Bertrand from reality. "How long does this take? Start to finish?"

"He's probably already been through primary initiation."

"Meaning?"

"Meaning he's probably undergoing confession."

"Confession?"

"Exorcising one's sins by professing them to the Prophet."

I was familiar enough with this. "You mean he shares his deepest, darkest secrets for Petrovich to use as leverage." I took her nonresponsiveness as confirmation. "And, we're at what? Ten days? Almost eleven?"

Zimmerman didn't respond. I considered my options and saw legal wrangling and denials, counterclaims of malfeasance against a worried mother. Weeks and months sliding by as nothing happened. There was only one course of action. "Okay. How do I break into the compound?"

Zimmerman laughed. "You don't."

I leaned forward. "Well, we're gonna change that. And, you're gonna help me, whatever that means."

* * *

It was after three before I pushed through the door at Foxx's office. It was always strange walking into a place after hours. The spotlight over James's desk shined down, leaving the rest of the silent office in shadow. It was both peaceful and creepy.

I showered and tossed my dirty clothes in a pile by the bed. I hung my jacket, lay on the sofa bed, and stared at the string chart. Was I going to get the chance to solve this case? Or would I ever come back from this ridiculously dangerous mission?

Would I ever see Mattie again? I thought about Bertrand, a grown-ass man who should've known better than to end up out there in a compound having his brain washed. Why should I risk never seeing Mattie again and all that would mean to her over him? But this wasn't only about Bertrand. This was about the hundreds or maybe thousands who'd met with his fate and the hundreds or thousands that would become victims if I did nothing.

I stared into the chart. When you join the force, you're usually young and single, ready to take on the world. You're prepared to take the risk, to sacrifice for others, even though you never truly believe you're gonna die. But when you get married and have kids, the badge grows heavier, and the only thing that keeps you kicking doors in is the knowledge that you're standing between the bad guys and kids just like your own. That's what I had to do tomorrow, put myself between the bad guys and a bunch of people just like Mattie.

A recent conversation I'd had came to mind, and I knew what I had to do. I pulled out a piece of paper and began to write:

Mattie,

I got your letter, and it's great you think so much of your old man. But the truth is, I was never around as much as I should've been.

You've given up as much to protect this city as I have, and that makes you and your mom pretty damned special. I don't know why you've tolerated sharing me with the scum of the city, but I'm glad you did it all the same.

Tomorrow, I have to go into harm's way. When I get back, I'm going to make uncomplicating this mess my one and only priority. I'm not spending another moment I don't have to removed from your life.

With All my Love,

Dad

I read the letter and cried myself to sleep, certain I would never see my daughter again.

Chapter Twenty-one

Tsaris walked into Jake's Coffeehouse looking fresh and spry. I'd grown to like this place. It was a great rendezvous spot when I wanted to keep away from the Loonies, the Upper City snoops, or the prying eyes of the TCPD. He sat without being invited. "You look like a man who needs coffee."

"Got some." My voice was heavy with fatigue.

"Care to tell me why you dragged me down here at this ungodly hour?"

"It's five thirty, Andy. All that eight to five Professional Standards duty making you soft?"

Tsaris grunted. "It's not as soft as you think. I get hauled out of bed when one of you clowns fuck up, same as any other detective."

The waitress set a cup of coffee in front of Tsaris. He thanked her. I watched him take a long, black draught. "I have a problem."

Tsaris chuckled. "You, Frank Parker, have more than a problem."

"I know you don't like me, and I can live with that. Truth is, you aren't exactly one of my heroes, either. I might have gotten lost along the way, but I never did anything that wasn't in the best interests of the citizens of Tycho City."

"Is that what you tell yourself, Frank? That violating people's rights is in the interests of the city? What are you gonna tell Allison Kramer's mom after framing Kelly Gordon? How are you gonna explain to her why her daughter is dead, so you could put your pet project behind bars?"

I looked away, but he pressed on. "What are you gonna tell the families of Gordon's victims? 'Sorry, I had to take shortcuts. Now, your attacker's back on the streets with millions in settlement money to boot?'" Tsaris paused. "You sure you wanna do this without counsel?"

"There's no time for any of that. I have a job that's liable to get hairy."

Tsaris tipped his head. "Is this a police matter, Mister Parker?"

"Not at the moment."

"Are you saying you're about to commit some kind of crime, Frank? I'm still a cop, you know."

I managed not to laugh. "I'm telling you my life is in danger. I can't keep running head on into these situations and expect to come out whole forever."

"So, turn it over to—"

"That doesn't work. I may already be too late, but some jobs take time to be done right."

"So, why the fuck am I here?"

"Mattie didn't do anything to deserve the spot she's in. Get her and her mother, put them in police custody, away from Katsaros and his thugs."

"In return for what?"

"I have a file on an unsolved case. It's probably not enough to get a conviction, but it'll show you where to look. You'll have to take it from there."

"Lenny Marquez."

"I didn't kill her. I was never planning any harm to that girl." I turned my eyes toward the window at the front of the shop. "Katsaros used me."

"And a streetwise cop like you didn't think he was capable of that. Right?" I didn't look at him. "Or, maybe you thought the great Frank Parker could handle this on his own, could be a one-man band. Right?"

I tried not to think of the times Dana Cooper urged me to take Marquez's info to the Seventh Precinct. "I was doing the best I could, given the circumstances."

"That gonna be your defense in court?"

"This isn't court."

Tsaris studied me with hard eyes. "No. That's not how this works, Frank. I'm not gonna be some kind of insurance policy."

I looked across the table. "If I get through this, I'll help you bring that bastard down, myself, the moment I get my daughter and her mother out of his clutches. But this has to be the way."

Tsaris glared at me, color rising in his cheeks. I decided to take a chance. "I've picked up another missing person gig. The kid's in trouble, way beyond the reach of the law. If I don't help him, he'll just be the latest victim of a powerful little machine that's exploiting disenfranchised kids. I know I'm doing the same thing I did with Lenny, but I don't see another way."

He said nothing and sat staring at me.

I leaned over, gritting my teeth. "Look, hate me all you want, but you are still sworn to serve and protect. Suzanne and Mattie are as innocent as Lenny Marquez or Bertrand Mellenburg."

"Mellenburg?"

I pushed on. "Katsaros holds on to them as insurance against my knowledge of his involvement in the Marquez murder."

"If you're such a liability, why doesn't he kill you?"

"I suspect for the same reason I tried to help Marquez on my own; he thinks he has things under control."

Tsaris took another sip, but his eyes never softened. "And, you think offering me Katsaros makes up for years of shady police work?"

"I'm not only offering Katsaros. I think I'm closing in on the people who murdered Rick Sanchez." He gaped at my words, and I pressed on. "I know you were investigating the Three-three for corruption. I know

Carson's role as a go-between. I know T-Van was under orders from Rocamora to set Rick up. And, I know Rocamora didn't kill him, at least not directly."

"You saying you have firsthand knowledge that the Rock had a hand in Rick's murder?"

"Secondhand, maybe third. I also know that Carson was a key connection to Rocamora and a bunch of dirty cops he called his 'cuff 'em or cut 'em' crew."

"You mean the same David Carson who worked as Rick's super?"

I sighed and watched the foot traffic roll by, suddenly regretting this conversation. "Yes."

A smug smile of gloat spread across his face. "Looks like it's not such a long walk from framing innocent pimps to helping scum like Rocamora. Eh, Parker?"

I glared across the table, but what could I say? Rick was taking ten thousand a shot from him in "poker" games. Of course, he was dirty. "Yeah, Rocamora must've thought Professional Standards was getting too close—" A new thought occurred to me, and I glared across the table. "How'd Rocamora know you were closing in, *Andy*? You find a way to throw your balls in his face the way you always do? You start bullying Rocamora as if he was one of the cops you harass?"

The smile on Tsaris's face fell. "Don't forget who you're talking to, Parker. You called this meeting, not me. I'd just as soon your family stay safe, but bad shit happens every day. I'm not gonna weep any louder for them than I do the rest of the city."

I wanted to snatch this guy by the throat, throttle him like the bitch he was, but he held Mattie over my head, and my usual subtle ways wouldn't do, here. "My point is, I know some things. Things you don't. I can give that to you and give you your shiny trophy. That's what you really want. Right? To be the guy who took down Rocamora's insiders?"

"My priority is in protecting the interests of the TCPD, Tycho City, and its citizens." His words were pretty, but I could smell the naked ambition coming off him. "Turn over any data you have and I'll— "

"That's not how this goes, Andy. If I get killed, you get my files. If not, we'll have plenty to discuss when I get back."

"Back?"

Tsaris wasn't as stupid as I sometimes gave him credit. I'd have to be more careful in the future. "Do we have a deal, or don't we?"

"I'll do what I can."

It wasn't ironclad, but it would have to do. "Fair enough." Shaking hands with this prick made me want to puke.

* * *

"You talked to him without me?" Foxx glared across her desk.

"I didn't have time—don't have time."

"You have a hearing in five days!"

"I might not live that long."

Janet sat up and studied me for several long moments. "Is there something I should know?"

I handed the letter I'd written for Mattie across the desk. "I know where Bertrand is."

She took the envelope. "But you don't have him, yet?"

"No."

"And, you intend to do an extralegal intervention to get him out of harm's way."

"It's the only choice."

"Care to elaborate?"

I caught her up on the events, focusing on Camilla and her role as a recruiter for New Sunrise. "Camilla is going to help me get in."

"She is? How's she doing that?"

"To start? She's setting up a fake ID to get me into the Sunrise compound. It's been fed into a super-avatar provided by a local hacker."

"Khatri?" I shrugged and she sighed. "And, this Khatri, is she going with you?"

"No."

"So, you're infiltrating an AI-enhanced, high security compound with no tech support and no advanced intel on where this kid is or if he's even still there?"

"Something like that."

"Not good, Frank. I was thinking all the PR from the Latham thing could help me get you a deal, but if this goes south—"

"That's why I had to talk to Tsaris, cop-to-cop."

"Cop-to-cop, huh? You think that shit matters?"

"If something happens to me, I want you to turn over all files pertaining to Lenny Marquez, Rick Sanchez, and Petrovich to him."

"Frank, I—"

"You make sure they take care of Mattie and Suzanne. Okay? You get guarantees of their safety and burn those bastards to the ground. Got it?"

She looked at me, her skin the color of moon dust. "How long before you're overdue?"

"A couple of days, maybe a week."

"I'll have to postpone the hearing."

"Okay, then." I stood and hesitated. "Janet, I—uh—"

"Just come back in one piece, Frank."

I nodded. "Sure," I said, and left.

Chapter Twenty-two

Maggie Mellenburg looked out her office window. "You're sure you're going to find him in Petrovich's resort?"

"As sure as I can be."

"And, this professor. This street urchin-turned-recruiter, you can trust her?"

"In that I have her back against the wall, yes."

"But she could have warned her employer, could be sending you to your death, so she can go about her business unmolested, or could just be an extremely good liar." We both knew Camilla Zimmerman had to be that, if nothing else. "And yet, you're going to act on her word without a second thought?"

"Oh, I've had second thoughts," I said. "But if I leave this to you and your lawyers or call the police, his lawyers get involved, his influence becomes a factor. This drags out for weeks or months, and eventually the reprogrammed Bertrand is brought forward to tell everyone everything is fine, he's just on this new and wonderful path, right before he slips back into the church, never to be seen again. Every second, every moment counts. Petrovich's AI has been molding him for almost two weeks. Damage has already been done. The question is will it be permanent?"

The words had the weight of a fist on Maggie's expression, and I thought she might cry. But she held back. "And, you're going over there on your own?"

"It's the only way."

"But— "

"Bertrand doesn't have that kind of time."

I could feel the woman's powerful mind churn, weighing her options. "And, this considerable money I'm giving you. It's going to this street urchin?"

"No, a third-party hacker. It's the only way to beat the on-site AI."

Another long silence stretched between us. "And, you think you can pull this off?"

"It's going to be difficult."

She turned from the window, her voice sharp. "You mean suicidal." I didn't meet her gaze. "For you and my son."

Lenny Marquez's cold corpse flashed through my mind. "No one said my raid has to be the only front in this operation."

* * *

I marveled at Doctor Camilla Zimmerman's office. It was spacious and neat and made the one Mary Hauser shared with her officemate look like a closet. I commented on the fact.

"A woman willing to do what she has to can get a lot of perks, Detective." I thought of Jorge Gomez and wondered how many other men she led around by the genitals. She read my expression. "Don't be so damned judgmental. I'm a survivor. Besides, I'm helping *you*, aren't I?"

Not by choice. I dismissed the thought and returned to business. "I need the ID info for the hacker."

She recced me the file. "You still haven't told me who this mysterious hacker is."

"And I'm not going to." I forwarded the file to Khatri.

"Still don't trust me?"

"I'm a survivor." We shared a grin, and I turned back to the matter at hand. "So, let's go over what I can expect."

The guilt clouding her features made me nervous. "I was only there, once, you know, and that was for a grand opening celebration, not initiation."

"I'll take what you can give me."

She took a deep breath and looked at the wall behind me. My pReC flashed again. A generic floor plan with large swathes of blind spots hung in my vision. "What can you tell me about these unmarked areas?"

"Restricted."

"You been in them before?"

"Some of them, but I wasn't exactly doing a tactical analysis of the place."

"Anything you can give me would help."

Zimmerman thought for several long moments. "Most of them are offices and such...I remember seeing a pretty sophisticated-looking security office."

"Does he lease out his security or—"

"Not in the sanctuary. They're all members of the church with unquestioned loyalty. Lots of current and ex-cops. They're all well paid and very competent."

"No volunteers."

"Not among the security."

"So, what can I expect? Procedurally?"

Another long moment of contemplation stretched between us. "They're going to sort you, interview you, compare you to the files I sent—I can go over that, if you like."

"Nah, I'll read over it on my own."

She nodded. "Once they get you sorted, they'll put you into classes, intense classes designed to reach out to your deepest, darkest insecurities. They have a pretty sophisticated AI that reads your body language and EEG. It will probe and probe and probe with messages of positivity, but I've heard there are subliminal messages layered within them that are designed to accentuate despondency and alienation."

"Making the students more dependent upon the church."

"In so many words, yes. Also, it's said the AI has the ability to influence dreams. So, keep that in mind, if you stay overnight."

"How much contact can I expect to have with other guests?"

"Very little. You do have joint classes, but much of it's virtual, and you'll be isolated from each other by firewalls."

I thought about the super-avatar Mickey Khatri was working on and wondered if it would be enough. "Group meals?"

"Not at first. The procedure is adjusted all the time, so there's no knowing, for sure, but that's how it was when I worked the rehab division." Rehab. "There are also the meds."

"Meds? Like for me?"

"Yeah, mostly injected stuff, cocktails of some kind."

"What kind of cocktails?"

"That was never my job. Strictly med techs and doctors dealt with the drugs. So, I couldn't even begin to guess."

Her words rang false, but I was in no position to dispute her. "And if I refuse?"

"The drugs?"

I nodded.

"You're trying not to be noticed. Right?"

I sighed. How the hell was I going to break into this place sleep-deprived and stoned on psych meds? "Sure you won't come along? I could use the help."

She shook her head. "Same reason as the meds. I never go to the sanctuary. Doing it now, with you, would draw attention to both of us."

She looked at the pic on the desk with sad eyes. It was the same woman from the end table, but teenaged Camilla was in the pic. They radiated joy with arms around each other. I had a moment of insight. "That's the deacon who saved your life. What happened to her?"

She drew a deep breath. "Darlene isn't in my life anymore."

"You're not a believer?"

She slipped a confident mask over her melancholy. "I told you; I'm a survivor, Detective. It was nice for a while, but you can't con a con. True colors always bleed through."

"But you do their bidding."

She shrugged. "Old habits die hard. Being with the Tabernacle has its perks, and, if they want to believe I'm a righteous servant doing their bidding out of love and devotion, who am I to tell them otherwise?"

I frowned and considered asking her to cooperate with the authorities if I didn't come back, but I could already hear her answer. *"I'm a survivor. Remember?"*

"Take care of yourself, Milly."

* * *

"Harrison Diggler?" Mickey Khatri, or the avatar portraying Mickey Khatri, absorbed the file Camilla gave me. This time she didn't resemble Dana Cooper, at all. She sported a perfect, golden-brown body, sun-kissed breasts barely contained by a skimpy, green bikini top that was more string than sling. Black hair danced across her face, driven by the crisp, salt breeze sweeping in from her right.

A hot, steamy jungle stood in for the precinct interrogation room. I had to admit it was a great improvement. We were looking down a cliff at a lagoon of clear water flanked on three sides by lush green. The metallic reflection of fish scales gleamed from below the surface as they danced underneath.

A hot, bright sun stared down through the break in the trees created by the falloff of the cliff. Puffy, white clouds tinged with shadows of grey crawled across a canvas of pale blue. And, low on the horizon, beyond the mouth of the lagoon, the crescent form of Luna, ghostly and white, looked back at me.

The heat assaulted my body, turning it slick with perspiration and making the air heavy with humidity. I'm not sure I would want to live this way all the time, but to a man who'd only read about these things or felt humidity in the shower, it was a feast of the senses. "Is this what Earth's really like?"

"Some of the nuisances have been filtered out, but the program was generated by real probes on site." I took in the wild beauty around me, so vibrant and full of life, and stopped thinking about this mission that was liable to be my last. Khatri brought me back, though. "I'm not sure how long I can guarantee your safety on this one. I've done some research into what you're likely to face. It looks to be a very aggressive program.

"Your one advantage is that it's going to try to work in the background, probing slowly to mask its presence. The more vigilant you are in feeling for it, the slower it's likely to progress."

"And how am I supposed to do that?"

"The unenhanced mind can only bear one thought at a time. So, keep it on something specific, something meaningful."

I remembered Camilla's warnings about dreams. "What if I go to sleep?"

"Don't."

"And drugs?"

"Depends on what kind of drugs they use. I can give you some agonist agents to counteract the meds, but the half-life is universally short. I could give you a couple of syringes, but..."

"If they found that, they might escort me to the nearest airlock." I shook my head. Prep was key in these matters, and I was being dropped into a snake pit with one eye gouged and my hands tied together. "I'll take the loading dose right before I step onto the transport. It's the best I can do."

She nodded. "Have you stopped to think that you won't be able to get out of there if it all goes to hell?"

Have I thought about it? "It's crossed my mind."

"And?"

"I have something in mind for that."

* * *

Shannon Lafave leaned in her pilot's chair; her round face pensive. "Lemme get this straight. You're offering me five thousand bills a day to hover around this surface compound and wait for your message to come pick you up and deliver you safely back here when you call?"

"Yes."

"And, that could be anytime between this evening and next month?"

I frowned. "If you don't hear from me in a week's time, you are to—"

"Get word to this lawyer, Foxx."

"Right."

"And the flight plan for Lunar Control?"

I grinned at her. "A little thing like a flight plan can't stop a former LDF pilot, can it?"

Shannon had provided me with taxi services during the Lenny Marquez case. I liked her, but she was an odd one. The last time we'd talked, she hadn't closed her mouth. Today, she was being downright cagey. "I could swing it—for an even fifty k."

"Fifty thousand?"

"It's the best I can do."

The best she could do. It was extortion. "That's some eighty-six alpha bullshit, Shannon."

Shannon laughed. She'd once been in the Lunar Defense Force. Eighty-six alpha was an old LDF code for situations deemed too hectic or dangerous to ride out and was transmitted when commanders wanted to break contact and regroup. It came to be used as any fucked up situation or behavior. "I'll have to reach out to my employer, but I'm sure she can swing it."

Shannon beamed, and I saw the chatty cabbie who'd staked out Allyssa Ramacci with me come to life. "Then, partner, we have a deal."

I smiled. Great.

Chapter Twenty-three

The address Camilla had given me was a repurposed warehouse in the same neighborhood as the flat Emily Harris rented and the notorious Drane Street hotel where Lenny Marquez met her fate. The church AI had a broad reach and tickled my pReC from half a block away. I injected the counteragent Khatri had given me, dropped the pneumo-injector into the trash, and strode up the block. I followed the signs that said "Intake" to a metal-framed glass door.

A short, mocha-skinned woman in a skirt suit sat inside at the counter. She stood and gave me her brightest smile. "Good morning, Mr. Diggler! I'm so happy to see you chose to join us!" Mr. Diggler. This AI was scary. I was suddenly aware of a crawling sensation in the base of my skull and soft whispers of platitudes in my ears. "Did you bring your tithes?"

My tithe was ten thousand bills. I transferred it from the expense account Maggie Mellenburg had established for me. Her eyes twinkled at the confirmation. "You're all set. Welcome to the family and have a spiritual awakening."

"Thanks," I said. "I'm just looking for a new purpose in life."

"Well, you will find it here."

"I'm sure I will." The wall panel to my right slid aside, revealing a short tunnel of soft black and the *drum-drum* noise of churning machinery. It was a state-of-the-art body scanner.

"Please step though." The baritone voice was dour and grave and would have been at home on an undertaker. It belonged to a monster of a man in navy blue coveralls who filled the exit of the passageway. A large, powerful face looked down from behind a tangled growth of white-flecked black beard. A smile touched his heavy lips, but it revealed no teeth and stayed so far from his walnut eyes. It might've belonged to someone else.

I stepped through the scanner, feeling naked and bare. The big man held out a massive paw. "Your bag, please." I handed it by the strap. He hefted it and gestured down the corridor with one python arm. "This way, Mr. Diggler." He let me pass and then followed. "All the way to the end."

The soothing whisper in my ears belonged to Petrovich. It had risen to a low, conversational voice that went on and on about the Grace of God and how wonderful it was that I had chosen this moment to turn my burdens over to Him. It talked about direction and purpose and meaning, and I tried to stop listening.

We reached the end of the hallway. A balding man with a medium build stood in an exam room. Patches of white and grey clung to his ears and wrapped the base of his skull. He didn't even turn from the meds he was gathering. "Have a seat," he said in a nasal voice. "I'll be with you in a moment."

The door behind me closed, and it was just the two of us. "That man took my bag," I said, trying to sound offended.

"For your safety and ours." His demeanor implied he addressed this complaint every hour of every day. He turned and looked at me. "Harrison Ryan Diggler, 22 October 2215?"

"That's right."

"Good." He nodded, turned toward the medical equipment next to my chair, and placed a few wireless probes on me. "Feeling okay, today?"

"A little nervous."

"That's all very normal—very normal." He smiled and stared at the readouts. His voice came off as distracted rather than supportive. "Excellent! Any allergies?"

I shook my head.

"Taking any meds?"

I shook it again.

"Okay." He reached for a pneumo-injector that made the one I'd just used look puny. "This'll sting a little." He pressed it to my arm and *pfft*. It felt like the gorilla with my bag had punched me.

"Ouch!"

"All done," he said.

"What's that?" I asked.

His eyes gleamed from below bushy, grey eyebrows. "A little something for the nerves." He didn't muss my hair, but his tone said he wanted to. *Run along to school, little Frankie!*

Another hidden panel at the back of the room slid aside, revealing an empty corridor with thick carpet and plain, papered walls. Pastor Wayne Petrovich stood there, plastic smile on his tan face. "Welcome to the flock, Harrison."

He wasn't real. It was an AI projection into my pReC, but damned if I'd have been able to tell the difference without advanced knowledge. I stood and left the man in the lab coat without another word.

The panel slid shut behind me, and the corridor became a windowed aisle with plants and trees brushing the outer surface of the glass. The whispers resumed, soft promises of grace and love playing backup to the words of AI Petrovich.

"Milly has told us all about you," said the fake preacher, his voice excited and energetic.

"I-I see," I said, trying to force real insecurity into my mind, supporting the work of Khatri's avatar. "She—she's a wonderful lady."

"She is." The AI turned and stared into me. "She thinks a lot of you."

He led me through a door, another sliding panel, into a waiting area. It was small, only a few seats. "You will board first. Please wait here." The AI passed through the door and disappeared.

I might have sat there for ten minutes. I might have sat there for hours. There was no way to know with the drugs and competing software waging war over control of my mind. I did have a lot of lucid dreams about Rick and Mattie and one disturbing hallucination about Camilla.

"Harrison." Petrovich's oily, bourbon-smooth voice broke me from the spell. His avatar stood in the door opposite the panel through which he had escorted me. "We are ready to seat you."

He led me through an open waiting room to an elevator that opened onto the roof and the landing pads. One hosted a Sydek Industries cargo hauler. It was a gross, ungainly looking beast with lots of cargo space in its rear holds that gave the monster its delta wing shape. But the front, nose section could be configured for passengers, and that's where a compartment door stood open with a long gangway reaching down to the scorched and stained landing pad.

A woman stood at the base. The blonde tips of her brown hair danced in the wash of the vertical engines. Her bright, toothy smile cast a beam, calling to me. The elevator doors closed, and AI Petrovich was gone, or at least the vision of him was. I could feel the AI poking and probing, whispering sweet nothings into my subconscious.

I strode across the pad, and the woman shouted over the whining engines as I drew near. "We're delighted to have you. Please, follow the red path to your berth." A red line like the one from Khatri's salon guided me up the stairs, toward the back of the craft, and into a private berth.

A flimsy pocket door had been cast open. A couch was crammed inside. My bag rested against the arm. I sat. Obeyed Petrovich's voice admonishing me to fasten my harness and listened to the whine of the engines rise.

My stomach lurched as the craft left the pad, and I told myself it was just the motion. But I wasn't kidding anyone, as my last delicate link to Tycho City and the safety it offered had been severed.

* * *

"Welcome and let God's Grace touch your spirit and guide you through this great process!" Petrovich's voice was a gentle hand on my soul, a reassuring blanket against the cold, uncaring world. I tried to shrug off the feeling of contentment and recenter myself, but I was losing the will.

I wondered without caring if this was the result of Khatri's antidotes wearing off, the power of the cocktail shot into my arm, or the relentless digging of the AI. "All of the above" seemed the most likely answer. The whine of the engines receded, and my seatbelts fell away. The flimsy cabin door slid open, and the same woman from the ramp smiled at me. "We're here!"

I smiled at her patronizing tone. "That didn't take long."

"Heavens, no! We're not that far away."

Just in a completely different biosphere, separated by kilometers of cold vacuum. "It'll be a nice getaway."

Her smile somehow brightened. "Oh, you don't know the half of it!"

I wondered if I'd want to. "So, what's first?"

She stepped aside and gestured down the corridor. "It depends on what group you're with. The system will guide you."

Another red ribbon appeared in my vision. Petrovich's voice was still low in my ear, babbling on and on until I barely recognized him. A shudder of fear rippled through me. This program was lulling me into complacency. I pushed back against the relentless AI, wide awake and on my fullest guard. But the morass of chemically induced apathy and fatigue were already pulling at me again.

I grabbed my bag, smiled at the woman, and strode toward the gangway. *"...ord doesn't want you to live in pain or fear. He wants you to be with Him, to be safe, to be under His very wing of protection..."* I followed the ribbon down the ramp.

I stood in a giant austere hangar, dark and dour. Unfinished moonrock walls looked out from all sides. Mirrored windows suggesting a control room shined in the wall at the rear of the spacecraft. A massive door had been cut into the wall next to it. It was all steel, reinforced by a thick frame, and looked to be a meter or more thick.

A buzzer sounded as I watched, and yellow lights to both sides began to pulsate. A loud *klack!* reverberated through the chamber, and the door began to rise with the growl of heavy machinery.

The vault had the feel of a military instillation, orderly to the point of religious devotion. Supplies had been stowed in metal cage lockers, keeping the floor clear of debris that might be a tripping or decompression hazard. I looked up at the heavy door in the ceiling, the inner door of the massive airlock through which we'd just passed.

"...care not for the burdens of this world," Petrovich was saying, *"it is all for naught next to His Kingdom..."* A group had collected at the bottom of the ramp. They gaped at their surroundings, looking as amazed and dumfounded as I felt.

"It is amazing what we can achieve when we do His work." The woman's voice carried over the cooling engines and bustling noise of the flight crew in a way that suggested AI enhancement. Her plain, unmade face was round and pleasant with a matronly quality. "He is so good. Is He not?"

"Amen!" said the rest of the crowd, or was that the AI talking?

I walked down the last couple steps to the bottom of the gangway and tried to blend. AI Petrovich continued to drone on in my subconscious, but I couldn't make out definitive words. There was an unsettling scratching and tickling in the base of my skull, like a beetle burrowing into wood, but I couldn't bring myself to be alarmed.

"I am Bonnie DeGigglio, counselor here at New Sunrise Outreach. I will be in charge of guiding you on your journey of spiritual enlightenment and with facilitating your greater bond with God and the Prophet Petrovich."

The Prophet Petrovich.

Bonnie led us across the concrete pad, past the scrambling ground crew, and toward the yawning chasm left by the door at the back of the hangar.

AI Petrovich filled the silence*"...giving yourself over to Him is the single most important part of cleansing the ugliness of this unclean world of our own making. It is only through Him that we..."*

Bonnie led us up a staircase built into the back wall of the hangar and into a small chapel, intimate and cozy. A gas fireplace burned at the front of the room. An arch of religious symbols was carved into the wall's face, and a picture of Pastor Wayne Petrovich smiled from the mantle.

"This will be our meeting place," said Bonnie. "Follow your tethers to your rooms and meet here in ten minutes."

New ribbons appeared, and we followed them to our rooms. My room was simple and plain, like the rest of the place I'd seen so far, but something about me wasn't happy about having privacy. I realized with alarm I hadn't spoken to another member of the retreat, and it made me feel sad, lonely, and isolated.

I missed Mattie and Suzanne and regretted the mess my life had become. I can't say where the tears came from, but they broke through without warning; memories of dead girls, of Candy Watkins, of the Adrieux kids, of Lenny Marquez rushed through my mind in an agonizing stream of consciousness that took my breath away.

My knees folded, and I crumpled to the floor in the soft gravity, alone, empty, and far from the world I knew. What was I going to do? How was I going to get out of this mess? What was going to become of me and my family?

Wayne Petrovich stood in the doorway. I'd never seen his smile look so sincere, so honest, so comforting. "It is so easy for us to feel alone when this world is against us. But I know the path. I am the Prophet. I can show you the way." He reached out a soft, manicured hand. "Let me show you the way."

I stared at him, panting, lost, and uncertain, adrift in a black sea of pain. "Help me find my way," I said, and reached out my hand.

* * *

"And, he told me..." Jenna Gould was tiny and frail. First glance suggested she didn't eat much, but the telltale tremble in her hands and the involuntary facial tics morphing her face spoke of M-plant withdrawal. "...I was not good, that no daughter of his would ever...use and slut around on his bills. A-and that's the day he threw me out."

The "he" Jenna was talking about was Ted Gould, a low-level politician on the staff of Judith Wait. Judy was a junior city manager who oversaw public safety and was a rising star in the city. I wasn't sure about Gould. His name was foreign to me.

Bonnie remained in her spot in the circle, the fireplace at her back. She offered somber nods. "It is a shame when the people we love let us down, a hard lesson for us to learn. The worldly cannot be trusted." She gestured towards Rodrigo, a previous speaker who'd been molested by his rich actor father and friends at terrible parties.

"Even those we love the most will betray us, use us, cast us aside. Only God's Grace never fails." I found myself nodding with the rest of the group, thinking of the people I had let down: Rick, Suzanne, Mattie—Lenny Marquez. "Even we fail ourselves and others when we shun God's Grace and step away from the teachings of the Prophet."

Her eyes fell on me, hard and knowing. "Is that not so, Mr. Diggler?"

"Tell us, child," AI Petrovich said into my ear. *"Tell us about that horrible day, how you tried, how you just wanted to be there for her, to help—and how it all went so wrong."* The memory of Lenny flashed through my mind; the dark room, the gory mess, her bloodless skin glowing in the gloom. I worked my mouth and tried to speak, but I couldn't.

Didn't I have another story to tell? Wasn't I here on a case? Mellenchamp? I couldn't remember. There was no room in my brain for anything but the blood and the pale, cold flesh of a dead girl I had failed. Hot tears stung my eyes. A soothing voice promised me, *"It's all right. You tell us. We're listening. We don't judge."*

And I did. Every word. From when I was placed on leave by Rodson and Tsaris to the final moment I found her body, slashed and torn. The group stared and nodded like zombies. And I realized they weren't here.

They were interacting with the AI and their own private hell.

Chapter Twenty-four

I stood in the old flat—my flat? Rick's? I wasn't sure. But Rick was there sitting on the couch drinking a beer. Some badge groupie knelt before him, her red head bobbing up and down in his lap. He held his beer up and smiled. "Blow jobs ain't cheatin', Frank."

I averted my eyes. "Sure." I hated when Rick did this, whoring himself to any slut who'd drop her drawers or get on her knees for a few minutes' pleasure, even if I did understand the temptation. "But I need to know, Rick. I need to know what you were doing out there on Fifteenth Street."

The blissful smile left his face, and he looked hard at me. "I told you, partner. Someone was watching."

The world around us morphed, and we were in the On the Border Bar, the day we'd put Kelly Gordon away. I was sitting on a stool, Rick across from me, leaning over the pitcher, still a quarter full of dark brown liquid. The still bliss from the apartment had been replaced by the wild look of a drunk. "You remember this, huh? Our last night together? You had to run back to that bitch, Suzanne."

"I-it wasn't like tha—"

"Leaving me here, too drunk to think straight, too drunk to be left alone. Killed me like that"—he snapped his fingers, his brown eyes clear and bright—"You left me here, too drunk to be trusted with my own life."

But I heard him in a memory. *"You see that girl? I'm gonna fuck her tonight."* The memory was gone, but it fueled my argument. "That's not true. You were chasing that barfly. I turned and saw her, blonde hair, nice ass. Sheila Tanner." The investigator inside me broiled with rage. "How could you be so stupid?"

He poured his double into the pitcher before him. "Thanks a lot, partner."

I blinked, and we weren't in the bar anymore, but in a small wedding chapel in the Upper City, a place called Carmichael's. It had once been the source of tears of joy, but the tears Debbie Sanchez wept as she knelt at the altar in her wedding dress were not happy.

Rick lay in his coffin dressed in his finest uniform, a salad of medals on his breast and a pair of white gloves over his dark hands. Giant invitations on easels flanked his coffin:

Ryan and Monica Tyre invite you to the wedding of their daughter Debra to Officer Richard Sanchez, tCPD.

Announcing him as Officer Richard Sanchez had been Debbie's idea. She once loved the job that tore them apart and had been proud to be a cop's wife. It drew my mind to Suzanne and the similar course we had taken over the years. In hindsight, we seemed such fools for thinking police work wouldn't tear our marriage apart.

Petrovich stood over Rick's body in his ornate raiment. His fingertips rested on the edges of the coffin, a broad, plastic smile shining down at her. "God takes all the pain. Trust His healing hand. Reach out to Him. Welcome Him." He turned his dark gaze to me, the smile becoming ferocious, the bright lighting of the chapel growing dark and ominous. His eyes glowed red and menacing. When he spoke, his voice was low and bottomless. "Isn't that right, Detective Parker?"

I swallowed in fear and fell through emptiness that appeared at my feet, careening down through the darkness and down and down and down.

* * *

"Wakey, wakey." It was a man's voice, faraway and hollow, as if calling from another dimension. "Come on, Detective Parker. Open those eyes."

I opened my eyes to a posh office with a large wooden desk and a thick rug over dark wood. Somewhere behind me, a grandfather clock ticked away the seconds, and before me an unbroken string of windows looked out at the green of Petrovich Manor. It was as the diorama had portrayed it in his church office, but much more magnificent in person.

Tall oaks with great grey beards of moss towered over the shrubs and grass. The yellows, whites, and reds of various flowers blazed over bushes and across fields of green. Trails of crushed moonrock cut discreet footpaths around the greenery, protecting them from the wear and tear of traipsing feet.

A great circle of people sat in an open-air sanctuary, dressed in bright, gay colors. They looked happy, singing and moving to music I couldn't hear. A clump of simple moonrock barracks marked their "campsite" and the entire scene was backdropped by acrylic windows looking out at the endless white of a moonscape under a black, starry sky.

Somewhere out there, Shannon waited.

"You're alive! I'm so glad. It was feared the Vretathol had killed you. My medical director can be a bit aggressive at times." Wayne Petrovich sat in a grey, collared pullover with New Sunrise Tabernacle on his breast. The mauve leather office chair threatened to swallow him. He leaned forward on the desk, dark eyes intent on me, his manicured hands crossed before him.

"We're alone," said Petrovich. The beetle was digging in the base of my skull, searching for hidden treasure. I tried to push back, but I was so weak and so tired.

Petrovich smiled. "There's no resisting, now, Detective Parker.

We've already gotten most of what we need. Your AI has proven very formidable, even without your conscious mind present. But Khatri always does a great job. Eh?"

I tried to hide my surprise, but Petrovich must've seen a tell. "Hackers are artists, Detective. Just as a connoisseur can recognize a musician's work from a few bars, so, too, can fellow hackers. And, you'd be foolish for not thinking I hire the best."

The faux pleasantry fell from his face and voice. "What are you doing here, Detective Parker? We both know you didn't come all the way out here for the wayward child of a self-important strumpet."

I didn't answer, and he said, "We can find the answers we seek through more...forceful means, but I fear the damage we do could be permanent. The drugs alone are—well, potent. Add in the effects of the AI probe..." He shrugged. "You might spend an eternity in your own private hell."

I tried to listen. It was hard. The beetle dug harder and faster. I could feel it damaging my brain and conjured up resentment. "With you as my very own Lucifer."

"I'm an angel, Mr. Parker. The Prophet of God."

"You mean you profit from God."

Petrovich bellowed with laughter and slapped the desktop in approval. "That's very good, Detective, very good, indeed, profit." He paused and regarded me with curiosity. "You think this is about money."

He spread his arms in display of his surroundings. "Do I look like I need more money?"

I shifted in my chair, and remembered Jenna, the politician's daughter, and Rodrigo, the actor's son, loose threads in the lives of people on the edge of power, loose threads that could be harvested into puppet strings in ten years' time. "You feed their addiction! Let them have whatever they want and extort them for favors. Money. Intelligence. Whatever you ask. But don't people get suspicious of you? Don't they figure out your—"

I looked out at the gathering beneath the trees; people in gaily colored clothes singing and laughing, roaming the tidy barracks of their camp, right here on Petrovich Manor. "*They* are your cover story. Scores of people singing songs and sharing the joy as cover for the darker, deeper secret of what your cult is."

Petrovich frowned. "I had hoped for better from you, Detective." He turned away and the floor opened beneath me, swallowing me and casting me down, down, down into the darkness.

* * *

I sat in a doorless cell under a harsh white light, staring at a grey wall. It occurred to me to move, to search these confines for sign of a door, a window, a way out, but my body was paralyzed, immobile. I was alone with my jumbled thoughts, the quiet beseeching of the AI, and the maddening ticktock of the grandfather clock to keep me company. Ticktock, ticktock, tick...

I tried concentrate on the case at hand, to find my way through the soup, but I remembered. *"We both know you didn't come all the way out here for the wayward child of a self-important strumpet."*

He doesn't think I'm here just for Bertrand! I buried the thought. *"The unenhanced mind can only bear one thought at a time."* I turned my thoughts to Mattie and Suzanne.

The beetle continued to dig, and Petrovich's soft whispers turned desperate. *"You can't hide from me!"* The grey panel in front of me popped open, and I wasn't in the cell anymore.

I was strapped to a stainless-steel chair, a bright light shining in my eyes. I squinted and turned my head: Andy Tsaris was sitting in a nearby chair, two days' growth on his face. We were in my tiny quarters.

"What happened? Foxx gave us the skinny. Sent us down here looking for you."

"What about Bertrand?"

"The ERT is rounding everyone up now." I could hear the authoritative voices of cops giving commands echo from the other room. Tsaris smiled. "So, Bertrand Mellenburg, am I to believe that's what brought you all the way out here on a limb?"

I didn't look at him. He snapped the light off and stood over me. "You're taking coin from Angelo Katsaros, and you want me to believe some spoiled little rich kid who lost his way is your main reason for being here?"

Katsaros? What the hell did this have to do with Katsaros? A white flash obliterated the scene, and I was filled with the sensation of rising from a great depth.

Chapter Twenty-five

"Frank...Frank, it's me, Camilla."

I opened my eyes, my head spinning, and my vision blurred. Something like a woman hovered in the foreground. She leaned forward out of the fuzzy backdrop, concern on her face. "Camilla?" My tongue was thick and heavy in my mouth, causing the words to sound more like "Kamiwa?"

The figure gelled into something like the recruiter I'd interrogated before coming here. Had that been yesterday? A week ago? There was no telling.

"Here, drink this." She pressed a beaker to my mouth. I gulped down a terrible, chalky concoction. Cold, wet elixir ran from the corners of my mouth. My stomach revolted and threatened to cast the nasty-tasting substance back up and into her face. But it was gulp or drown, and I choked down as much as I could before pushing the container away. "What is this?"

"An antidote of sorts. Blocks the drugs New Sunrise has been pumping into you. You're not supposed to drink anything this soon, but I don't have time for your gut to settle." She pushed the beaker back to my lips, and I drank more of the bitter brew. Something drove deep into my arm, and I yelped, spilling antidote on my shirt. "Ow!"

"Ssshh," she said. "You trying to get us killed?"

I watched her face come more into focus, my scrambled brain running in slow motion. "No."

"Then let me bandage your arm. We're going to have to get out of here."

I gulped down the mixture and braced myself against the urge to vomit. "How long have I been here?"

"Twenty hours."

"Twenty hours?"

She sighed. "I knew there was no way you could pull this off, so I got some antidotes drawn up and came up here on the next shuttle."

"Why?"

"I have my reasons. Let's go."

I rose on unsteady feet and my gut lurched. The antidote spewed from my mouth and nose, searing my sinuses with its acid wash. It splattered all over the floor, splashing me and Camilla and painting the floor with its grey-white color. Another wave rose and splattered against the floor, adding a second coat.

I wiped my mouth on my vomit-stained shirt. "Sorry." Camilla shook her head but smiled. That's when I caught sight of the boy. "Bertrand?"

He was pale, and thinner than his pics. He trembled, his once sad eyes glazed and unfocused. Camilla brushed a lock of hair from his forehead. "I had to get him first. It's going to take them moments to realize you've been liberated. After that—"

"After that, they shut the whole place down."

"Right."

I tried not to be panicked, to see her as my escape route, but there was a wrongness here. Something I was missing. My scrambled instincts could feel it. I reached for a needle on the counter and gripped Camilla by the hair. I thrust the needle against her neck at the base of her jaw. My hands had lost a lot of their coordination and I pressed too close, drawing a trickle of blood. "Is that how this works? Keep fucking with my mind until there's nothing left?" Camilla remained calm and kept her voice even. Bertrand stared.

"Frank," she said. "I came here at great risk to myself. Petrovich's people will find out and will kill us all, you, me, the boy. Unless that's what you want, I suggest you let me go and follow me out of here."

I eased off the pressure, but there was nothing I could do about the shaking. "Follow you out? Where are you going to lead me to next? Pandrom Prison? Some crime scene from my memory?" My head spun, and I couldn't say what was real and what was a construct. "Are we even here?"

"Oh, Frank," she said, "this is reality, and we're losing time. If you don't—"

A calm voice filled my head. *"The facility is on alert."* It was Rick's voice, and I knew without being told that my avatar was warning me. I didn't let Camilla go. "My AI says the alert has gone out."

She deflated. "Then the shuttles are locked down."

"Shuttles?"

"I was hoping to stow away, but—"

I tried to smile, but it felt wrong to my drug-soaked brain. "Can you get me to the surface?"

She looked at me with confusion. "You mean beyond the biosphere?"

"Yeah."

A long moment of thought passed. "I suppose."

I smiled at Bertrand. "I've made arrangements."

* * *

We left my room and moved down the corridor toward the chapel. It was empty and quiet. No classes. No confessions. A fresh wave of nausea crested from the exertion, and I began to think I'd leave a trail of vomit for our pursuers to follow.

Bertrand made whimpering noises.

"Which way?" I asked Camilla.

"Here." She led us down a corridor toward a section of the facility not even on my bare-bones diagram.

The soup doing duty as my brain tried to make sense of this. "I thought you didn't know your way around."

"I did some recon during my search for Bernie. Here!"

I nodded, trying to figure out if my suspicion was from all the mindfucking I'd endured, or if there was something truly wrong. The corridor emptied into an elevator lobby. The light over the center car lit up, and the bell dinged. I stood in the middle of the floor with Bertrand, staring at the doors about to open.

Camilla grabbed us both, dragging us into a janitorial closet. Something about the place seemed familiar. A fresh-churned memory rose in my brain. I looked at my feet and saw JJ Adrieux staring up through the strands of a mop, single shot through his chest. I put my hand on the wall and tried not to be sick. I started to pant, and my chest hurt.

A gentle hand on my back brought me back to the moment. Then JJ disappeared, and Camilla's voice, soft and reassuring, spoke. "Are you okay, Frank?"

My chest still heaved, and my chest still ached. I held a deep breath and nodded. "I'll make it."

"The coast is clear. Let's see if we can get that elevator before someone else claims it."

There was a problem with that plan. I could feel it, but I couldn't put it into words. "Okay."

The elevator door opened to her touch, and some of the problem with the plan took shape. "The elevators should be on lockdown. I—"

"Not for me, Frank," Camilla said. "I'm a bona fide recruiter. Remember?"

I leaned against the wall and tried not to hurl when the elevator started to rise. I was still breathing hard. I rested my head on the cool elevator wall and looked at Bertrand. "How are you, Bernie?"

He looked at me, something like life in his eyes. "Who are you?" The words came out slurred.

"A friend."

"It really is about Bernie. Isn't it?" Camilla looked at me with admiring wonder. "All this danger and crazy risk. It's all to get this one kid you don't know out of harm's way?"

I managed to meet her gaze and felt some of my strength return. "It is. But I'm shutting down this entire operation." I glanced at Bertrand. He seemed to be coming out of his trance, too. "They're not doing this to anyone else. I promise."

We shared a smile, the elevator stopped, and the door opened to an empty lobby. I glanced at the front corner of the elevator and the camera that had to be there. What was I missing? How could they be letting us walk out of here?

Camilla turned right and led us down a corridor, and I saw the emergency evac sign. At the far end, big red letters proclaimed: EMERGENCY EXIT AIRLOCK

"It's a long way to Tycho," she said. "You have a plan?"

My coordination was improving, and I didn't feel as nauseous. But I was a long way from normal. "Yeah."

We made it to the airlock antechamber. It was empty of people. The door was metal-framed clear acrylic that slid on a track, similar to the mantraps in the detention centers I'd spent so much of my life in. It was clean and maintained, and I could see our reflection in the immaculate acrylic; a ghost of Camilla helping Bertrand into a rigid EVA suit. It was orange, with a tracker. How far were we going to get?

I looked past them at the reflection of the corridor to the elevator. Empty. I turned to look directly, my suspicions tingling. Was this another dream? A probe of my mind? An attempt to get me to lower my guard? And the pieces came together. *"It really is about Bernie. Isn't it?*

All this danger and crazy risk. It's all to get this one kid you don't know out of harm's way?"

I accessed my pReC and one of the enhancements Khatri had installed. "Shannon, you there?"

There was a long, agonizing pause. "I'd begun to think you'd forgotten!" Her voice was scratchy and distant.

I closed my eyes. "Eighty-six Alpha, Shannon. You copy that? Eighty-six Alpha."

There was another long, staticky pause. "I hear ya." Her voice was quiet and sad.

Bertrand screamed. I opened my eyes. The airlock door reflection was no longer empty. Camilla stood motionless, looking at me with sad eyes. The corridor that had been empty all the way to the elevator lobby was full of beefy security agents in blue jumpsuits. Three had pushed through the door behind me, and I could see evidence of more beyond.

"I'm sorry, Frank. I know you deserve better."

I looked at her and felt more of my composure return. "I know. Just a survivor. Right?"

Chapter Twenty-six

The goons took Bertrand. He screamed and fought until they loaded him with something from a pneumo-injector. Then, he grew quiet and slumped against the wall. I took a step forward, but a cherry-faced guard with red hair dissuaded me with something more lethal.

"I wouldn't do that, Mr. Parker," said a familiar voice.

Deacon Remy Frey stepped into the room. He wore an undertaker's suit and a wolf's smile. "We've gone through a lot of trouble to take you alive. I'd hate to see that wasted now."

I frowned. "Is this the part where you take me to your leader?" Redface slapped me.

"Show the deacon some respect." But Frey only smiled.

"Now, now, Mark. The Lord has delivered Mr. Parker to us. Let us not sully him before the Prophet has had a chance to talk with him."

"As you say, Deacon," he said, but neither the look on his face nor the tone of his voice expressed pleasure with the decision.

Frey looked out into the corridor. "You two, deal with the kid." He looked at Camilla. "You, my dear, are coming with us." He led us back down the hallway toward the elevators.

We—me, Camilla, Frey, and two of his gorillas—squeezed into the car. One gorilla was a hatchet-faced man with craters on his cheeks. The other was Mark. No one spoke during the ride, but I noticed with pleasure my stomach hadn't lurched when the car started to rise.

The doors opened to a beautiful foyer that seemed aesthetically familiar. A dark wood floor was covered with a red rug. A bookcase rested against the wall to my left and a large, Old World globe took up floorspace on my right. A huge skylight provided a view through the transparent biodome and into the dark sky. The Earth wasn't in view, and I missed it.

Two guards in suits flanked a pair of inner doors. They were thick, with mahogany veneers and tight tolerances. I'd seen doors like these on Janet Foxx's remodeled office, the ones equipped with magnetic seals. They opened and revealed a familiar office. Old World richness with a space age view.

Petrovich sat at the same desk from my interrogation, in the same chair that had threatened to swallow him. He wore the same grey shirt with the logo, and I found myself wondering if I hadn't actually been here earlier, but there was no telling. There was no sign of a smile on his face, plastic or otherwise. Anger pinched his features and a furious thundercloud roiled in those green eyes.

Frey pushed past me and strode up to Petrovich. The pair had a hushed exchange. I couldn't make anything out, but I didn't think Frey was having a good time of it. The huddle broke, and Frey stood tall, taking up station behind Petrovich, his expression dour.

Petrovich let the moment stretch into long seconds. "What are you doing here, Detective?"

I managed to stare back. "Oh, you know, life has been hard. Figured I could use some of that Old Time Religion."

Petrovich made no motion, but a hard overhand came down from my left, the spot Mark had taken up. So much for being left unsullied.

Petrovich continued in that honey-sweet pastor's voice. "I would think you, of all people, would know what we could do to you, if we wanted. I can turn your brain into pink-grey mush, if I have to." He leaned forward, blood rushing to his cheeks. "Now, what the fuck are you doing in my home?"

"I think he's telling the truth," said Camilla.

Petrovich looked at her as if she'd just risen from the dust. "I'm sorry. Did you say something?"

She held her ground. "I-I think he really came out here for Bern—Bertrand Mellenburg and only Bertrand Mellenburg."

Petrovich's eyes moved to Frey, but the man offered nothing. He turned back to me. "That right, Detective? You here risking everything over one lost soul?"

I was suddenly sure if I told him I was, he would kill me. "You tell me, *Prophet.*" I put as much mockery in my voice as my condition would allow. "You think Katsaros only cares about some spoiled brat who lost his way?"

Mark kicked the back of my knee and followed with an overhand chop where my neck met my shoulder. White-hot pain exploded, and I toppled to the floor.

Petrovich seemed to like that. He chuckled and rose from his chair. He leaned over the desk propped on his hands. "That's more like it, boy. What is Angelo after? What's his business with me?"

I stared past him out the window, trying to come up with something to offer this man, anything to give me ten more seconds. He strode around the desk, walking in slow, deliberate strides, and loomed over me, his shadow blocking the light from the windows.

I looked up and met his gaze. Mark karate chopped me in the shoulder again.

"Don't you look at the Prophet!"

Petrovich said nothing. Those empty eyes regarded me for several long moments, then turned to Camilla. "You led him here. Helped him break through our security and broke your covenant with me."

Camilla took a knee and fixed her gaze on the floor. "I-I warned you,

Prophet. I reported his breach as soon as I could do so, earned his trust, and helped bring him here before you." There was a note of contrition in her voice, the pleading of a believer to her god. "I did what I could."

The scratchy sound of our conversation rose from hidden speakers.

"You're not a believer?"

"I told you; I'm a survivor, Detective. It was nice for a while, but you can't con a con. True colors always bleed through."

"But you do their bidding."

"Old habits die hard. Being with the Tabernacle has its perks, and, if they want to believe I'm a righteous servant doing their bidding out of love and devotion, who am I to tell them otherwise?"

Her face morphed into horrified terror, but Petrovich cooed a soothing banter. "No. No, sister. There's no need to fear. We understand. You need conditioning, remediation. Yes?"

Her face said she had doubts, but relief swept it away, and she smiled. "Yes, Prophet."

His smile was pure sunshine, but I felt the danger in it. "Then rise, child. God loves a sinner come to repent."

Camilla smiled, tears staining her eyes. "Thank you, Prophet. You won't—"

"Camilla!"

Phwep! Phwep! Hatchetface's needle gun coughed two rounds into the base of her skull before her brain had time to process my warning. Her body stiffened and pitched forward in the time it took for Mark to bring his chopping hand down on my shoulder. The wooden floor offered a hollow *thenk!* when she hit.

Her body convulsed as if it was still trying to figure out it was dead. She breathed several slow, snoring breaths, let out a long sighing moan, and fell silent.

Petrovich stood over me, head cocked, his arms held out in a gesture that said, *What are you gonna do?*

I turned my face away.

Petrovich wasn't giving me any time to grieve. "You walked in here with ten thousand bills in security software and Vretathol blockers. You didn't come here without a plan. What did he send you for?"

I tried to put Camilla out of my head. I needed a Katsaros connection now, or that letter to Mattie would be my last. I closed my eyes and let my instincts go. "He knew you were moving against him. He thought those nights partying together made you nervous, especially after the Lenny Marquez thing." My mind raced, trying to put together a good story, and I wondered how much of this was based in fact and how much was fantasy. "The way you broke off your associations with him made him worry. Mellenburg was a smokescreen, a chance to get a peek behind the curtain."

Petrovich glanced at Frey and back to me. "It wasn't really the whore, though the thought that Angelo's network had been penetrated by a pair of do-gooder pirate reporters did provide me with the last bit of incentive I needed to change things."

He cocked his head sideways, regarding me with a cold predator's gaze that stayed far from his broad, plastic smile. "I can understand his concern. But I probably won't be able to tell that tale to the police." I didn't even pretend to act surprised. "Poor Camilla, here, is the only one you got to before—"

"There are records!" I said, and glanced past his hip at the black Luna sky. "You kill me, it all gets released."

The smile froze. "What are you talking about?"

"Camilla was quite the street rat—very smart." Petrovich's eyes narrowed. That meant he was listening, and I was breathing. I pressed on. "You thought she was a believer, but you heard what she said. You can't con a con. She saw through the curtain." I remembered the picture on her desk and where I had seen a much older and more haggard version. "After what you did to Darlene Hurt, could you even pretend to be surprised?"

The smile finally faded. I pushed on with my educated guesses. I couldn't be getting the details right, but if there was enough of the big picture, he might not notice. "Milly told me all about Hurt, how she was recruited after Hurt caught Milly ripping off the church. But this wasn't some hundred-bill score from the collection plate. It was a real job, grand larceny." That was the only way TCPD would have bothered with the case.

My eyes drifted across the empty sky behind Petrovich. "The way I see it, Hurt saw first-class grifting potential in Milly and sold the recruitment idea to you. After all, what are you but a guild of grifters operating under the flag of religion? Am I right?"

Petrovich and I shared amused smiles. I continued. "I guess it never occurred to you that even a grifter can develop loyalty beyond herself. But Camilla keeps"—I looked at the body on the floor—"kept pictures of those formative days on her desk at work and her house." I glanced around the room, taking stock in locations and stances. "I think she took it hard when you came down on her hero like you did."

Disgust spread over Petrovich's features. He leaned down over me. "If she was so loyal to you, why did she run to me first chance she got?"

"Because she knew you were watching, like you do all your people." I glanced over his shoulder and saw new, brighter stars on the horizon. "You provided the room, got her the job with the university, and paid for all of her expenses. How could she not think you were watching? That you wouldn't be reading her mail? You can't con a con, right? That's why she went to you, because she had no choice, but there is a treasure trove of records; contracts for her flat, the way her salary was deposited into a church account, so you could offer her a meager stipend, and, of course, your wire transfers that coincide with drug purchases made by Milly."

Petrovich's face burned bright red. His eyes bulged. "You're a liar!"

The stars over his shoulder grew bright.

I smiled. "I am, but the trail is still there"—I motioned toward the window over his shoulder—"for them to find, and they know about it."

He gazed out the window behind him. The faraway glow of the closing shuttles loomed large through the dome windows beyond the biosphere.

The AI spoke over an open pReC channel, its voice robotic and formal. "Prophet." Even the AI called him Prophet. "The Tycho City Police Department is transmitting to us, demanding permission to land. They are also communicating a warrant signed by a Magistrate Howard."

I knew Wanda Howard, a solid judge who could be both fair and tough but had an understanding that police work required latitude. Her signature probably meant they had done a little judge fishing to get their writ.

Petrovich seemed incapable of speech for several long moments. "What? Rec Greg Leichman!"

I stood, pushing hard off the floor, driving myself backward into Mark. I guessed at where his face might be and lashed out with my head. I caught a cheek, but my shoulder sent him spinning in the low G. I grabbed at his body, my hand searching for the butt protruding from his shoulder holster. I found his back instead and pushed him down, turning back to Petrovich.

Hatchet Face had already cleared leather and was drawing a bead, but I'd stood Petrovich up and hidden behind him. I gripped his neck in the crook of my right arm and did a quick search of his belt and chest. No weapons. Leave it to a guy like Petrovich to have those around him to do the dirty work of violence.

"Put him down!" shouted Hatchet Face.

Frey produced a pistol from inside his suit. "Step aside!"

I kept Petrovich between us and tried to get real small. Frey might've been ruthless, but he wasn't trained. Hatchet Face had more of a clue. He stepped to his right, the ominous gaze of his pistol staring me down.

I wasn't going to be able to cower with Petrovich between me and both of them for long.

Petrovich was screaming for his guards. The doors burst open and the men appeared.

I made a quick decision, grabbed Petrovich behind the scruff of his neck and the back of his belt, and drove him forward. I pushed him hard, trying to drive him through Hatchet Face. There was no time to see what the result was. Frey shouted in concern. "Prophet!"

I grabbed his gun hand and lifted it away with my left. I brought my right elbow into his chin. I felt no crack, but I felt the strength go out of his posture and pulled the gun from his grip. His guards were just getting their bearings, but Hatchet Face was shoving Petrovich to the floor and bringing his gun to bear. I stepped forward, shoved Frey's pistol into his face and blew a hole in his right cheek. He made a wet gurgling noise and collapsed.

I knelt and fired a few rounds at the door in the same instant Mark found his feet and blasted away at the space I'd just occupied. His rounds screeched over my head, and the guards at the door sought cover. I dove forward and tracked Mark with the handgun. I managed three rounds before colliding with a rising Petrovich.

Mark grunted and staggered backward, the pistol *klonking* to the floor. I stretched out over a prostrate Petrovich and fired a few more rounds into the doorway to discourage his guards. I grabbed the Prophet by the scruff again and stood him up. I hid behind him and pointed the gun over his shoulder. "Come in here and you'll see parts of your boss in a whole new light."

Petrovich let out a whimper, and I couldn't resist. "Tell 'em, Prophet. Tell 'em to take a deep breath or you're gonna look like big ugly over there." He glanced at the gurgling body on the floor.

"S-stay outside." I'm sure he was trying to sound prophet-like, but I don't think he'd spent much time having a gun stuck in his ear. "N-no one come in here. He will kill me."

I remembered the heavy, veneered doors with the tight tolerances and leaned close. "Order the AI to seal the inner doors."

"What?"

I gripped him tighter, pulling him closer. "Don't play games with me, Petrovich. I saw the reinforced doors on the way in. If they rush this room, you and I will be on that chariot to Heaven together. Close the doors and seal the maglocks. Now!"

The doors slammed and the loud *clack!* of the maglocks filled the booming echo. Mark writhed on the floor, moaning and gripping the right side of his chest at the shoulder. It would be a few weeks before he could use that arm to beat another unarmed man. I took a chance, strode over, picked up his pistol, and looked down at him.

If Petrovich was smart, he could coordinate with the AI to unlock the door and let the guards in, but I was willing to bet the consequences of a miscalculation would give him pause. "Hurts, don't it?"

He scowled up from the floor. "Not as much as when I get—"

I stomped on his shoulder, and he howled. "Why don't you do it, right now?" I did a quick search with one hand. Mark was clean. I pointed to the far corner of the room. "Get your miserable ass up and sit in that corner. Then, you can die whenever you want."

"Fuck you!" I shot the floor, showering him with expensive wood fragments. He yelped. "The next one goes through your hard head. I don't have many options and don't make the mistake of thinking I'm going to spend a lot of time on this one just because it keeps more blood off my hands. Now, get your ass up and sit in that corner, like I said!"

He rolled, grunting and crying as he did. I stepped closer to Petrovich and motioned him up the stairs toward the loft I assumed was his private suite. My gun hand stayed trained on Mark. We were halfway up by the time he slumped into the corner. Petrovich found some indignation. "He's dying, and you're marching him around the room?"

I studied the stricken man. He wasn't looking good. "You, of all people, are gonna moralize on issues of killing and slaving?"

He offered a soft chuckle. "Is that what you think of me? Some kind of slave master? There's a reason these people call me Prophet."

We reached the top of the stairs, and I looked over a loft of ostentatious beauty. A gorgeous dining table sat on a rug thick enough to sleep on. It looked out over the biosphere and through the windows beyond. A wood-paneled partition wall and matching doors sat to my right. The gold-handled behemoths sat ajar, revealing a bathroom twice the size of the flat I'd shared with Suzanne. A gold-handled tub sat on the far side of the massive chamber, the immaculate glisten of pale ceramic accentuating the room's magnitude. His bed was immense and enjoyed the same view as his dining table.

I motioned him toward the table. He smiled and followed my direction. "Drink?"

"Pass."

Petrovich shrugged, as if to say *suit yourself,* and poured a healthy dose into a tumbler. He drew a sip and sat into his chair with a flourish. TCPD cruisers were finding the ground outside, kicking up moon dust as they touched down. I watched them and looked back to him. "They're coming for you."

"You sure about that, Detective?" Petrovich's honey voice was bright and gay. His plastic smile was back on his face. "I'm a powerful man."

"I know. Risen on the power of faith and extortion." I glanced at him. "Is it that easy? Promise them eternal life and have them offer you everything? Fortune? Secrets? Loyalty?"

"You make it sound so cheap!" His voice was indignant. "I bring these people purpose, meaning! I fill the hole in their lives." I thought of a lewd joke and passed on it. "What were they before I found them? Lost sheep! Rudderless wretches! What are they now? People who get up in the morning belonging to something. With direction and purpose.

Disciples of God!"

"You mean *your* disciples."

His expression asked if there was a difference, and I was awed at the man's hubris. I turned my head and watched cops in reinforced containment suits dismount and charge the airlock. "You know what I find about powerful men?" We shared a glance, and I offered him a smile. "They have powerful enemies."

He drew a long sip, but something like worry touched those green eyes. "I have good lawyers. And leverage! Lots of leverage!"

"I'm sure you do, but I have an instinct about these things, and you know what I notice about all this?" Blue-black officers were deploying across the green grass. There was no sign of resistance. "They're coming with a writ. I'm guessing with the legal authority to search for evidence of kidnapping, extortion, fraud—you know, your bread and butter."

The smile left his face, and I could see him interacting with his pReC. Was he looking at the transmitted copy of the warrant?

"You know what that tells me?" There was nervousness in his glance, and I offered a predator's grin. "That someone as big as you are is pushing this." I let that notion take hold of him and said, "She's got kind of a cold touch, but Maggie Mellenburg loves that boy. And I took it upon myself to pass along all the dirt I could manage and point her in the direction of disgruntled allies. I think she knew what to do with it."

He looked at me. "These people are all adults!"

"And, this invasive AI, casting its voodoo spells the whole time I was here?" I paused and made a show of gesturing at the air around us. "The one subdued by the TCPD cyborgs?" Cyborgs was our pet name for the cybercrime nerds. I'd never found them to be robust physical specimens, but they knew their way around programming. "I bet they're already having quite a time reading your protocols."

He looked at me, mouth agape, eyes wide with terrifying realization.

I gave a voice to his fear. "It'll take months to go through this place and log all the felonies you're committing just by being here. And, when they go to your church and outreach centers..." I shrugged.

"We're a church! I—"

"You take donations from people under the influence of outlawed AI, *Prophet*, and that's just the beginning."

A loud *clack!* echoed through the chamber. The office doors opened. I gripped the pistols in my hands.

"TCPD!" called several authoritative voices.

I glanced over the lip. And saw navy blue body armor. "Up here!" I looked at Petrovich. "That lawyer? It might be time to see if he can cut a deal to keep you from walking the plank."

The cops reached the top of the stairs, their weapons trained on both of us. "Drop the weapons!" I did as they commanded and put my hands up. "Pastor Wayne Petrovich. Step aside."

He offered me a victorious grin. "Of course, officers."

They kept their guns on me. "Francis Derek Parker! You are under arrest for violating a protective order of the Second District Court of Tycho City." A pair of cops covered me as another approached with handcuffs. He snapped the steel bracelets around my wrists and droned about my rights under the Tycho City Charter.

Petrovich beamed a glorious smile. "I thought they were coming for me?"

A new voice broke in. "I asked them to wait for me. Rank has its privileges." The smile fell, and we both turned to see Sergeant Darren Norrington at the top of the stairs. A pair of silver handcuffs dangled from his grip. "Would you please turn around, Mr. Petrovich?"

Chapter Twenty-seven

"Well," said the doctor, returning to the exam room. "Your physical state seems fine, but there appear to be some corruptions in your pReC software that might need attending to, and there's no way to know what kind of psychological trauma all those drugs and torture might've done. I recommend you consult with a software psychiatrist at your earliest opportunity and let your primary know about this stunt." She thought I had a primary.

She passed through the door, leaving Foxx in the exam room.

"You came through."

The image of Petrovich standing over Rick's coffin with red, robot eyes leered from the recesses of my mind. "Yep! Doing great!"

I must've overplayed my hand. Foxx looked at me with skepticism. I tried accessing the files on my pReC, but everything was jumbled and foreign, as if Petrovich had left his funk on all of it.

"Dammit, Frank, did Angelo murder that girl?"

I cast the files aside and looked away. "I can't prove it, but yeah."

She let out a long breath. "Maybe not, but that file you left is a shitload of probable cause. You could have let me in on some of this. I am your lawyer, you know."

"I know," I said. "But, at the time, you were a Katsaros agent."

She glared at me with glittering blue pain. "That's a helluva thing to say!"

It was, and she deserved better. "I need to get Mattie and Suzanne to safety. After that, we can burn him to the ground."

"Deal."

"What deal?" Darren Norrington strode into the room with Lacy Hammond right behind. "I was told you had information that I would find interesting, information about an ongoing case of ours."

I glanced at Foxx, and felt Norrington deflate. Hammond's thin mask of patience shattered, and she flew into a series of curses. "I told you he was jerking your chain. I say we take him, right now."

"Have an arrest writ, do you, Detective?" It was Foxx.

Hammond glared at the lawyer but managed to hold her tongue.

Norrington looked at me. "I thought we were getting somewhere, but you're stringing us along again."

"Look, Darren—"

Norrington laughed. "Darren! Don't you Darren me, Parker. Your lawyer"—he glared at Foxx—"promised me information on the murder of Lenny Marquez, said you could paint a great picture for me, you knew I would vouch for you with Pro Standards, that I would back your story and put you on the side of the angels and that you could be trusted. That we would pull your fat out of the fire."

"You did get a nice collar out of this, Sergeant," said Foxx.

Hammond chuckled at that. "You mean Chief Conrad got a nice collar out of this. We're just doing the grunt work."

"Look, I still have those issues I told you about."

"But you sure as hell didn't mind having your lawyer give me a song and dance. Did you?"

I frowned. "I'm not reneging on my plans to help, I just—"

"Refuse to do it now. I'm done being used, Parker. Consider this bridge burnt." He shared another glance with Hammond and nodded. "Lace, you've earned this."

A malicious smile stretched across her face. "Frank Parker, you have the right to remain silent..."

* * *

"This wasn't the deal," I said.

Tsaris's grin wasn't quite as bright as Hammond's, but there was a wolfish quality to it. "It wasn't my idea, but I like Norrington's style."

"But I—"

"You're the one who wanted nothing in writing. So, you got nothing in writing and no protection."

"You're actually charging me with Lenny Marquez's murder?"

He took a deep breath. "No, that was Daysha's doing." Daysha Poole was the Upper City prosecutor. "But the idea of real charges pending appeals to me. It gives me what you'd call—leverage." Leverage. I was hearing that word a lot, lately. "You can still work with me, give me what I want. In return, I can try to help you with your circumstances."

"And, the million-bill bond?"

Tsaris grinned. "Judge Howard has a powerful sense of justice." He didn't tell me Katsaros would know I'd been charged. Nor did he suggest that knowledge could make me and my family a liability. He didn't have to. "You said you might be closing in on Rick's murderer. Now might be the time to talk about that."

I stared for several long moments and weighed my options. I had to pick a path, right here and now. Cyborg Petrovich flashed through my memory, and I made my choice. "You'd turned Rick in your investigation into the Three-three. He was gonna tell you everything. Wasn't he?"

He gave nothing up. I pressed on. "But Rocamora got wise and killed Rick before he could say anything."

He sneered at me. "I thought you said you were closing in on Rick's murderers. How are you going to come to me with this bullshit and convince me you aren't lying your ass off?"

I looked into his face. "So, what've you got?"

Tsaris laughed. "You know better than that, Parker. *You* tell me what *you* know and *I* see what I can do for you with your charges."

"And what happens to my family?"

"Same agreement we made before. I do all I can to help them."

I considered the resources likely to go into backing that promise and Katsaros's means. "No. If I'm in, I'm a partner. Period."

Tsaris laughed. "A vigilante cop and partner to Suspect Number One, and you wanna be directly involved? My case would be tainted in every court in the land. No deal."

"Then I can't help you."

"And when I leak that you're cooperating with me? How long do you think it'll take for Katsaros to find that out? How long before the Loonies are planning a topside trip? Or maybe your family takes an unexpected journey straight down?"

I couldn't believe this guy. "You're a cop! You—"

"Don't tell me you haven't been on the giving side of this exchange, Parker." I thought of a pimp named "Fast Eddie" Perkins and the unsolved murder of Candy Watkins. "Sorry if you don't like the shoe on the other foot, but that's not my problem. You help me and get something, or you don't and what happens, happens."

There weren't many options. I looked at the door and back at Tsaris, victory all over his face. "What do you want?"

The muffled sound of voices passed through the door, and it opened. Janet Foxx's feisty voice poured inside. "Please give me an excuse to sue this place. I'll buy the Olympian and rename it in your honor—Officer Derry."

Tsaris turned, a frown on his face. "Can I help you, Counselor?"

"Yes, my client made bail hours ago. What the hell are you doing still interrogating him?" He stuck out his jaw but said nothing. "I can rename the Olympian the Tsaris Fuck Up as easily as the Officer Derry."

Disgust morphed Tsaris's face, and he moved his head. "Let 'im go."

* * *

It took less than twenty minutes to process me, and we were striding out onto the landing pad on the roof. "Did you pay my bond?"

Janet shook her head. "Someone else insisted on it."

The door slipped open and Maggie Mellenburg sat in the compartment. She smiled, her eyes damp with grateful tears. "Detective Parker."

"Maggie. How's Bertrand?"

"He's getting the best care money can buy." I wondered how much of the damage Petrovich's people had done was permanent. The same worries dominated Maggie's features. "Words can't do justice to how grateful I am."

"So, you were able to press the cops to raid Petrovich's compound."

"Janet did most of the real work, but it was your pilot who reported a murder in progress that lit the fire under their ass." Foxx nodded her agreement. "I can't imagine what would have happened if you hadn't intervened."

I chose not to point out any competent investigator could've done this work, but she seemed to read my doubt. "How many would have taken on this suicide mission of yours?" I smiled, and shared a knowing glance with Foxx. "We both know you went above and beyond."

"It's my job." She smiled but added nothing. The whine of the engines lowered, and the craft began to descend. "I appreciate you bailing me out. I'll pay you—"

"Don't you dare, Frank Parker!" Maggie's glittering eyes bordered on indignant. "You brought my son back to me and helped me see what a shit I was married to. I'm a woman of means. This is the least I can do. It would be my pleasure to fund your defense."

I wanted to tell her I didn't need her help, but I also thought about Suzanne, Mattie, and the sentence worse than death hanging over their heads. "Thanks."

The craft set down on the roof and Maggie grabbed my wrist. "There is one thing you can do for me, Detective."

We stared at each other across the tiny compartment. "Sure. Anything."

"This situation complicating things between you and your daughter. Uncomplicate it."

* * *

I dreamed about Android Petrovich standing over Rick's coffin, invitations from Mr. and Missus Tyre flanking him, his red, glowing eyes staring from my traumatized mind. "This isn't over, Detective. A man like me isn't vanquished so easily."

I opened my eyes. *"This isn't over, Detective."*

I rose from the bed and tried not to think about what a man like that could do to my family. *"A man like me isn't vanquished so easily."*

I tried to leave my fears behind, to sweat Android Petrovich away, but my broken mind moved to Tsaris's threats. *"And when I leak that you're cooperating with me? How long do you think it'll take for Katsaros to find that out? How long before the Loonies are planning a topside trip?"*

I remembered how Rick and I had bluffed Fast Eddie and tried to convince myself he was bluffing, too. But there was too much at stake to find comfort in the hope. I finished my workout in Foxx's gym, showered, and made coffee. I stood in the early morning quiet, looking at the string chart, and realized something was there, something new, or rather, a new light shined on the case, but my broken mind couldn't see it. I sipped at my coffee and read the chart from the center out. Rick, his cases, David Carson, Rocamora, Monique Benson, and on and on, but it wouldn't come.

My pReC flashed, but my second sight was empty, save a single word: UNKNOWN. Alarm rose in my soul and I was certain the message carried ill tidings. A simple text scrolled across my vision. "Condolences..."

My mind raced for the attached stream link with the ominous title "Tragedy in the Upper City." A holo of a sheet-covered body stared out from my second sight. Grief rose in the certain knowledge that Katsaros had killed my family, had taken Mattie.

I fell back in time to a low-rent flat on Drane Street and the butchered bodies of Lenny Marquez and Tommy Henson, but the faces belonged to Mattie and Suzanne. Pale, lifeless Claude and Claire Adrieux stared from the shadows, the tiny faces of their children between them, accusation in their eyes. They were joined by Allie Kramer, Vicky Mickelson, and Sassy Harrelson. Lenny Marquez and Tommy Henson were there, too.

The stream swept the visage aside, replacing it with the scene of an Upper City street; a body lay in the street's center. I broke into the stream mid-sentence and braced myself for the landslide of tragedy. "—orities aren't saying much about this crime, but..."

The Adventure Continues...

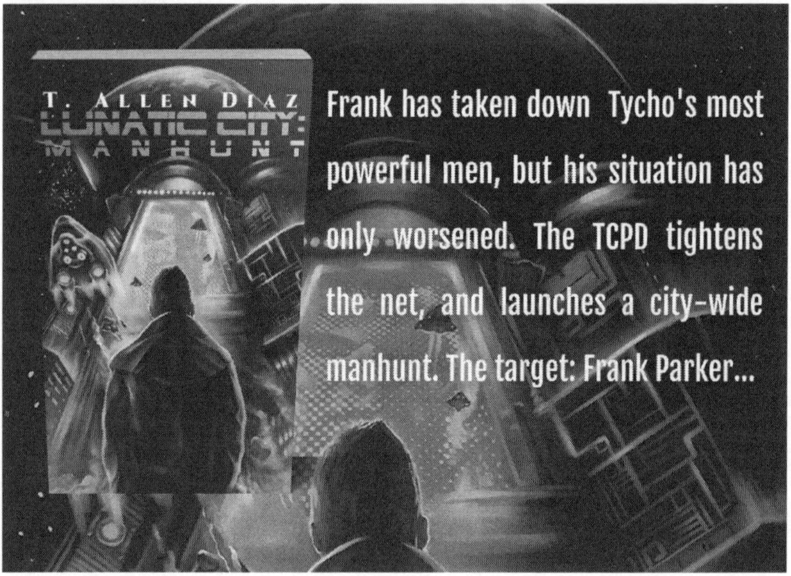

T. ALLEN DIAZ
LUNATIC CITY:
MANHUNT
Frank has taken down Tycho's most powerful men, but his situation has only worsened. The TCPD tightens the net, and launches a city-wide manhunt. The target: Frank Parker...

Don’t forget your free e-book!

Read about Frank’s early detective days FREE when you join the T. Allen Nerd Crew at Tallendiaz.com!

Acknowledgements

Lunatic City: Manhunt couldn't have been written without the help of others. I know I will fail to include some deserving soul, but I will strive to include you all.

Earl Emerson, thanks for proving that a firefighter can also become a commercially successful writer. I cannot tell you the influence that has had on me. I am also humbled that you would take the time to return the emails of an aspiring writer from across the country. I wish you good health in your retirement and success with your future writings.

Merritt and Pam McClamma, I am truly humbled by the unconditional support and unsolicited help you have both offered me. I look forward to sporting your new stuff at my next book signing or show. I could not imagine better friends or role models. "Thank you" just doesn't do it, but it's the best this struggling artist can do, for now.

Alvin Epps, your art work is amazing. I envy your talent and am so fortunate to have the opportunity to work with you. I love the way you bring these covers to life and look forward to working together in the future.

Aysha Rehm, I am so grateful to you for your keen editor's eye and the insight you bring to these books. They could not be the polished product they are without you. You are a pleasure to work with, and I look forward to many more collaborations in the coming years.

Mom and Heather, thank you both for believing in me and supporting me, even when you didn't understand me. A big part of who I am today is because of you two, and I'm very grateful to have you both in my life.

Dave Butler, you are one of the classiest guys in this business or any other. I'm so excited for you and your success and look forward to many great Dave Butler works.

Kevin Anderson, words can barely express my gratitude for this wonderful opportunity you and WordFire have given me! I only hope that this book lives up to your expectations and that it's the first of many to come.

Melanie Bettis, it's no secret that I would still be schlepping books from my corner booth struggling to break even without your faith and influence. I love you, baby, and am very grateful to have you in my corner.

About the Author

T. Allen Diaz is a self-professed nerd and author of speculative fiction. The moon-based, cyberpunk noir, *Lunatic City* series typifies his gritty, no-nonsense writing style and flawed, relatable characters, while the *War of the Gods Saga* delves into the deep lore of a fantastic, post-industrial civilization wrestling with the rise of an ancient evil and the moral pitfalls of empire. His first series, *The Proceena Trilogy*, is a space opera with the grit and sci-fi military action of *Battlestar Galactica* and the tumultuous, revolutionary setting of *Les Misérables*.

T. Allen lives in the Tampa Bay area with his wife and two of his three kids (one has flown the coop.) He has served as a firefighter in the region for more than twenty-four years and intends to retire as a fire company captain in the coming months. He is diligently working on new material and looks forward to dedicating his full energy to his writing.

Made in the USA
Columbia, SC
27 June 2024

37522728R00148